What a silly little fool Mina had
been for thinking that
Roger de Montmorency might be
any different from every man she
had ever known.

She had been a dolt to feel anything for him.

The idea that Sir Roger could make her swoon with
ecstasy without even trying was enough to make her
grind her teeth in anger. The boastful, vain, pompous
creature! No doubt all the women he had made love to
so far had been serving wenches or peasants who
believed there was something special about a nobleman,
or who wanted something in return, like money or
advancement.

Well, she knew better. Noblemen were men first, and
seldom noble. If her betrothed thought he could just
crook a finger and find Mina Chilcott waiting patiently
in the nuptial bed, he would soon learn otherwise....

Dear Reader,

Kathe Robin of *Romantic Times* had this to say about award-winning author Margaret Moore's new Medieval, *The Norman's Heart:* "A story brimming with vibrant color and three-dimensional characters. There is emotion and power on every page." We hope you enjoy this delightful story of the marriage of staid Sir Roger de Montmorency and the willful Lady Mina Chilcott.

Taylor Ryan's first book, *Love's Wild Wager,* was part of our popular March Madness promotion featuring talented new authors. With her second book, this month's *Birdie,* she returns to Regency England and Ireland to tell the touching story of a woman of noble blood who was raised on the streets.

Our two other titles for the month include *Man of the Mist* from Elizabeth Mayne, the sweeping tale of a Scottish officer who finally returns to claim his young bride, now a grown woman. And from longtime Harlequin Historical author Lynda Trent, *The Fire Within,* a haunting story of lovers who must choose between the past and the future.

Whatever your taste in reading, we hope Harlequin Historicals will keep you coming back for more. Please keep a lookout for all four titles, available wherever books are sold.

Sincerely,

Tracy Farrell
Senior Editor

Please address questions and book requests to:
Harlequin Reader Service
U.S.: 3010 Walden Ave., P.O. Box 1325, Buffalo, NY 14269
Canadian: P.O. Box 609, Fort Erie, Ont. L2A 5X3

To the independent Warren women and the
self-confident men who married them.

**Books by Margaret Moore**

Harlequin Historicals

*A Warrior's Heart* #118
*China Blossom* #149
*A Warrior's Quest* #175
+*The Viking* #200
*A Warrior's Way* #224
*Vows* #248
+*The Saxon* #268
*The Welshman's Way* #295
*The Norman's Heart* #311

Harlequin Books

*Mistletoe Marriages*
"Christmas in the Valley"

*Warrior Series
+Viking Series

## MARGARET MOORE

Prior to embarking on her writing career, Margaret Moore studied English Literature at the University of Toronto, taught basic military training in the Royal Canadian Naval Reserve and worked for every major department store chain in Canada.

Margaret is married to a man whose eyes really change color. They have two children and live in Scarborough, Ontario.

# Chapter One

Rain pelted against the stone walls of Montmorency Castle and drummed on the closed shutters. The wind moaned softly about the battlements, and heavy clouds scudded across the full moon.

Inside the hall, Sir Roger de Montmorency paced impatiently, ignoring everyone, including Sir Albert Lacourt, who leaned against one of the many trestle tables, his arms crossed and his head bowed as if deep in thought. An occasional sharp glance at Sir Roger betrayed some anxiety on his part as well.

A huge fire burned in the new hearth, and most of the wedding guests huddled near it, awaiting the lavish evening meal intended to welcome Sir Roger's bride. The bright banners of the visiting nobility hung from the walls; fine beeswax candles burned upon the linen-covered, flower-strewn tables, and in honor of the festive occasion, fresh herbs had been sprinkled over the rushes on the floor.

Dudley, the steward, a Saxon who had been in the service of the de Montmorencys his whole life, looked about to have an apoplectic fit as he scurried between the kitchen corridor, the tables and the door. The maidservants, idly waiting to serve the food, stood near the corridor and whispered among themselves. Dudley signaled them to hush before he peered again into the rain and the dark of the night, running his hand over the few remaining white hairs on his nearly bald head. The question in his eyes and the unspoken words on the tip of his tongue were obvious to all present: What was keeping the bride?

Sir Roger, his usually inscrutable face full of annoyance, suddenly stopped his pacing. "We have waited long enough," he announced. "Everybody sit down."

The wedding guests glanced uncertainly at one another, for this was a serious turn of events that did not bode well for the future alliance between the de Montmorencys and the Chilcotts. On the other hand, they had been waiting for some time and were very hungry, so they moved to their respective places. The movement of the crowd revealed an elderly and frail priest who was sleeping slouched on a stool, his back against the wall.

"Father Damien, give us your blessing," Sir Roger called out as he strode to take his place at the high table on the raised dais. When the priest did not respond, Sir Roger bellowed his name again.

Dudley hurried to the priest and gently shook him awake. "The blessing, Father," the Saxon said quietly and respectfully, although he glanced uneasily over his plump shoulder at Sir Roger. "It's time for the blessing."

"What's that? Is she here at last?" Father Damien asked, peering about myopically. "Where? I don't see anybody."

"She's not here, but we will not wait," Sir Roger said loudly.

"Ah, my son," Father Damien said in his high, cracking voice, "shouldn't we wait—"

"No!"

Everyone in the room jumped a bit and Father Damien immediately started to mumble a brief blessing.

His duties finished, the priest moved to his place at the table with surprising alacrity, and Sir Roger turned to his oldest friend. "You sit here, Albert," Sir Roger said in a tone that would brook no denial as he indicated the seat that was to have been his bride's.

Sir Albert did as he was told with obvious reluctance.

The servants also moved swiftly, and Dudley seemed to relax somewhat as the first course arrived, apparently none the worse for the delay.

Albert looked at Roger, an expression of condemnation in his usually mild brown eyes. "Your guests could be delayed by the storm, Roger, and—"

"And if that is so, they should have sent a messenger on ahead to tell us."

"I understand your impatience, Roger. I, too, would be far from happy if my future bride was delayed. However, let us hope they have stopped at an inn to wait out the storm."

"That would be the sensible thing to do," Roger said as a roasted capon was set before him by a buxom serving wench whose shapely lips fell into a pout when he ignored her.

Roger stabbed the meat angrily. "Unfortunately, Chilcott is *not* a sensible man. They could be anywhere between his estate and mine."

"At least he has the sense to pick a fine husband for his half sister."

Roger snorted with unsuppressed contempt. "Save your flattery for someone else, Albert. He might have made no end of trouble over his broken betrothal to my sister if I had not agreed."

"So why did you not insist that Madeline marry him? You could have stopped her marriage to that

Welshman. He impersonated Chilcott, after all. I must confess I expected you to kill the fellow, Roger, right there on the steps of the chapel. When you offered to knight him—God's blood, I almost dropped dead myself. It's a good thing he refused. Think what Baron DeGuerre would have said!''

"If the Welshman had sworn fealty to me, the baron would have been appeased. Besides, I wanted the guests to enjoy themselves after I had gone to such expense for the feast. They were all sitting there like statues until I made the offer. But it doesn't matter now." Roger wiped the trencher in front of him with a piece of bread. "For the first—and last—time in my life I acted like a softhearted fool."

"Or as if you *had* a heart," Albert mumbled under his breath as he pulled the wing from a roasted duck.

"What did you say?" Roger demanded.

"I understand your predicament," Albert replied. "Still, Baron DeGuerre will be pleased that this alliance is going to come about after all."

A foot soldier appeared at the wide doors of the hall. Because Roger had heard no cry of alarm, he assumed that the matter was some minor household trouble. Dudley hurried toward the man and listened to his words.

For a moment, Roger felt some pity for his steward. Dudley was not a young man, and between the anxiety over the preparations for his lord's wedding, which he had planned with as much care as if Roger were the king, and this unaccountable delay, he had aged considerably.

Roger's anger at Chilcott grew even more. It was an insult to him and to his steward that Chilcott didn't have the courtesy to arrive on time.

Dudley came bustling toward the high table as fast as his plump legs would carry him. "My lord!" he said, looking as if he feared the castle were about to fall down around his head, "they are here! In the inner ward! Lord Chilcott and his half sister and their retinue!"

Albert gave Roger a censorious look, which grew deeper when Roger made no move to get up, let alone leave the hall, but Roger didn't care. "Have the servants show them to their quarters," he ordered brusquely. "They can have wine and fruit there."

Dudley wrung his hands and chewed his lip. "Forgive my impertinence, my lord, but should you not greet them? Or at least invite them into the hall to dine? They have journeyed a long way, and—"

"Arrived too late. If they wish more to eat, they may join us at the table. Or not, as they please. I am not interrupting my meal for latecomers who do

# MARGARET MOORE

# the Norman's heart

## Harlequin Books

TORONTO • NEW YORK • LONDON
AMSTERDAM • PARIS • SYDNEY • HAMBURG
STOCKHOLM • ATHENS • TOKYO • MILAN
MADRID • WARSAW • BUDAPEST • AUCKLAND

ISBN 0-373-28911-1

THE NORMAN'S HEART

Copyright © 1996 by Margaret Wilkins

not have the courtesy to advise me of any unexpected difficulty."

With a baleful look at Albert, who gave a slight, resigned shrug of his shoulders, Dudley nodded and hurried out of the hall, wringing his hands with dismay.

"Just what do you hope to gain by this discourtesy?" Albert asked quietly.

"Are you accusing me of incivility?"

"Yes. There could be many reasons for their tardiness. If you had only waited a little longer—"

"I don't care to hear their excuses."

"She is your bride, after all."

"You don't have to remind me."

"Aren't you curious to see her at all?" Albert asked, impatience creeping into his voice.

Roger looked at his friend with some surprise. "Not in the least. I daresay she's like that popinjay Chilcott, a vain, overdressed, affected young lady whose spending habits will cause me some grief before I train her out of them. Nor do I intend to encourage tardiness from my future wife, now or at any time. If you're so interested, why don't *you* go and greet her?"

"Because I am not the groom," Albert replied.

"And because it's raining hard enough to put dents in the stones," Roger added laconically.

Albert grinned slightly, then frowned. "It still doesn't make it right for you to be rude."

"I'll be seeing the woman for a long time to come," Roger said in a tone that signaled the end of the discussion. "And this meal was too expensive to be ruined with delay."

Lord Reginald Chilcott, knight of the realm, lord of several manors, whose ancestors had sailed with William the Conqueror himself, stood shivering in the dark courtyard of Montmorency Castle gazing mournfully at Sir Roger's steward. Rain dripped off his bedraggled velvet cloak; his once finely perfumed and dressed hair hung limply about his narrow shoulders, and he wiped his aquiline nose, which was now dripping from within and without. Behind him, his men muttered discontentedly and his wagons were soaking. The smell of damp horse was nearly overwhelming.

"Not coming to greet us?" Chilcott repeated incredulously for the fourth time. "You are absolutely certain?"

"Yes, my lord. You must understand, the hour grew late and Sir Roger does not like to be kept waiting. If you had sent a messenger—"

"We did not realize Sir Roger keeps his bridges in such poor repair that a summer's storm would wash them away, or we would have," a woman's voice interrupted. Dudley tried to see past Lord Chilcott to what appeared to be a cloaked and hooded woman mounted on a rather inferior beast.

"Mina!" Chilcott chided, his tone between a plea and a warning as he turned toward the woman.

The woman dismounted. "It is true, Reginald, and you know it."

She faced Dudley, who tried to see beneath her hood without being overly obvious. "My lord has told me to show you to your quarters, where wine and fruit will be brought to you," he offered.

At that moment, one of the servants left the hall. The light from the open door poured into the inner ward and was reflected in the many puddles. Simultaneously they heard the chatter and raucous laughter of those assembled in the hall, as well as the clatter of wooden dishes and metal goblets, no longer muted by the heavy oaken door.

Mina Chilcott slowly turned toward the steward. "The evening meal is not yet finished," she observed.

"No, my lady," Dudley mumbled, not quite sure what to do.

"We cannot go into the hall looking like *this!*" Reginald Chilcott said in a voice that was almost a screech. "We're soaked to the skin! My clothes are nearly ruined, and your skirt is covered with mud."

"Surely that is not unexpected, given the weather. Nevertheless, Reginald, I will go to the hall of this most courteous knight," the bride said with what sounded suspiciously like sarcasm.

This did not seem the type of gentle, soft-spoken woman able to win any man's heart, let alone Sir Roger's, Dudley thought despondently.

"I would suggest, Reginald, that you tell the men to stable the horses, then go to the kitchens and make sure they are fed before bedding down for the night wherever this fellow says. Your name, sir?" she suddenly asked.

"Dudley," he replied, taken aback by the unexpected courtesy in her voice. "I am the steward here."

She nodded, then tilted her head up. "It's stopped raining," she noted, and threw back her hood.

Finally Dudley saw her face, and he wanted to moan with helplessness. The baron could not have chosen a more unsuitable bride for Sir Roger if it had been his intention. Why, this woman had red hair—not auburn, not red gold, but brilliant red, like the barbarian Irish—and, worse, freckles! Above all else, Sir Roger liked an unblemished complexion. She was tall, too, nearly as tall as her intended husband himself.

"Thank you, Dudley," she said, turning to face Lord Chilcott, who was sniffling again. "This place is smaller than you led me to believe, Reginald. Still, what is that saying? Beggars cannot choose? And I daresay Sir Roger sets himself a good table. Since I am hungry, I am going to eat."

"But Mina," Reginald spluttered, "you cannot simply walk into Roger de Montmorency's hall unannounced!"

"Do you not believe my betrothed will be pleased to see me?" she asked with an undisguised sneer. Without waiting for an answer, Lady Mina Chilcott turned on her heel and went toward the hall.

Dudley let out a low whistle, which he cut short when he realized the lady's relative was still there.

"Exactly," Chilcott muttered. He faced his men. "Do what she says, oafs, before you catch your death from a chill!"

"What do *you* wish to do, my lord?" Dudley asked deferentially.

"Follow her, of course, to make sure she doesn't ruin everything," Chilcott said helplessly. Then he glanced down at his wet garments. "After I change my clothes, of course."

Mina stood uncertainly inside the entrance of the hall of Montmorency Castle. It wasn't as large as her father's hall, yet it was very brightly lit, warm and decorated with pennants and flowers. Several well-dressed nobles were sitting at long tables, eating. The smells greeting her made her mouth water, and she took a step farther inside.

Then she realized the handsome man sitting at the center of the high table was staring at her. From his position of importance, she knew he must be Sir Roger de Montmorency, her betrothed.

But such a look! Cold, appraising, arrogant. He must know who she was, yet even now, he did not rise to greet her. He simply sat and stared at her with those dark, forbidding eyes.

Did he think he could intimidate her with that look? She was no spoiled young girl raised in sheltered gentleness. Nor was she a peasant to be overwhelmed with any nobleman's rank and wealth. She was Lady Mina Chilcott, and she could be just as self-confidently arrogant as any man. Her father had raised her to be that way, even if that had not been his intention.

So she stared back. Her betrothed was extremely well formed, with muscular shoulders and a broad chest that narrowed to a slender waist. He wore a simple tunic of dark green with no ornamentation of any kind, nor did he wear any jewelry. It struck her that he had no need for extra adornment.

Surprised by this observation, her gaze returned to his undeniably handsome face. Unexpectedly, he did not wear his hair in the conventional Norman manner, cut around the ears as if a bowl had been overturned on his head, the way Reginald did. Instead, he wore his hair long, like the wilder Celts. Indeed, he seemed to have more in common with those brazen warriors than Reginald or the other noble Normans she was used to.

Despite her bravado in the inner ward, her refusal to be alarmed and her very real hunger made worse by the abundance of food around her, Mina wondered if she had made a mistake by not taking the steward's advice to go to her quarters.

*No, I am in the right,* she thought resolutely. He should have greeted them in the courtyard and offered them the hospitality of his castle. Instead, he had left them outside as if they were merchants or traveling performers, not honored guests.

With that thought to bolster her courage, she took a deep breath, lifted her chin and reminded herself she was the legitimate daughter of a knight, even if her mother had been a Saxon. Then she marched straight down the center of the hall between the tables.

The gray-haired nobleman on Sir Roger's right rose, a welcoming smile on his pleasant, careworn face that warmed her as much as the blazing fire. One by one the other men and women who were gathered in the hall fell silent, waiting expectantly.

Only an elderly priest seemed not to notice the interruption as he continued to eat.

Still Sir Roger only looked, although his brow lowered ominously. What would he think of a woman who dared to embarrass him in front of all these people? No matter how she felt about the arranged marriage, Mina had given her word. Was it wise to anger her future husband?

Mina slowed her steps and lowered her eyes demurely. When she reached the dais at the far end of the curved hall, she made a deep obeisance. "Forgive my intrusion, Sir Roger," she said softly. "I fear, however, that no one informed you of our arrival."

Finally, *finally,* Sir Roger de Montmorency got up, still fixing her with his dark, measuring stare. His thigh-length tunic was belted about his waist and exposed long, lean legs. She noticed that his hands were slender and sinewy, obviously strong and surely capable of handling the heaviest weapons with ease.

"You are late and sent no word," her betrothed said in a voice as unfriendly as his expression. "We could not wait the supper."

"The bridge not five miles from here has been washed away...my lord," she added, with just enough of a pause to give her time to glance up at him. Let him see *her* eyes, too. Let him realize that she knew he had been unforgivably rude to herself and to her half brother, who was of a higher rank.

A vein in Sir Roger's forehead began to pulse, and she surmised she had scored a hit. "I'm sure it is not your fault," she said sweetly. "Underlings are often all too anxious to take advantage of a kind and generous lord." *What a lie!* she thought as she waited for him to respond. She could well imagine how he would treat his tenants. They would probably all welcome a mistress who understood what it was like to be mistreated.

Sir Roger made no answer, nor did his expression alter.

A particularly colorful curse rose to her lips. How could he continue to be so rude, with all these people watching? Was he that sure of himself that he did not fear their censure?

Looking at him, she thought he probably was.

"May I sit?" she asked, though it was not a request.

"My lady, please, take my chair." The gray-haired knight moved quickly aside. He smiled again, a kind but knowing smile. "I am Sir Albert Lacourt. Naturally we are delighted by your arrival, but you are quite wet through. Are you certain you would care to—"

"I was most anxious to meet my future husband," Mina interrupted calmly as she came around the table, removed her cloak—and suddenly realized that her soaking dress was clinging to her body like a second skin. She felt her face flush with embarrassment, and a quick glance at the assembly proved that she was making a spectacle of herself. Even the ancient priest was looking at her as if he had never seen a woman before. Considering she might as well be naked, perhaps that was not so far from the truth.

Nevertheless, she said not a word and took her chair as if nothing untoward had occurred.

"I, um, trust your journey was most pleasant except for the final portion," Sir Albert said.

"Yes, it was," Mina replied.

A serving wench with enormous breasts and a brazen manner that suggested her duties did not end with the hall but probably extended to the lord's bedchamber, as well, set down a platter of meat with a clatter.

Mina turned to Sir Roger and realized his gaze was fastened on her own breasts. "I see you are hungry, too," she remarked evenly.

A disgruntled frown flew across her intended's face before he turned his attention to the trencher before him.

"The storm was so severe, we were sure you had taken refuge somewhere along the road," Sir Albert observed after a moment of awkward silence.

"We would have, but Reginald was most certain of a kind welcome here and insisted we continue," she answered truthfully, keeping any hint of irony from her words.

Reginald finally appeared at the entrance to the hall. The reason for his delayed arrival was apparent immediately. He had changed his clothes and dried his hair as much as he could. Now he wore a long tunic of a heavy brocade that seemed to emphasize his thinness rather than make him look sturdier, which, Mina suspected, was its intention. He stood there awkwardly, frantically trying to curl his hair with his fingers.

To Mina's considerable chagrin, Sir Roger immediately stood up and strode toward her half brother. "Lord Chilcott!" he cried, his deep voice decidedly pleasant. "How pleased I am to see you again!"

Mina tried to stifle the flush she felt coloring her face. She rose immediately and spoke to Sir Albert. "If you will excuse me, sir, I fear I am greatly fatigued after all. Good night, Sir Albert. It was a pleasure making your acquaintance." Her gaze fixed on the buxom serving wench, who was once again making her way along the table refilling wine goblets. "I wish to be shown to my quarters."

"Of course, my lady," the wench said, her air of insolence noticeably diminished. Mina heard the men approaching, but she did not look at them or say anything.

Instead, she followed the maidservant, who tossed her long, honey brown hair and led the way toward the stairs leading upward to what Mina assumed was the upper hall.

Once away from the crowd, Mina smiled to herself, for she was certain that whatever else she had accomplished in the hall, she had shown the mighty Sir Roger de Montmorency that she could not be completely cowed.

As Roger walked back to his place with Reginald Chilcott at his side, he watched his future bride glide toward the stairs behind Hilda. She had not waited to be excused, or even said a farewell. God's blood, what kind of woman had he agreed to marry?

"Sit down and eat," he growled at the over-dressed Reginald, who blushed noticeably, his face turning nearly as red as his scarlet tunic. His elaborate garments were quite a contrast to the severely plain gown his relative had worn. Either Mina Chilcott was not nearly as vain as her half brother, or her garments were merely an extension of her frigid personality.

His almost brother-in-law cleared his throat awkwardly. "Mina is . . . she is not an easy person sometimes, Sir Roger," he explained haltingly, "but she was most competent in managing my father's estate in his final years when he was not able to do so himself. Perhaps once you are married, she will...mellow?" he finished hopefully.

Roger thought it highly unlikely that a woman of Mina Chilcott's coloring and temperament could ever be made to "mellow." He caught Albert's censorious eye and pushed some particularly savory venison in a rich, spicy sauce toward the younger nobleman. "Please, eat."

With a grateful smile, Reginald started consuming an astonishing amount for one of such slender build. Mercifully it seemed that Reginald would rather eat than talk. Albert, too, stayed quiet, and most of the guests talked softly among themselves.

At last Reginald belched delicately and said, "A very fine meal, my lord. My compliments to your cook. Now, if you will excuse me, I believe I, too, shall retire."

"If you wish, I shall have someone bring you some mulled wine to your bedchamber," his host offered with more graciousness, since Reginald was leaving. Roger signaled for Dudley to come toward the table.

Reginald's eyes widened and he nodded. "Yes, Sir Roger. I would like that. Thank you very much."

Roger kept his amusement to himself, though it seemed the young fool was taking an offer of mulled wine in much the same way another man would take an offer of a vast estate.

"Excuse me, Sir Roger," Reginald continued as he rose to follow Dudley. "Thank you." Reginald and Dudley headed toward the stairs, with Reginald pausing to greet some of the guests on his way out of the hall.

When they were gone, Roger took a large gulp of his wine.

"That was an interesting display of childishness, Roger," Albert noted dryly, "although I was pleased and surprised to see that you were not totally without some manners."

"Is it childish to make it plain that I do not care to have my meals interrupted for any reason? Is it childish to expect to be informed of a delay? Nor do I consider it childish to be less than impressed when a person I do not know dares to chastise me in my own hall about my tenants and my bridges."

"I've warned you often enough about that bridge. Besides, they are your guests."

"Bridge or not, they were late."

"If the bridge is out, they couldn't have sent a messenger on ahead."

"So they should have stayed at an inn."

"She said she was anxious to meet you."

Roger's only response to this observation was a derisive grunt as he reached for more wine.

"Granted she's not very attractive, but there is a certain something—"

"She's a shrew. Or a harpy. Call her what you will. I hate red hair and blemished skin."

"She knew she was in the right, and she acted like it," Albert said firmly as he eyed his companion. "I found her rather refreshing. And those are freckles, not blemishes, and there were only ten."

"You counted?" Roger raised one eyebrow speculatively. "If you think her such a prize, why don't *you* marry her?"

Albert flushed and looked away. "You know why not. Besides, you made the bargain, not me."

"With that buffoon Reginald. I must have been mad."

"You could always break it off."

"It is a tempting thought."

"She has a fine body," Albert noted while his attention wandered to the huntsman, Bredon, who was tossing bones to his favorite hounds. The dogs yapped and scrambled through the rushes for the tasty titbits.

"A fine body she displayed to the entire hall," Roger replied, still sounding annoyed. In actuality, he was recalling her exquisite shape. Indeed, she might have been nude, the way that soaking gown clung to her body, with her nipples puckered from the chill.

"It could be worse, you know," Albert said. "She could be much uglier."

"She could be much prettier, too." Roger shoved back his chair and stood up. "With *courtesy* in mind, I believe I shall see that my guests have been attended to properly. Is Dudley back yet?"

"Here, my lord!" the steward replied, rushing forward.

"Where did you put them?"

"The two new chambers in the upper hall, my lord."

"Good. Now have something to eat and get yourself dry or you'll catch your death. I have no desire to find myself another steward."

"Aye, my lord."

Ignoring the rest of his guests, Roger strode toward the stairs leading to the new upper hall, added within the past year. His castle was not a large one, but he had been expanding it since he had come of age and been confirmed as lord dependent upon swearing fealty to Baron DeGuerre.

His plans had not included marrying the half-Saxon half sister of Reginald Chilcott. To be sure, Reginald was willing to be generous to get her off his hands, but Roger didn't doubt that with his looks and reputation, he could have married a very wealthy, influential woman instead of this red-haired termagant.

Did she think him as foolish as Reginald, to be tricked by that little act of ostensible contrition? He had seen the determined, haughty look in her eyes as she came toward him in the hall. Those big green eyes of hers said everything: that she was a stubborn, arrogant creature who had been insulted and meant to let him know it. It had only been toward the last that she affected the docile woman's role.

She would soon discover that he was not so easily fooled, although he had to admit that she had been wise enough to be subtle with her criticism.

But God's teeth! She was not the type of wife he wanted. He wanted lineage, wealth, beauty and submissiveness. He wanted a wife who would understand who ruled this castle.

Of course, there would be compensations for such obedience, not the least of which would be provided by her husband's prowess in the nuptial bed. Every woman Sir Roger de Montmorency had ever made love to had said he was the best.

Mina Chilcott would have to learn that he would not countenance another such performance as she had given tonight, and the lesson might as well start immediately.

Roger took the short flight of stairs toward the upper chambers two at a time and strode along the narrow corridor, the resounding thump of his boots on the wooden floor sounding like a drumbeat heralding the start of battle.

As for Mina Chilcott's compensation, that would have to wait.

# Chapter Two

Roger rapped once on the door to his betrothed's bedchamber, then shoved it open. He had not bothered to check the preparations for this guest chamber, but a quick glance assured him that all was ready and quite comfortable, from the brazier that provided some warmth against the chill to the new tapestries on the walls and the thick coverings on the bed. He had even purchased a carpet for this room, an almost unheard-of luxury that he intended to have moved to his own bedchamber after the wedding.

Hilda stood inside. She half turned and giggled when she saw who was in the doorway. Roger looked past Hilda to encounter the frosty gaze of his bride. Clad only in her wet white shift, Mina Chilcott glared at him while she reached for her gown, which had been laid out to dry on the only chair. He had thought her soaking gown had displayed her body outrageously; he instantly realized that a wet linen shift was truly next to nothing. He could see the pink tinge of her nipples and the reddish triangle between her legs.

He suddenly realized he had never made love with a redheaded woman, and the idea was not completely distasteful to him.

Mina grabbed hold of her gown and held it against herself in a futile and late attempt at modesty. "Sir, what is the meaning of this intrusion?" she demanded.

Roger forced his expression to remain impassive as he returned his gaze to her face. His bride was not as unattractive as she had appeared before, now that she was no longer chilled. Her skin was smooth and pale, pink tinged with a blush that hid her freckles. Her drying hair no longer hung limply about her slender shoulders, but waved and curled about her heart-shaped face. Her eyes, which had looked green in the hall, appeared bluish gray in the flickering light of the candles. They dominated her features and offset the luscious fullness of her lips. Perhaps he had been too hasty in his judgment of her.

"Hilda, go below," he ordered, his tone tempered by his continuing appraisal of the woman who was to be his wife.

With a toss of her head, Hilda obeyed. However, she came much closer to him than necessary on her way to the door as if to remind him of the countless nights of mutual pleasure they had shared. Unfortunately for Hilda, he had already decided to end their liaison. For one thing, as aptly demonstrated by her departure, the serving wench was becoming far too impertinent. For another, once he vowed to be faithful to his wife, he had every intention of abiding by his pledge. His honor would not allow him to do otherwise, even if he didn't particularly care for the woman. He simply would not break any vow, for any reason.

"Sir Roger, what is the meaning of this intrusion?" Mina Chilcott repeated, her tone calmer and her eyes much more enigmatic than they had been at their first meeting, or even moments before.

Sir Roger de Montmorency was reminded that he had intended to put his betrothed firmly and forever in her place. He was used to unquestioning obedience, respect or fear, and his wife was not going to be any different. "Perhaps I came to assure myself that my servants were attending to you properly," he said. "You implied that I was somewhat remiss in my supervision."

She held the dress a little higher. "Hilda seems quite competent. In a number of ways, I suppose," the young woman finished casually, although there was a brief flicker of condemnation in her eyes that Roger did not like.

He walked toward her slowly and deliberately. "I am the master here," he said in a commanding tone that was not a shout, but deep and resonating, nonetheless. "I will do as I wish, within the bounds of honor, and it is not for you to criticize, *ever*. When you are my wife, you would do well to remember that I am used to obedience. I will accept nothing less."

"And I am used to being chastised, Sir Roger," she answered quite calmly. "For the present, I am neither your lackey nor your wife, so I ask you again, will you please have the goodness to leave?" Then, to Sir Roger de Montmorency's considerable chagrin, Mina Chilcott had the effrontery to turn her back to him.

His anger turned to shock when he saw the marred flesh above the neckline of her shift. The white, silky skin was covered with long, thin scars, as if from a lash or a switch. For a moment, he was speechless at the thought that anyone could have inflicted such damage on this woman. Any woman. "Who did that to you?" he demanded hoarsely.

"A man who wanted me to obey," she replied matter-of-factly, twisting to look at him over her shoulder. Her face was expressionless, except for her remarkable eyes. They were full of defiance, and such resilient inner strength that he could not quite believe those flashing blue gray eyes belonged to a mere woman. "Good night, Sir Roger," she said.

Astonished by what he had seen, and not quite sure what to say, Roger left the room, slamming the door behind him.

A deep shudder of released tension shook Mina's body as she slowly lowered her arms and threw the gown back over the chair. She rubbed her arms to restore some warmth after clutching the cold, wet gown. Still shivering, she stoked the coals in the brazier, fighting the memories from her past, especially the horrible years after her beloved mother's death, which always brought a chill to her.

She slipped out of her damp shift and hung it over the chair, as well. Taking the heavy coverlet from the bed, she wrapped it around herself and went to the narrow window, where she looked out at the rainy night. Clouds now completely obscured the moon, and everything beyond the nearest wall was in darkness.

This castle was not at all what she had expected, considering the awestruck way Reginald spoke of Sir Roger. Her half brother was forever reminding her what a favorite her betrothed was with the powerful Baron DeGuerre and how long the de Montmorencys had held this land. She had expected something much more impressive than this simple structure with only one round curtain wall and the interior buildings lining the walls. Indeed, when they had first entered the inner ward, she had thought they were merely in the outer wards, not the courtyard.

As she watched the moon appear at the edge of a cloud, it occurred to her that if there was anything impressive about Montmorency Castle, it was the master, not the place itself.

Sir Roger de Montmorency was not quite what she had anticipated, either. He was as vain and arrogant as any man, but in his case, not without some cause. Nor was it a surprise that he expected unwavering obedience.

She sighed softly. She was used to such expectations, which did not mean she intended to give in to them. Or to him. For too long she had been at the mercy of others. She had learned to endure in silence and to pray for the day when she would be free.

But what freedom was there for an unmarried woman? None, she had discovered after her father's death, and even less respect. She was merely a valueless commodity to be disposed of in marriage with the least trouble possible, or sent to the seclusion of a convent.

Marriage had seemed by far the lesser of two evils. As a nobleman's wife, she would at least share in the respect due her husband.

Sir Roger obviously demanded and commanded a great deal of respect, so her plans were being fulfilled in one way. However, it remained to be seen if he could earn such a response from her. Thus far, she didn't find that likely.

Still, things could be worse, she reflected as she walked back to the brazier. Sir Roger had ambition, another quality she had wanted in a spouse. It had to be ambition that would cause him to join with the Chilcotts, whose greatest asset was not wealth or power but the value of their ancient name. She was ambitious, too, or at least eager to better her lot.

She could also appreciate her future husband's self-control, perhaps better than any other noblewoman. Despite his anger, Sir Roger had not hit her. Her father would have beaten her for considerably less aggravation, but then, her father often beat her for nothing at all.

A greater mystery, perhaps, was what Sir Roger made of his bride. She had angered him, and he had understood all too well that she acted not as she truly felt in the hall below, but as might be expected of a woman in her position. It was something new to discover that somebody had seen through her deception.

She recalled the unexpected tone in Sir Roger's voice when he asked who had scarred her back. He had sounded angry, yet it was a different kind of anger, as if he wanted to punish the person responsible.

Or was it pity? She frowned and crossed her arms. She didn't want or need pity. She wanted a place in the world. And she wanted respect.

Mina went toward the bed. She surveyed the linens and lightly brushed her hand over the fine coverings. Her gaze roved over the other furnishings, simple but finely made, chosen with a discerning eye. The hour was growing late, and she suddenly realized she was exhausted. She blew out the candles and prepared to get under the covers.

Then she heard a woman's giggle and a man's low voice in the corridor. Sir Roger's voice, she thought. Curious and quite used to listening at doors to avoid future trouble, she got out of bed, drew the coverlet around herself again and opened the door a crack, peering along the corridor. Someone had taken the torch from the iron bracket outside her door and doused it in a nearby bucket of sand, so the only light was provided by another torch flickering near the spiral stairs.

Mina could discern two shapes, one a woman with her back against the wall, the other, larger one obviously a man—and obviously Sir Roger. The woman laughed, low and guttural, as she slid her slender arms up his muscular ones. ''I thought you were planning to do without," she whispered, and Mina recognized Hilda's sultry voice.

Sir Roger's bride turned away and closed the door softly, her mouth a hard, grim line.

Roger removed Hilda's hands from his shoulders. "No," he said quietly but firmly. "It's finished between us."

Hilda gasped, and even in the darkness he could see the panic in her eyes.

He suspected she had been waiting for him, to see where she stood now that he was to be married. He had no intention of punishing a woman who had pleased him by sending her away from her home. "You need have no fear," he said. "You may remain as a servant in the hall."

"I can't, my lord!" Hilda protested, starting to weep and covering her face with her hands. "She'll not allow it! She hates me already, I think. The looks she gives me! She knows about us, or guesses—and rightly, too, as you well know. I'll have to leave here!"

Roger grasped Hilda's upper arms and waited until she uncovered her tear-streaked face. He spoke slowly and deliberately, so that she would hear his sincerity. "I say that you may remain in this castle. You are a good woman, Hilda, and a fine servant. No one may force you to leave. Do you understand?" He thought of the stern condemnation he himself had received from Mina Chilcott's censorious eyes. He let go of Hilda and stepped away. "Nevertheless, you had best keep your distance from me in the future."

Hilda nodded and smiled tremulously. "I . . . I will, my lord. Thank you, my lord." A little of Hilda's usually seductive manner asserted itself. "We had some good times, didn't we, Sir Roger? If she don't treat you right—"

"I will be faithful to my wife, Hilda."

"Yes, my lord. I should have known." She sighed again as she turned to walk away. "I hope you'll be happy, my lord."

Roger didn't answer. What was there to say?

"Would you be so kind as to order an escort for me?" Mina asked Sir Roger as she joined the men at the high table the next morning to break the fast. The mass had been mercifully brief, yet something of a trial, for Father Damien mumbled and even fell asleep at one point.

A seat had been left vacant for her beside Sir Roger, she noted, which was an improvement from the previous evening. Sir Albert sat beside the empty chair, and again she was warmed by his pleasant countenance and kind smile. Reginald sat to Sir Roger's left, and seemed rather over-

whelmed by his host, to judge by the constant in-
gratiating grin on his face.

As for Sir Roger, she did not really know what
his expression might be, because she did not deign
to look at him after the first glimpse, which had
made her blush and remember all too well the last
time she had seen him, when he'd been enjoying his
lustful rendezvous with the serving wench. Apparently she was more ashamed of his conduct than he.

The unbridled arrogance of the man, to practically make love with another woman right outside
his betrothed's bedchamber door! She would be
relieved to be away from him.

"I wish to ride out today," she announced,
"since the storm has ceased. We were unable to see
the land around the castle last night in the rain and
the dark."

"I cannot waste my time riding about the countryside," Sir Roger said brusquely and not unexpectedly. "I have business to attend to."

Mina was glad the hall was not as crowded as last
night. She didn't particularly want everyone to see
the curt manner with which Sir Roger treated her.
"Of course," she answered with seeming affability. Truly, she didn't desire any company. She
wanted to get away by herself, as she often did when
she was dispirited, which had to be because of the
tiring journey in yesterday's rain and the unfamil-

iar bed, nothing else. "You must oversee the repairs to the bridge," she continued just as pleasantly, "as well as any other edifices that may have crumbled in the storm."

Hilda sauntered by the table and set a platter of bread and fruit in front of her. "And perhaps you are tired," Mina added innocently.

Sir Roger gave her a black and questioning look, and Hilda scurried away. Mina kept a sly, triumphant smile from her face as she took an apple and bit into it, enjoying the sweetness and juiciness of it.

"I will be happy to—" Sir Albert started to offer.

"I need you," Sir Roger interrupted.

"I thank you for your concern, Sir Albert," Mina said with a smile, "but I am quite comfortable going out alone." She daintily dipped her fingers in a bowl of scented water beside Sir Roger and delicately wiped them on her napkin before rising. "Good day, gentlemen. I shall look forward to your gracious company at the evening meal, when I have returned from my ride."

"I will not provide an escort," Sir Roger reiterated.

"I understood you the first time, sir," she replied evenly. She caught sight of Reginald, who was desperately shaking his head and winking as he tried to warn her to acquiesce to Sir Roger's wishes.

She could easily ignore her half brother.

Sir Roger shot a glance at Reginald, who flushed bright red and cleared his throat awkwardly. "Mina, perhaps it would be better if you were to stay here today. It was a long and difficult journey, and the rest will do you good."

"How kind of you to think of my well-being, Reginald. I appreciate it all the more for its rarity. Now I bid you a good day," she replied, curtsying with maidenly modesty.

Roger wasn't deceived. He saw her slightly stubborn smile and the hard gleam of determination in her eyes.

He recognized that look on her face. The best knights had it, for it revealed an unyielding desire to win in any situation. Inflexible fortitude was an admirable quality in a nobleman—but certainly not in a woman. There was only one kind of desire he wanted in a woman.

Then Mina Chilcott swept out of the hall without so much as a backward glance. God's blessed blood, she was like no woman he had ever met before. Thank God.

Reginald cleared his throat again. "There, you see, my lord," he said eagerly. "She can be reasonable."

"Good," Roger replied, but he was far from convinced that Mina Chilcott had any intention of obeying either him or Reginald. That smile, that superior little smile—the man who had trained him in the arts of war had always smiled like that when he expected Roger to fail, and that smile had too often proved prophetic. He had come to hate that smile of Fitzroy's very much.

"If you excuse me, my lord," Reginald said, "I have not much of an appetite this morning." He got up and wandered in the general direction of the outer door, then into the courtyard.

"If he consumes that much when he has little appetite, I fear for the contents of my larder," Roger said sarcastically.

Albert shifted in his chair. "Your betrothed has spirit, my lord," he offered. "Very stimulating, and surely suggestive of a passionate nature, too."

Roger looked at his friend with some surprise. "What's this, Albert? I haven't heard you comment on a woman in years."

"And *you* seem to be going to great effort to be unpleasant," Albert noted.

"I am the way I am," Roger replied. "If she's going to be my wife, she had better get used to me."

"I've seen you be quite charming toward other women, Roger," Albert chided gently. "I should think you would make an effort for your betrothed."

"It is precisely because she is my betrothed that there is no need for any exertion on my part. She will be in my bed on our wedding night whether she wants to be or not. Or whether I want her or not, for that matter."

"You are a heartless creature, Roger!" Albert said with very real dismay.

"I am the way I am," Roger repeated coldly, getting to his feet. If he had no heart, that was not his fault. It was God's, or fate, or the whim of nature that had taken his parents from him too soon. And it was the fault of his parents' friends, who had decided it was best that Roger go to Castle Gervais to learn the ways of knighthood while his sister Madeline was sent to a convent.

"I didn't mean to upset you," Albert said. "I just thought you could be a little friendlier to her. I've heard some things... I don't think she's had a particularly easy life."

Roger thought of the scars on Mina's back, and although to a casual observer his face would have seemed expressionless, Albert saw that his words had affected his friend.

"Very well," Roger said. "I will make an effort to be polite, if that will please you."

"It will, indeed."

Roger gave Albert the ghost of a grin as they headed to the door. "I daresay it's quite a trial shepherding Reginald."

Albert chuckled companionably.

"We had best see what damage the storm brought about," Roger said. "I am especially concerned about the mill. If the water was strong enough to ruin a bridge, it might have damaged the wheel." He halted abruptly when he looked into the yard.

Mina Chilcott, attired in a long blue cloak that made her chameleon eyes look like the sky in the first days of spring, sat upon her horse with absolutely no escort in sight. Her mount was a broken-down nag who had obviously seen better and younger days, quite a contrast to the splendid stallion Reginald rode.

Reginald hurried up behind them. "I say, Mina!" he called out nervously. "I won't give you an escort, you know."

"Don't fret, Reginald," she said with an infuriatingly cool smile directed at Roger. "Unlike some people, I have learned to do without."

Roger stared at her, very well aware that Hilda had used similar words when she had waylaid him in the corridor the previous night.

He marched toward Mina Chilcott. He would not provide an escort, and no woman—not even this one—should ride alone and unprotected. Before he could reach her, however, she kicked her horse's side and went galloping out of the gate, the beast moving with more speed than he would have thought possible.

"Stop!" Roger shouted, running a few steps after her, but she either didn't hear him, or, more likely, ignored him and rode on.

"Saddle my horse!" he called to one of the lads gawking out of the stable door, suddenly cognizant of the humiliating spectacle he had made of himself. When the boy rushed to do his bidding, Roger turned and glared at Reginald. "Your sister has seen fit to disobey both of us," he said through clenched teeth. "I am going after her and when I find her, I fully intend to make sure she understands that was *not* a wise decision!"

# Chapter Three

Mina smothered a pleased laugh as the troop of mounted men thundered past her hiding place in the grove of beech trees beside the road. She could see well enough to catch the grim expression on Sir Roger's handsome face, and the frightened one on Reginald's. He hated a pace faster than a walk, so this headlong gallop after her had to be terrifying.

Poor fellow! There was no need for Sir Roger to insist upon his presence, for she was quite sure Reginald had been compelled to go either by a direct order, or the force of Sir Roger's malevolent glare.

The other soldiers simply looked intent upon keeping up with their lord. She could well imagine the harsh words with which Sir Roger would upbraid them if they fell behind.

When the sound of the horses disappeared in the distance, Mina took off her stiffened headband and wimple and walked her horse along a narrow path

through the unfamiliar woods. The land around the
rise on which the castle stood was flat and even, but
a short distance away, the forest began, as well as
the slight swell of rounded foothills. Squirrels
scampered overhead, and she caught the occasional call of a jay nearby.

As she continued on her leisurely journey, she
realized her future home was located in very pretty
countryside. The path wound close to tended fields,
and she could hear snatches of conversation among
the peasants. They spoke of the coming harvest and
their families, and they made jokes. Sir Roger must
be a good lord, she thought, or she would hear
complaints and grumbles from people thinking
themselves unheard by anyone from the castle.

Soon she reached a babbling brook, its banks
covered with purple scabious, ladies' bedstraw and
rushes. She bent down to drink the clear and delicious water. Sitting back on her haunches, she
sighed contentedly, taking in the beauty of her sur-
roundings and her few moments of peace. Long
ago she had learned to savor such rare moments,
and to store them in her memory to recall again
when her life grew more difficult.

How many more such solitary rambles would she
enjoy? Very few, probably, unless she could convince Sir Roger that they were safe and enjoyable to
the point of being a necessity. That might be pos-

sible, although she was quite certain that Sir Roger would never see it that way. Surely he never stopped to admire a lovely, sunny summer's day, or watch the birds and squirrels preparing for the winter.

Was there anything he enjoyed simply for the pleasure it gave him? She could easily think of one thing, she realized with a frown, her mood spoiled by the remembrance of Hilda in her betrothed's arms. Yes, that no doubt gave him pleasure. But did it give him peace?

Wrapped in her thoughts, she slowly walked the horse back toward the main road, stooping periodically to pick a bouquet of wildflowers. How sweet they smelled, the various scents blending in the warm air with the odor of the thick carpet of earth and leaves beneath her feet.

A rabbit peeped cautiously out of the undergrowth, making Mina smile. Was it a mother rabbit looking for food? Or a male rabbit looking for a mate?

Suddenly the rabbit dashed across the pathway as if it had been frightened. Then Mina heard the sound of horses on the road.

As she suspected, it was Sir Roger, Reginald and the soldiers. Since she had accomplished her goal, she did not try to conceal herself.

"Mina!" Reginald called out, relief in his voice as Sir Roger gave the signal to halt. "Where have you been?"

"Picking flowers," she answered calmly, ignoring Sir Roger's glare. The other soldiers shifted nervously in their saddles. "There was no need for alarm."

Sir Roger swung down from his horse and marched toward her, his frowning lips matching his glaring black eyes. "It is dangerous for a lady to ride out alone." His forbidding gaze seemed to bore into her.

"Really, Sir Roger? Your lands are not safe? Outlaws do not tremble to hear your name?"

Roger stared at this foolish young woman with the limpid eyes who dared to imply that he could not maintain the safety of his people. "No forest is safe for a lone woman."

"Of course. How stupid of me to forget."

She went to go past him, but he grabbed her arm and pulled her close. Her horse's reins fell from her hand, and the flowers she carried in the other were crushed against his chest. "You are *not* stupid, but you *are* a lady. And if you want to be treated as one, I suggest you act like one." He pulled her even closer, so that her breasts were pressed against his hard chest. "Or would you rather I did not treat you like a lady?" he whispered huskily. "I could, you know. Do you think that simpleton Reginald would come to your aid if I dragged you off into the trees. Or perhaps that is what you would like?"

"You would not dare—"

"I dare whatever I like, my lady. This is my land, and you are to be my wife. If you do not wish to anger me again, I suggest you do as you are told."

"Or you will what? Rape me?" she demanded, her voice low so that the others could not hear, but so intense he couldn't doubt the passion and the conviction behind them.

She twisted away from him as he gaped at her, stunned by her blunt words. He had only been trying to frighten her into obedience.

"My lord, I can believe you are capable of *anything,* and if I am to act like a lady, might I suggest you act like a gentleman?" She tossed the destroyed flowers aside and crossed her arms. "You are right about Reginald. I know that as well as you do. Better, I daresay. Rest assured, Sir Roger, when we are married and in public I will be a docile, obedient wife. But do not ever try to take me against my will, because if you ever attempt to destroy the one shred of dignity I have left, you will regret it." She grabbed the trailing reins of her horse and moved to mount.

He yanked her around and her gaze darted from his strong, lean fingers on her arm to his stern face. "You are hurting me, Sir Roger."

He let go of her. She mounted quickly and spurred her horse into a gallop, heading down the road toward the castle.

Roger stalked to his waiting horse, too angry and distressed to notice the curious, astonished expressions of the others. God's blood; she had surprised him—and not just with her words.

A woman who was not afraid of him, even at his most domineering. How did she get that way? From what source did that incredible resolve and the fierceness in her glowing gray eyes come? She was undeniably shocking. Even more surprising, perhaps, was his other reaction.

He liked her. He admired her poise and her assurance. More importantly, he could respect her.

He put his hands on his saddle, ready to leap onto his stallion's back, when another response besieged him. He wanted her. The perception of his desire was nearly as shocking as its magnitude.

But there could be no denying what he felt. What he had first experienced the moment he had brought her body into contact with his. There in the woods, with the scent of flowers about her, her hair loose and unkempt and her cheeks flushed, she seemed wild and untamed. Free. Passionately free.

God's teeth, if he could but turn a portion of that passion to himself...

"I must apologize again for my sister's outrageous behavior," Reginald said. Startled, Roger glanced at the gathered men and mounted his horse. "She is an independent creature, despite my father's attempts to subdue her."

"How did he attempt it?" Roger asked as they nudged their horses into a walk. "Did he try beating her?"

"Of course," Reginald replied, obviously believing that Roger intended to use that method of correction himself. "But I am afraid it had little effect."

"I suppose he starved her, too."

"He thought fasting was good for the soul. Everybody had to, or so he said. Fortunately, my uncle took me to France and I escaped the old villain's eccentricities."

Obviously Mina had not escaped such severe eccentricities. The beatings would explain the scars. What kind of man could beat his own child so viciously?

"You...you aren't planning on calling off the wedding, are you?" Reginald asked when the castle came into view.

"No," Roger replied curtly, reflecting that it was a good thing Gaubert Chilcott was already dead, or he would be tempted to teach the fellow something about pain.

That night, Mina sat in the place of honor at Sir Roger's right hand. She was trying to concentrate on the food, but she was all too aware of the man beside her. She could smell the scent of the crushed wildflowers that lingered about his clothing, an evocative reminder of their confrontation that day.

After what had happened, she had expected to see Reginald hurrying toward her with the news that Sir Roger had decided not to marry her. Instead, her betrothed was sitting beside her as if nothing at all untoward had taken place, and Dudley had already begun preparations for the wedding feast the next day. The ceremony would be at noon outside the chapel, presided over by Father Damien.

Nor was she the only one anxious in the hall, she realized. Everyone assembled seemed to take their cue from Sir Roger, and his silence was most unnerving. She had to remember that her actions might influence his mood and thus the tone of the gathering in the hall. It was not a responsibility to be taken lightly. Nevertheless, at this particular time, she could not bring herself to speak, especially when her gaze kept being drawn to Sir Roger's right hand and the lean, sinewy fingers that had gripped her arm that morning, the slender fingers that tomorrow night would touch and perhaps caress her.

Unbidden, her gaze strayed to his handsome profile. The black-browed eyes. The straight nose. The full lips. The strong line of his jaw.

Suddenly Sir Roger turned to her. With a flushed face, she quickly looked away as he spoke, his inflection as placid as his countenance. "I have arranged to have an escort at your service whenever you wish to ride out again," he said, his voice deep and low in her ear.

"That will not be necessary," she answered, staring straight ahead.

"I am afraid I must insist."

"I thank you for your kindness, Sir Roger, but I believe I will have too much to do to allow me the pleasure of a ride anytime soon."

"I see."

Was he disappointed? A strange and unfamiliar pleasure at the thought that she could make him feel any disappointment whatsoever made her heart miss a fraction of a beat. She hadn't thought it possible this simple and quite honest refusal would have any effect on him at all. "I fear I am going to be too busy settling into my new duties and responsibilities," she explained.

"Are there any other requests you would care to make?" he asked after a moment.

"None, Sir Roger," she answered truthfully. Then she made a little smile. His lips twitched slightly, as if he wanted to return her smile but wasn't sure how—or perhaps how such a thing would be received.

For the first time since she had arrived, Mina felt that Sir Roger was not looking at her as if she were an article he had paid too high a price for, or a creature that filled him only with fury. She imagined...hoped...he was looking at her the way he usually looked at a woman he was attracted to.

The notion excited her, a flame kindling in the region of her heart and spreading outward until her whole body felt warmed by its glow. She yearned to tell him how a favorable response from him would please her, yet she could not, with all the people in the hall.

Instead, she reached out and touched his hand lightly. Instantly he pulled it back, then grabbed his goblet. His action had more rebuke in it than anything he might have said. He had reacted as if her touch were leprous.

The burning heat of shame washed over her, and she quickly returned her attention to the food, to Reginald, to Sir Albert, or to anything other than Sir Roger.

After the last of the fruit was cleared away, a minstrel and small group of musicians appeared bearing a lute, tabor, fithele and harp. Sir Roger didn't seem the type of man to find solace or enjoyment in music and, indeed, when the opening chords were struck, he appeared quite bored. She was in no mood for entertainment, either, but she gave the men her attention as if enthralled.

The minstrel was a very thin young man with a pockmarked face and straggly blond hair. Every other minstrel Mina had ever seen had been as vain as Reginald. She could only assume that this minstrel's voice would supply the beauty his visage lacked.

She discovered that she had surmised correctly about the minstrel's voice. It was deep and rich, and he infused the appropriate emotion into every word. Nevertheless, her interest flagged considerably when he began a long lay about a woeful knight trying to win the heart of his lady. The knight sounded like a dolt for persisting where he was so obviously unwelcome, and the lady seemed a vain, dishonorable creature for believing the fellow's flattery and finally giving in to his constant pleas, thereby committing adultery. If that was love, she could certainly do without it.

"My lord!" Dudley whispered, appearing at Sir Roger's elbow. "The Baron DeGuerre has arrived."

Sir Roger stood at once, mercifully cutting short the minstrel's verses, which seemed composed entirely of the knight's exclamations of his lady's perfections. "Is his chamber prepared?" he asked, with the merest hint of anxiety as he hurried to greet his overlord.

Mina looked at the table, hiding her satisfied expression as excited murmurs raced through the hall. So, even the great Sir Roger de Montmorency could be intimidated.

When the baron entered the hall and received the kiss of greeting from his host, Mina could see why he would be. The two men looked quite capable of defending Montmorency, or any castle, single-handedly.

The baron was a formidable man, with piercing, icy blue eyes, a powerful build and brown hair that, like Roger's, fell to his shoulders. He wore a long tunic of unrelieved black, with no ornamentation of any kind. Suddenly everyone in the hall looked vastly overdressed, except for Roger. Even the little bits of embroidery around the neck of her own gown seemed ostentatious.

She also noted that whatever anxiety Roger had felt before, it disappeared—or was very well hidden—when he was in the baron's presence. They seemed much more like two good friends, perhaps even brothers, than overlord and underling. The other wedding guests rose and bowed as they passed by.

Mina stood as the men approached the high table, wondering if this new gown were quite fine enough. It was the nicest one she possessed, apart from the dress she was to wear to her wedding, yet she found herself wishing she had more jewels, blond hair and no freckles, especially when the baron ran his eyes over her as if she were a mare brought to market.

She straightened her shoulders. She was not a horse, and her father's family was of higher rank and greater antiquity than the baron's. She knew exactly how the baron had risen in the world, so she would not allow herself to be dismayed by him, either.

Reginald hurried around the table and made a deep, obsequious bow. "Baron DeGuerre, I am honored to meet you at last!" he exclaimed, acting as if the baron were the king instead of an upstart born in obscurity who had fought and married his way to a higher station. "Allow me to present my sister, Lady Mina Chilcott."

The baron nodded at Reginald and stopped in front of the table. Mina made her obeisance, not once taking her eyes from the baron's face.

"Lady Mina," the baron said, his voice low and mild. There was a very shrewd look in his blue eyes, though, and she guessed the mildness was a deception.

"I am honored," she replied softly, darting a glance at Roger, whose mien was annoyingly inscrutable.

Roger continued to introduce the baron to the wedding guests, starting with Sir Albert, who had evidently met the baron before. As they made their way through the hall, Mina sighed and sat down, still watching them. So, that was the great Baron DeGuerre. He was certainly an impressive man, and one, she guessed, like Roger—used to unquestioning obedience.

Nevertheless, there was something rather sad about his eyes that for a fleeting moment had made her sense he was one of the most unhappy men she had ever seen.

However, the baron's troubles were of considerably less importance to her than her own, and when the men returned to the high table, she soon felt out of place and very lonely. She didn't know the people they spoke of, or the places they had been, so she rose and excused herself.

Sir Roger didn't seem to notice.

* * *

Roger was not quite drunk, even though he had consumed several goblets of wine, and he wanted to be. Usually he was quite proud of his ability to drink without getting stupid or sleepy, but tonight he wanted to drink himself to oblivion even if that meant embarrassing himself in front of the baron.

He had to do something to drive Mina Chilcott out of his thoughts. He should be listening to the baron and his news of the doings of the court and other nobles, but her one light touch had nearly driven him mad with desire.

He should not be remembering how lovely she had looked in the woods, or how much he had wanted her. He should not be envisioning Mina naked beneath her coverings, or trying to decide what he should do first on his wedding night. He should not be thinking of her unyielding pride as she had stood before the baron, unwavering. Unafraid. Worthy in every way to be a nobleman's wife.

At least Reginald, that fawning, embarrassing dolt, had finally stumbled off to his chamber, one arm draped around the ever-helpful Hilda. Where had Hilda been during the evening meal? Not that he had noticed her absence particularly, until she had suddenly appeared after Mina had retired. Was she afraid of Mina? By God, she should be. Mina Chilcott jealous would probably be a sight to see.

Would she ever care enough about *him* to get jealous?

"Falkes de Bréauté's mercenaries continue to behave like untamed beasts," the baron continued. "I think the king will have to get rid of the man somehow, although—Roger?"

"Baron?"

"Forgive me, Roger," the baron said indulgently. His eyes, however, blazed with irritation, which got Roger's undivided attention immediately. "I was forgetting this was the night before your wedding. Perhaps I should stop telling you the news and allow you to retire."

"My apologies, Baron," Roger said, instantly and truly contrite. "I was listening."

The baron nodded, and his vexation seemed to evaporate. "Be that as it may, your wedding is tomorrow, and I have kept you here far too long. This news can keep." The baron moved conspiratorially closer. "She is quite different from Reginald, isn't she?"

"Yes."

"God's blood," the baron said, shifting and leaning comfortably against the back of the chair, "I'm glad of it. Reginald's a harmless enough fellow, but I couldn't imagine living with him. She is a shapely wench, isn't she? I must confess that red hair took me by surprise. I can only surmise she has a temper to match."

"I believe so, my lord," Roger acknowledged.

"Well," the baron said, rising and stretching his muscular arms over his head, "if anyone can handle a tempestuous woman, Roger, it would be you." He looked shrewdly at the younger man. "If you don't want her, you have only to tell me. I have discovered that the Chilcotts' property is not what I had been led to believe."

It occurred to Roger that the baron's second wife, who had been some years older than the baron, had recently died. Although Roger admired Baron DeGuerre, he knew the man was a clever schemer who might have some unknown reason for wanting Mina Chilcott for himself.

That idea did not please Roger at all. "I have made an agreement with Reginald," he said. "I intend to keep it."

The baron smiled, a truly warm expression of satisfaction he rarely bestowed. "Good. I believed you to be a man of your word, and now I know it is so. A long and happy life to you!"

"Thank you, baron," Roger said with great politeness. Inside, he was seething with rage. The baron had no need to test his honor, not after the years Roger had spent in his service, and after he had agreed to tie himself to a useless fool like Chilcott with a marriage that the baron had proposed. Baron DeGuerre should know that for Sir Roger de Montmorency, disloyalty was more terrible than any of the mortal sins, and worthy of the most ghastly hell imaginable.

"I did not mean to offend you, Roger," the baron said sincerely. He looked down at his own powerful hands, which had fought so many times and killed so many men. "I was thinking of your happiness. If you would rather not marry Mina Chilcott, I will not take it amiss."

"Are *you* interested . . . ?" Roger let his deliberately tranquil voice trail off suggestively.

"Gracious God, no! I have no wish to marry again," the baron responded with unquestionable sincerity.

"I have no complaint to make about the arrangements," Roger said, his suspicions allayed, though he was somewhat unhappy for his overlord. Baron DeGuerre's two marriages had given him wealth and status, but perhaps, Roger thought, perhaps that was all.

What was wrong with that? What other reasons could a man have for marrying? "I do have one cause for some trepidation," Roger said in a more jovial tone. "I fear that on my wedding night, my bride may be harder to pierce than my shield."

The baron chuckled. "I do not doubt your ability to kindle passion in even the coldest maiden."

Roger raised his goblet in acknowledgement, and the two men shared a companionable laugh.

They did not see Mina, standing on the stairs in the shadows, a deep frown on her face.

Unable to sleep, Mina had waited for the noise in the hall to cease. The cacophony had died down, but she had not heard Reginald and wondered what was happening to keep him below. Then she thought she heard Hilda's giggle. She had tried to tell herself it didn't matter what Sir Roger was doing, or with whom. They were not married yet. Even then, many men had dalliances with women other than their wives.

She had looked out the door anyway, to see Hilda supporting an obviously drunk Reginald and helping him into his room. Mina tarried a little longer and soon saw Hilda leave Reginald's chamber and go below. Perhaps looking for Sir Roger?

Again Mina tried to convince herself that it didn't matter, and again she didn't quite succeed. She crept down the steps, listening carefully. When she drew near the hall, she realized that most of the guests had also retired for the night. Hilda was nowhere to be seen, nor the ubiquitous Dudley. Only Sir Roger and the baron were awake and talking together at the high table.

She had turned, prepared to go back to her chamber, when she caught mention of her name. Slipping into the shadows, she stayed and heard them talking about her as if she were no more than any common wench. To Mina, they seemed like grotesquely leering jesters making sport at her expense.

What a silly little fool she had been for even starting to think that Roger de Montmorency might be any different from every man she had ever known. She had been a dolt to feel anything for him. He was like all the others.

She began to walk back to her chamber, recalling what she had overheard. The idea that Sir Roger could make her swoon with ecstasy without even trying was enough to make her grind her teeth in anger. The boastful, vain, pompous creature! No doubt all the women he had made love with so far had been like Hilda, serving wenches or peasants who believed there was something special about a nobleman, or who wanted something in return, like money or advancement.

Well, she knew better. Noblemen were men first, and seldom noble. If her betrothed thought he could just crook his finger and find Mina Chilcott waiting patiently in the nuptial bed, he would soon learn otherwise.

# Chapter Four

Sir Roger de Montmorency's wedding day dawned gray and unseasonably cool, with a heavy drizzle and chill breezes that made it seem as if an October day had somehow found its way to July by mistake.

"What are you going to do?" Albert asked the groom, who stood at the door of the hall staring gloomily out into the inner ward. "You could have the blessing in the chapel rather than outside the doors, I suppose."

"I suppose," Roger answered. "But the chapel is too small. All the guests won't be able to go inside, and those who do not fit will probably feel insulted." He sighed deeply as Dudley bustled about the hall behind him, admonishing the servants or mumbling to himself. "God's wounds," Roger snarled, "this wedding is too much trouble. And it's costing a fortune, too."

"Chilcott's paying for most of it," Albert reminded him. "And the baron's pleased."

"He should be," Roger muttered.

"She's not as bad as all that."

Roger didn't respond except to close the door and turn around just as Hilda sauntered by. She gave him a tentative smile. "Has Lord Chilcott managed to crawl out of his bed?" he asked the maidservant, mindful of the goblets of wine the young man had ingested, and grateful that he wasn't the one paying for it.

"Aye, my lord," Hilda answered with a throaty chuckle. "But the poor fellow looks like a corpse."

"And his sister?"

"She's not come out of her chamber, and I don't think she intends to until the wedding. The door's locked and she's not letting anybody in. Says she wants to be alone. To pray. I, um, didn't think I should wait."

Roger had no idea what Lady Mina was doing, and he was in no humor to try to decipher her mood. "See that Lord Chilcott is well cared for. I don't want him too sick to attend the ceremony."

"Aye, my lord." Another less cautious smile, and Hilda was gone.

"If he can't drink well, he shouldn't drink at all," Roger remarked grimly.

"Not everyone has your capacity, Roger."

"Then he should have gone to bed, like you."

"What do you suppose the bride is doing?"

"What does it matter, as long as she's at the blessing on time."

Albert cleared his throat deferentially. "What are you going to do about Hilda? It's well known that you two have been rather intimate."

"So what of that?"

"So you're getting married today. I don't think your bride will appreciate the knowledge."

"I don't care what she thinks. Besides, it's finished."

"Perhaps it would be better if you were to send Hilda to one of your smaller estates, at least for the time being."

Roger gave Albert a disgruntled look. "I think I'm capable of making my own decisions."

"Very well," Albert said with a shrug. "Do as you wish."

"I intend to." Roger eyed his friend. "For a man who has never married, you seem to be quite adept at dispensing advice to the prospective groom."

When Roger saw the torment in his friend's eyes, he regretted his hasty words. He knew the sad story of Albert's youth and the reason he looked far older than he actually was, and he realized he had been cruel to speak to Albert in such a way.

Rather than admit he had acted cruelly, however, he said, "If the weather doesn't clear, we'll have the ceremony in the hall. It can be decorated early, I suppose."

"Would you like me to tell Dudley?" Albert offered, and Roger was relieved to see that apparently all was forgiven.

"No. Let's wait awhile. In the meantime, I'll make sure the guests' men and animals are being well treated."

"As long as you're not late for the wedding," Albert said.

Although Albert's tone was innocuous enough, Roger slanted him a suspicious look. "I won't be," he said firmly before he marched from the hall.

When Hilda and Aldys, one of the older and more experienced maidservants, arrived to help Mina dress for the wedding, they were surprised to see the bride sitting serenely in the small chair. She was already attired in a lovely gown of rich, dark green velvet girdled with a supple belt of bronze links and delicately embroidered about the neck and long dangling cuffs with fine gold thread. Beneath the gown she wore an undertunic of thin golden silk. Her thick, wavy hair was brushed and ornamented with a slender circlet of gold. In her hands she held a fine coverlet of embroidered linen.

Hilda and Aldys glanced uncertainly at each other, wondering if they were going to be chastised for being tardy.

"This should go to my lord's bedchamber," Lady Mina announced, nodding at the coverlet. She pointed at a silver carafe standing on the table nearby. "And that wine, too. They are marriage gifts from my relatives."

"My lady," Hilda said, "forgive us for not coming sooner." She bit her lip and wiped her perspiring palms on her homespun gown, for she knew, despite Sir Roger's guarantee, that she should still be wary of Sir Roger's wife. "We were busy with the preparations below and did not know you were waiting for us, and—"

Lady Mina held up her slender hand, and Hilda was quite taken aback to see how work worn it was. Why, this fine lady had hands like a scullery maid. She was no pampered, spoiled person, Hilda thought, impressed, and Lady Mina's next words confirmed her estimation of her new mistress. "I prefer to dress myself, not being used to maidservants. Is Lord Chilcott well enough to attend the blessing?"

"Yes, my lady," Hilda answered softly and with true respect, taking the coverlet. It was very soft and she resisted the urge to rub her cheek on it.

"Good. Go now, and fetch me when it's time for the ceremony."

"If you're sure you don't need any help..."

"I am quite sure I have everything prepared," Lady Chilcott answered, her eyes on the carafe that Aldys hurried to pick up.

When Hilda and Aldys left the chamber, they paused and looked at each other. "What do you make of her?" Aldys asked. "She didn't look angry."

"No, she didn't," Hilda replied thoughtfully. "She's a deep one, she is. Did you see her hands?"

"She's done some work with them, that's for sure, and not just sewing," Aldys said solemnly.

"I think I'm going to like her."

"She hasn't had you sent away yet, at least."

"Why should she?" Hilda demanded with more bravado than she felt.

Aldys gave her friend a skeptical frown as they went up the spiral stairs to the tower bedchamber. "You know why."

"She needn't know about that. Besides, those days are done with," Hilda replied.

"I wouldn't want her angry at me," Aldys remarked forcefully.

"Sir Roger rules here, not her," Hilda said as she pushed open the door of Sir Roger's large bedchamber and quickly laid the coverlet where Lady

Mina had directed, a slight sigh escaping her lips.
The linen didn't reach all the way across the plump
feather bed.

Aldys, who had never been in the room before,
moved much slower and took her time looking
around.

The walls were plain, undressed stone. There
were no tapestries, although there were hooks, in-
dicating that tapestries might be hung there in the
colder weather. A huge chest with a painting de-
picting Daniel in the lion's den stood in one corner, a bronze brazier was in the other, and in the
middle of the room was a round table and one
heavy carved chair. There was only one other item
of furniture in the room, and that was the im-
mense bed, with tall posts carved to look like trees
covered in vines, and thick bed curtains surround-
ing it.

"Come," Hilda said, giving the coverlet a final
look. "Dudley will be having seven fits if we're not
back soon."

Aldys, still overwhelmed by the size of the bed,
only nodded in response.

Several minutes later, Reginald Chilcott knocked
softly on the door to Mina's bedchamber. The bride
herself opened it, attired in the wedding finery that
he had given her as part of his wedding gift. If Mina

had her way, she probably would have worn any old rag, despite the presence of numerous noble guests and Baron DeGuerre. Her hair, loose and adorned with the thin circlet, framed her unusual face in a most becoming manner.

He noticed as he entered that she was quite alone. "Where are the maidservants?"

"I sent them away. Is it time?" Mina asked, neither her face nor her voice betraying anything except mild interest.

"Nearly," he replied, not sure what to make of her. He hadn't been able to fathom her since he had arrived from France to find this decisive, stern woman in place of the wistful child he had known. "You look...you look quite lovely," he said encouragingly.

She gave him a skeptical frown as she sat down on the only chair.

"No, Mina, I mean it. I really do. That gown suits you perfectly. You...you look like your mother in that color."

Mina smiled at Reginald, overdressed and with his hair overcurled as usual. She wasn't sure what was most ridiculous—the long, lavish plume on his brightly embroidered cap, the incredibly bright color of his green tunic or his parti-colored hose. And yet, as he stood there excited and eager to see her pleased with his gifts, she saw again the bewildered, insecure boy being taken away to France with his uncle to avoid any taint from his father's Saxon wife. She had not been very old then, but she remembered that of all her half brothers, Reginald was the only one who had ever said a kind word to her. "Thank you for providing it."

"That's not what I meant," Reginald answered sincerely as he stood awkwardly by the door. "I always liked your mother, you know. The first time Father brought her home, she kissed me and said she hoped I would be her friend. Her voice sounded like music. I was quite sorry to say farewell to her when my uncle took me away with him." He came a little closer, toying with the heavily decorated leather belt around his waist. "I know it wasn't easy for you, with my brothers and sisters. I'm sorry I wasn't able to help. But, Mina, I think Sir Roger will be a good husband for you. I truly do."

Mina rose and went to the window. "He'll be a *husband,* and more than that, I don't expect."

"He's not the cold brute he seems, really. He was most kind after those horrible ruffians left us in the woods. He was even polite to the abbot who was captured with us, and I assure you, that was no small feat. I mean, for a man of God, you should have heard him! He acted as if Sir Roger had been personally responsible for his discomfort. And it was Sir Roger who suggested this marriage, you know."

"I thought it was the Baron DeGuerre."

"No!" Reginald came a little closer. "He suggested only that I marry Madeline de Montmorency. It was Sir Roger who came up with the alternative."

"He only thought of it to please the baron," she said.

"Mina, you mustn't take such a cold view of this. I mean, if Sir Roger didn't want to marry you, he wouldn't. He and the baron are such good friends, I'm quite certain the baron wouldn't hold it against him if he changed his mind."

"You're forgetting the value of our family name, Reginald. The baron needs your goodwill as much as you seek his."

Reginald did not look convinced.

"I suppose the baron will be trying to make another match for you one day soon," she said matter-of-factly, trying to alter the course of the conversation.

"What?"

"You would be a great prize, Reginald." Not for a woman like herself, perhaps, who despised weakness, but he was a harmless, good-hearted fellow, and many a woman could do worse.

"I'm ... I'm not ready after what happened last time," he stammered.

In the next moment, however, he was pensively fingering one of his carefully arranged curls, and she had to suppress an indulgent smile. "Well, I would take care some woman doesn't try to seduce you into marriage."

"I will," he answered solemnly. Then he blushed and cleared his throat. "Since you've raised, um, the subject, Mina, is there anything you need to know ... about the wedding night?"

"I know what is expected of me," she answered just as solemnly.

Reginald looked very relieved. "Well, that's good. Excellent."

She might have been tempted to smile again at her sibling's comical discomfort, except for the sudden vision of a naked Sir Roger waiting for her in bed, his dark eyes watching her. Her pulse started to race, and it took some deep breaths to restore her calm.

"When do you return to France?" she asked.

"Oh, that," he said. "Well, as a matter of fact, Mina, Sir Roger's offered to let me stay here for a while. Southern France is so hot this time of year, and the travel would be so uncomfortable, I've agreed. And—" he lowered his voice and knit his brows together with genuine concern "—I do want to make sure he's kind to you. I've heard how Father was near the end, and I think I owe you that much.''

Mina suddenly felt rather remorseful for the unflattering things she had thought about Reginald in the past. ''Thank you,'' she said quietly.

There was a loud rap at the door, and Hilda's head appeared. ''It's time, my lady,'' she announced solemnly. Her gaze ran over Reginald. ''My lord,'' she said with some awe.

''Well, Mina, shall we?'' Reginald asked, holding out his arm to escort her to her wedding.

''Yes, Reginald,'' Mina replied, and with a purposefully blank face and a heart lacking any expectation of true marital felicity, she went.

# Chapter Five

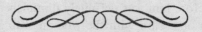

Roger surveyed his hall while taking small sips of the expensive wine imported from Agincourt. He was glad that the weather had cleared enough to allow the wedding ceremony to be held outside the chapel. Everyone had been able to see the bride and groom as they stood in front of the doors and pledged their troth, albeit barely looking at each other. For his part, Roger's gaze had been fastened firmly on doddering Father Damien, who seemed blissfully unaware that the couple he was joining in holy matrimony didn't seem particularly thrilled by the idea.

At least the guests appeared to be enjoying the celebratory meal. Dudley had compelled the cooks to outdo themselves. Every dish of meat had a special sauce, and many smelled of an extravagant use of spices. The bread was wonderful, the fruit as fresh as could be, and the wine the best.

The decorations in the hall had been enhanced, too, with more flowers and linens. Reginald had provided a multitude of candles, so that the large room would continue to be brightly lit as the evening wore on.

Unfortunately, Roger's pleasure in regarding the scene before him was definitely diminished by his growing obsession with the woman sitting beside him, now his wife.

He had expected his bride to be a vain, foolish woman of no particular beauty. He had anticipated finding his wedding ceremony no more exciting than any trade arrangement, and his wedding feast to be simply an expensive extension of the transaction. He had thought that he would take more pleasure in the baron's company than anyone else's, and find his new wife's presence less distracting than that of a horsefly.

Instead, he had discovered that Mina Chilcott was quite unlike any other woman he had ever met. As she sat beside him tonight, he couldn't help noticing how the green gown she was wearing enhanced her eyes and brought out the subtle purity of her skin beneath the few freckles, or how the gold circlet emphasized the golden highlights in her astonishing red hair.

His first impression of Mina, though, which had been rapidly corroborated, was of her fortitude and astounding inner strength, not usually qualities that excited one about a woman.

Tonight, it dawned on Roger de Montmorency that to win Mina Chilcott's respect would be no common thing, and to have her desire him would be worth any effort it might take. He didn't doubt that later, when they were alone in bed and he caressed her with his expert hands, he would bring her such ecstasy as she had never known. Yes, he would earn both her respect and her desire. More than that, he didn't need or want.

Harboring such thoughts, Roger slipped into a companionable mood. Now he could overlook Father Damien's mumbling of the blessing outside the chapel that had made him a married man, although at the time he had ground his teeth with frustration. Instead, he remembered the moment he had put the ring on Mina's slender finger and repeated Father Damien's words. She had not trembled or blushed, but thrust her hand toward him with a vigor he found exciting. No timid wench, Mina, and he hoped she would do everything with such enthusiasm.

Glancing at her seated to his right, he noticed that she was not eating, despite the plethora of fine foods placed before her. Well, he supposed many brides lacked that kind of an appetite.

"A bountiful feast," the baron, who was seated on Roger's left, remarked, as if he had been reading his host's mind. "You're not eating much."

Startled, Roger looked at his own trencher and saw the baron's observation was not without merit.

"I regret I cannot stay beyond today," the baron said.

"I, too, my lord," Roger responded.

"Reginald told me you have invited him to remain with you?"

Both men turned and looked to the other side of Mina, where Reginald Chilcott was already displaying every sign of getting drunk. "I'm glad," the baron said quietly. "He's a nonsensical young man, but I have hopes he might improve under the proper supervision."

"I've invited him to stay until after Michaelmas."

"Excellent. And then he plans to return to France?"

"I believe so."

"Try to persuade him to stay in England over the winter. As I said, I have hopes for Reginald, but I am not so sanguine about his brother, Herwin, whom I understand is getting quite a reputation for viciousness." Roger remembered Mina's scars and wondered if this Herwin was responsible for any of them.

Hilda sauntered over to the table and began to clear away the trenchers and platters, moving very slowly, with her eyes demurely lowered. She took a very long time when it came to the remains of the baron's food, and as she finally moved off, the baron turned to Roger with a questioning look.

"What's her name?"

"Hilda, my lord."

"Is she married?"

"No, my lord." By now, Roger was very aware that Mina was watching them, and that she had been watching Hilda, too.

"Send her to me later."

Hilda overheard the baron's order and stood motionless, her face pale and her eyes wide. Roger knew Hilda enjoyed being pursued, once she had made her desires known, but this blunt command was not the same. The baron's order made Hilda look like a common whore and Roger feel like a pander. Still, this was the baron....

Mina, her green-gray eyes flashing with what could only be anger, broke into the men's conversation. "Baron DeGuerre," she began softly so that only those closest could hear, yet so firmly that there could be no mistaking her outraged feelings, "if you would care for sport, I suggest you find a brothel. My home is no such place, and I will not allow any man to treat it like one."

The baron's eyes narrowed and Roger waited with bated breath, too shocked and angry to speak. No one had ever, *ever*, dared speak to the baron in such a manner in all the years Roger had known him, not even those nobles closest to the king. Although he quite agreed with Mina, he wasn't sure this was the appropriate response to the powerful Baron DeGuerre's command.

Fortunately, the baron did not seem overly annoyed as he rose slowly and took Mina's hand in his. "Forgive me, my lady. It was not my intention to offer you an insult." With great deliberation, he kissed her hand—and Roger was suddenly, absolutely convinced the baron wanted Mina.

God's blood, he himself had barely touched her, and she was his own wife! But that look in the baron's eyes—Roger had seen it before, and he knew what it meant. Baron DeGuerre lusted after Mina even more than he had for Hilda!

To think he had idolized this man, given him all the respect due a king, only to have the lustful, base villain dare to look at his wife that way....

The sly speculation in the baron's eyes disappeared with a rapidity that made Roger question its original existence.

The baron glanced at Roger, who, though somewhat relieved, had to struggle to keep his face impassive. "If you will excuse me, Roger," the baron said with a far too astute expression, "I have a long journey to one of my more northern estates tomorrow, so I shall retire." His gaze shifted to Mina. "Alone, my lady."

In a small show of defiance, Roger took his time getting to his feet as the baron made a bow to Mina. Then, to Roger's even greater astonishment, the baron smiled at his wife with what seemed like brotherly affection. Perhaps that had not been lust at all in the baron's eyes but, incredible as it might seem, simple admiration. "I envy you your obvious good fortune, Roger."

"I thank you, Baron DeGuerre," the groom replied, thankful he had not voiced his earlier objections.

Everyone rose and bowed as the baron strode out of the hall. Roger sat down heavily and turned to Mina, who remained standing. He didn't know what to say, although he had every intention of remarking upon her unladylike brazenness. Not tonight, perhaps. Tomorrow would do well enough.

"I believe I, too, shall retire, my lord," she said flatly.

Roger had planned on remaining in the hall for the lavish entertainment that Dudley had arranged and Reginald paid for. However, he had never liked either minstrels, with their ridiculous fantasies of love, or dancing, and there was the nuptial bed awaiting, so he was quick to stand before she moved away. "Good night, everyone," he said loudly. "Stay and enjoy the music. My wife and I are going to go to bed."

Some in the hall gave each other knowing looks. Several of the soldiers raised their cups in a silent salute. A few of the noblewomen, and not just the younger ones, sighed softly.

Filled with a growing sense of excitement and anticipation and quite ready to forgive his new wife's insolence—at least for one night—Roger grabbed Mina, lifted her into his arms and carried her from the hall.

Whatever Mina had expected at the end of the wedding feast, it certainly had not included being swept up into Sir Roger de Montmorency's arms and carried off like a piece of baggage, or with several of the wedding guests cheering like an unruly mob of peasants in the marketplace.

But they were *not* peasants, and she was not some peasant wench. She was a noblewoman from a more important family than many of those gathered in the hall.

Afraid of falling, she clung to Sir Roger tightly as he took the stairs two at a time, until she realized that she seemed to weigh no more than a piece of cloth to him. He had to be very strong. Extremely aware of the powerful arms around her, she struggled to breathe normally and was relieved when he finally reached the topmost chamber in the tower adjoining the hall. He kicked the door open and then set her down. Slowly. With a meaningful smirk on his darkly handsome face.

She still couldn't breathe properly, which was quite absurd.

"Don't be afraid," he said quietly, and then he smiled. A superior smile. A vastly knowledgeable smile.

She stepped away and turned, spying the carafe of wine on the small table. Then it was her turn to smirk, and be thankful that she had taken care of her sick father. From a necessary habit of frugality, she had kept the remainder of the sleeping potion the alchemist had prepared for him. It had little taste, and the strength of the fine wine should easily mask it. "Would you care for some wine?" she asked, approaching the table and reaching for one of the goblets.

"If you will join me," he replied, coming close to her. Much too close. His proximity made her hands shake as she poured the wine into both goblets. With a tremulous smile, she held one out to him.

His hand brushed hers as he took it. Quickly she stepped away. Roger picked up the other goblet and gave it to her, saying, "Please, my lady. You look as if you need it."

She pretended to sip the wine, and watched carefully as Roger downed a large gulp. "This is very good," he commented.

"It is a gift from Reginald."

He set down the goblet. "Come here, wife."

*When would the drug take effect?* she wondered desperately. It had worked quickly on her father, but he had been old, thin and ill. Perhaps she had used too little.

Roger reached out and took hold of her goblet, setting it down beside his. "I said, come here, wife." He grabbed her hand and pulled her close, so that she was pressed up against his muscular chest.

She couldn't look at him and didn't know what to do. She had little experience of men in general, and none of men trying to bed her. Was she supposed to feel this way, her heart pounding, her legs weak, her body hot? Frightened and excited at the same time?

He ran his strong, slender hands up her arms, then tilted her chin so that she had to look up into his face and his intense, hungry eyes. "You don't have to fear me tonight, Mina. I will be gentle with you."

How many other virgins had he said that to? How many other women had he taken into his bed?

Did it matter?

Then he kissed her. Gently, tenderly, as if he cared for her.

Mina had never been kissed in her life, either. Indeed, she had never known a gentle touch of any kind since her mother's death when she had been but five years old. At once, a flood of emotions poured over her—surprise, delight, exhilaration—then all were swamped with a single devastating fear.

He was making her weak.

She had vowed that she would *never* let anyone make her feel weak and helpless ever again.

Mercifully he pulled away, a confused and uncertain look on his face as he shifted slightly and put a hand to his forehead. He walked slowly to the bed as if he were on the deck of a ship, and sat on the bed's edge. "I don't...I feel ..."

"Are you ill?" she asked.

"Help me with my boots," he replied dully.

Slowly she went toward him and bent down to take hold of one of his feet. Suddenly he grabbed hold of her arms and yanked her into the bed, then rolled so that his weight was on her and she couldn't move. His lips crushed hers, and his hands fumbled with the lacings of her gown.

What was he doing? What was happening? Why was he being so rough? Did he suspect?

She could smell the wine on his breath, knew he had drunk from the goblet. Unsure of what to do, she could only lie still, submissive, convinced her plan was a failure and hoping it would be over soon. She would not struggle. She would not protest.

Hot tears stung her eyes as he continued to tear at the lacings impatiently. One hand reached inside her bodice to caress her roughly.

Then he gave a low moan and was still, his body a dead weight on top of hers.

For a long moment, Mina could only lie panting heavily, relief slowly replacing her terror. Afterward she cautiously eased herself out from under her husband's slumbering body and stood, looking down at him.

The great Sir Roger de Montmorency, brought low by a woman. How vast was her satisfaction, until she remembered the response his kiss had inspired. She hadn't guessed a simple touching of the lips could affect her so.

Perhaps it was only because it was the first time she had experienced a kiss that she had enjoyed his embrace. Roger certainly hadn't felt anything approaching her awe, not to judge by his subsequent loutish behavior. Maybe that was typical of grooms on their wedding night.

Mina didn't know, and she didn't care to find out. He had bragged to the baron of his manly prowess, and she had set out to destroy that overweening male pride, to prove that she was more clever than he, and she wasn't finished yet.

She went to the table, took the carafe of wine and poured the remainder out the window. With more haste she emptied both goblets there, too. She went to the bed and started to disrobe her husband, going carefully at first, then with less gentleness when it was clear he was not going to wake with every movement. Finally he was naked.

Feeling somewhat guilty but more curious, Mina allowed herself to look at her husband's body. Again she noticed that he was extremely well built, with powerful shoulders tapering to a narrow waist. His long, lean legs were no doubt developed from years of riding and hunting. As for the other parts of his body, she had little with which to compare, but she would not be surprised if he felt qualified to brag about that, too.

She went around the bed and drew back the covers, exposing the clean white linen. Taking Roger's dagger, she pricked her finger and squeezed out a few drops of blood, watching bright red fall onto pure white. Then, she shoved Roger under the covers and pulled them over him.

She stood beside the bed and wiggled out of her torn dress, reflecting that although she hated to see such a pretty garment destroyed, it was in a worthy cause. She crumpled it up and tossed it across the room. With even more regret, she took hold of the neck of her silk tunic and jerked, tearing it, too. Going to one of the goblets, she dipped her fingers into the small bit of wine left and rubbed some spots on her arm, staining the skin so that it looked like purpling bruises.

Her preparations finished, she sat in the chair to wait until Roger awoke.

Roger moaned softly and rolled over in the bed. His head hurt as if he had been trampled by a horse. Several horses. Big destriers, too. What had happened? Wine had never affected him like this before.

He ran his hand over the bed. Where was Mina... his wife. He had vague yet pleasant memories of kissing her last night. Yes, a gentle, delicate kiss to lessen her anxiety. That was what he had meant it to be. He had expected her response to be in keeping with what he already knew of her—cold, unfeeling, as if performing nothing more than a necessary duty.

Instead, to his surprise, her reaction had been tentative and vulnerable. Absolutely virginal, but not without more than a hint of passion. A completely breathtaking sensation of genuine desire had come over him. He had been shocked by that, too, so astounded he had felt light-headed and had to sit.

Once safely on the bed, he had looked at her again, expecting to see that virginal innocence in her eyes. Instead, he had perceived a calculated expectation there, a shrewdness that made him certain the emotion of the first kiss had been a fraud.

Then he had recalled the way she spoke to the baron, his overlord. Was it her intention to rule here? To take command, starting in the bedchamber? He had decided at once that must never happen.

So he had called her to him and kissed her again, forcefully. And then . . . and then . . . everything seemed a blank in his memory.

Slowly and cautiously, he opened his eyes. The first thing he noticed was Mina's wedding dress, a disheveled heap on the floor opposite the bed, with her obviously torn shift beside it.

Then he saw Mina sitting in the chair, her hair covering her face and her head leaning against her hand as if she had slept in that position. Her feet were bare, the nails tinged blue from the cold floor.

She wore a gown that he had not seen before, a plain and simple blue one with long, tight sleeves.

"Mina?" he asked hoarsely, shifting to a sitting position and realizing he was quite naked beneath the sheets.

She slowly turned to him, a questioning look in her bluish gray eyes and a frown on her full lips. God's holy rood, he must have been mad, imagining that initial maidenly yet passionate response to his kiss. "Yes?" she inquired defiantly.

"What time of day is it?"

"Dawn."

"Why aren't you in bed?"

"Because *you* are there."

There wasn't loathing in her voice, or indeed any strong emotion at all, which made her simple, unexpected reply worse. It was as if only an idiot would welcome sharing his bed, and perhaps other things, as well. "It's my bed, and now it's yours," he replied, trying not to sound annoyed.

"You hurt me," she said flatly.

Maybe she was merely upset because of the perfectly normal consequences of losing her virginity. "The pain was not so very bad, was it?" he asked not unkindly, quite certain that even if he had been blind drunk, his skill would still have made her wedding night bliss.

"Which one?" she asked sarcastically.

He sat up a little straighter. "I'm referring to the...to the loss of your maidenhead," he said, feeling an unfamiliar discomfort at having to discuss the subject.

"That is not what I was referring to." She shoved the sleeves of her gown upward and he saw purple bruises.

"God's wounds!" he gasped, truly appalled. "I've never hurt a woman in my life!"

"Perhaps knowing I was your legal wife made a difference," she observed, pulling her sleeves back down. "I am going to go to mass, where I will pray for you."

He got out of bed, noticing the drops of blood on the linen as he did so. The marriage must have been consummated, and apparently he had been a wretched brute. "I don't want your prayers. I was simply acting like any husband would after your insolence to my overlord," he lied defensively. He saw his own garments scattered about the floor and yanked on his chausses.

Her lip curled scornfully. "Baron DeGuerre was a guest in my house, and if you don't care if he respects your home, *I* do. I am not so blinded by admiration that I don't see his arrogance."

"If I admire him, it is because he is deserving of it."

"Is he? This man who treats your servant as his whore, and who dares to do so at your wedding feast—this man is worthy of your complete devotion?"

"I have sworn my allegiance to him." Roger tugged his tunic over his head.

"Have you sworn away your judgment, too, then?"

"No!" he growled as he put on his belt.

"Neither did I when I made my marriage vows. I am mistress of this castle now, and I will be respected, by everyone. Including you, Sir Roger de Montmorency. And with that in mind, I tell you, if you touch me again as you did last night, you will rue it."

Roger grabbed his boots and shook them at her. "I am the master here, woman, and you had best take care not to forget that! And if anyone rues anything, it is I who rue agreeing to marry you." He came close, standing nearly nose to nose with her. "Rest assured, since the marriage is already consummated, I will not touch you again—until and when I am ready to. Then you had best submit, Lady Mina *de Montmorency,* because I will not allow you to refuse!"

Still holding his boots, Roger marched from the room.

## Chapter Six

Slumping onto the last stair at the bottom of the tower, Roger shoved his bare feet into his boots. The action made his head throb, and with a disgruntled sigh, he rubbed his temples.

"What's this?" Albert said, getting up from his place on a nearby bench where he had obviously slept. "Do my eyes deceive me, or has Sir Roger de Montmorency finally been defeated by a goblet of wine?"

"It must have been that imported wine of Reginald's," Roger growled in response.

Albert came closer. "Are you all right? You sound sicker than Bredon's old dog. The poor thing died last night—and you look like you should have. I didn't think you found your bride that attractive."

"Where the devil *is* Bredon, anyway?" Roger asked. He hadn't noticed the huntsman in the hall last night. However, he had not been paying strict attention to the guests, other than the baron. He had heard of the dog's illness, and should have expressed some concern. Bredon was the finest huntsman in the land, partly because he doted on his dogs as if they were his children.

"He's in the kennel, I expect."

"He'll mope in there all day if I let him. Some hunting might do both of us good. Can't do me any harm. I should also see how the training of my newest gerfalcon goes. Fetch the falconer, too."

Albert gazed at him shrewdly. "Do you really think you're well enough to ride and hunt, Roger? You truly do look sick."

"Thank you for the compliment, Albert," Roger responded sarcastically to the knight's genuine expression of concern. "Where is the baron?"

"I believe he's in the inner ward waiting for his horse. He's leaving soon, of that I'm sure."

"Fine." Roger hauled himself to his feet. "Be a friend, and find Bredon and Edred. Tell Bredon I'm sorry about the dog but I want to hunt, and see if Edred wants to try the new falcon, or use the tiercel. Then order the necessary preparations for the hunt."

Albert didn't obey at once. He stood awkwardly beside the stairs, adjusting his tunic unnecessarily.

"Well?"

"Aren't you going to go to mass?" Albert asked.

"No. My head would burst in the stuffy confines of that chapel. I need to be in the open air."

"What about Lady de Montmorency?"

Lady de Montmorency. Roger wanted to grumble that he didn't have the first notion what to do about Lady de Montmorency. Instead, he said, "She's still in bed. I imagine she can find plenty to do today without me underfoot." Then, deciding that he had a reputation to uphold, he winked at Albert lasciviously. "*If* she gets out of bed at all."

Looking somewhat relieved, Albert chuckled companionably and set off toward the kitchen corridor, presumably to find the huntsman and falconer. Roger watched him go, then with a grim and set expression went out into the inner ward. As Albert had reported, the baron was indeed there, pacing impatiently and glancing overhead at the sky. Roger squinted at it, too, and wondered if the clouds were leaving or arriving. He couldn't quite tell.

His gaze returned to the baron, and he told himself his admiration for his overlord was well-founded, whatever Mina Chilcott—de Montmorency—thought. It was his duty to be loyal and to obey. It was to his credit that the baron treated him as he did, and if the baron wanted to sleep with Hilda, that was his privilege, too.

Of course, Mina was right that Montmorency Castle was not a brothel and shouldn't be treated as such, but it was not her place to upbraid the baron.

It was his, and he should have done it.

"Roger! How good to see you before I go!" the baron called out.

Roger hurried toward him. "I'm sorry you have to leave so soon after arriving," he said. "Perhaps when you have completed your business in London, you can return."

"Perhaps," the baron said, "if your wife will allow me to set foot here again."

"I assure you, my lord, that you will be only too welcome."

"Don't be so angry about it, Roger," the baron said amicably, drawing Roger aside from his mounted men. "She was quite right, you know. I wish I could say that the wench addled my wits, but the truth is, I forgot myself and my manners." He surveyed Roger shrewdly. "She is a very special woman, I think, Roger, although I suppose you have already discovered that for yourself. I truly envy you." He ran his gaze over Roger again, and Roger tried not to scowl. He was no article on display in the marketplace!

"You had best take care to get more rest, Roger," the baron said. "I rely on you, you know, and will take it amiss if you fall ill, for whatever reason."

The baron was talking to him as if he were a child, not a nobleman, Roger thought indignantly.

"Now if only I could find a suitable wife for Reginald, eh? That won't be easy, though. I mean, he's not at all like you."

Meaning that *he* was an easier prize to dispose of? Roger wondered. What was the baron doing, spending his days as some kind of noble matchmaker as if he were a gossiping old woman instead of a man who had won so many tournaments nobody could keep count?

A towheaded stable boy appeared leading the baron's magnificent stallion, bearing fine accoutrements of red and silver. "Ah, ready at last," the baron said before swinging into the saddle easily. "Thank you, Neslin. I bid you farewell, Roger. Give my good wishes to your charming bride." He leaned down and spoke quietly. "If I had known Chilcott's sister was such a fine woman, I might have been tempted to marry again myself."

Roger didn't have time to respond before Baron DeGuerre signaled his men and rode out of the gate, for which Roger was grateful. He feared he might have said something he would regret later. Nevertheless, he didn't trouble to hide his frown as he watched him go. Could Mina have been right in saying that perhaps his overlord was not deserving of the unquestioning devotion and respect Roger bestowed upon him?

Mina didn't know the baron as he did, Roger told himself. She had never served him, ridden with him, hunted with him, fought with him, wenched with him. Roger knew that the baron was one of the finest men he had ever met—brave, just, worthy of admiration and emulation.

For a moment, he was tempted to call the baron back and tell him to take Mina, if he found her so enticing. Let the baron deal with her inscrutable ways and sharp tongue and unfathomable moods. Let the baron try to decide if the sentiment that seemed to be in her kiss was genuine, or only a trick.

Maybe the baron wouldn't care if he hurt her or not, and surely the baron wouldn't feel unclean and impure for acting like little more than a loathsome beast on his wedding night.

*He* didn't like having his world shaken to its foundation. Not again, not after it had taken him so long to rebuild it after the shattering experience of his parents' untimely death and the breaking apart of his family.

"Oh, God help me, I'm dying!"

Roger spun around, grimaced with pain from his aching head and glared at Reginald Chilcott, who came staggering out of the hall as if he had been wounded in six different places. His hair hung limp and uncurled; his clothing was disheveled, and his hose bagged at the knees.

"What's the matter?" Roger demanded unsympathetically.

"My head hurts, and my mouth is as dry as...as the bottom of a dry well, and my stomach feels—" He didn't have to finish describing his stomach, because he was promptly sick all over his brightly painted leather boots.

"Dudley!" Roger bellowed.

The steward, his face wreathed with smiles now that the wedding feast was over and the baron gone, hurried out of the kitchen. "My lord?" His smile disintegrated when he saw Reginald Chilcott.

"Take Lord Chilcott inside and see that he's attended to."

"Yes, my lord," Dudley murmured, turning paler. "I'll fetch one of the servants at once."

Mina appeared in the doorway, scanned the inner ward, ignored her husband and Dudley and rushed to Reginald's side. "Come inside, Reginald," she crooned.

To Roger, she had been as cold as the brook during the spring thaw. He would never have guessed she could sound so solicitous. And to think it was not for him, her husband, who had awakened far from well. If he had been kinder to her last night—God's teeth, if he could only remember what he had done to her!—she might have been speaking in those soft dulcet tones to him.

No, she was his wife, the marriage consummated. He didn't need her hushed words or kind-hearted . . . pity. Yes, pity was what she was giving Reginald. Therefore, he did not need it, or her. Nor did he want her arm around him.

Roger marched stoically toward the stables, too annoyed to notice that his head was not aching quite so much. "I'm going hunting as soon as Albert finds Bredon," he announced, ostensibly to Dudley.

Mina ignored him while she assisted Reginald back inside the hall.


Reginald groaned pitiably as Mina helped him into the hall, much more pathetically than Roger had that morning, although her husband had been paler and even somewhat green. However, she could find it in her heart to have pity for Reginald. He didn't have the stomach for wine, as she had quickly discovered on his return. She had considered that strange, since he had spent so much time in France, but not so strange when she realized the poor fellow was quite ignorant of his own weaknesses.

She got Reginald to the closest bench. Hilda came out of the kitchen corridor with a broom, clearly intending to clear away the rushes and the remains of last night's feast before mass. She dropped the broom and hurried to Mina's side.

Together they laid the enfeebled young man down. "God, just let me die in peace!" he moaned. "Send for Father Damien. I haven't got much time."

Mina had to smile, although she turned away to hide it. Every time Reginald drank too much, he was convinced he was on his deathbed. Reginald gave another groan and thankfully, Hilda was ready with a bucket. "Leave him to me, my lady," she said quietly. "I'll look after him."

Mina nodded. She had had quite enough of tending to the ill, and she knew there was nothing seriously wrong with her half brother, just as she had known there was nothing seriously wrong with Roger. The effects of the drugged wine would soon wear off.

Suppressing a sigh, she got up to leave Reginald in Hilda's competent hands when Hilda laid a detaining hand on her arm. "My lady!"

"Yes? What is it?"

"Thank you. For last night, I mean. With the baron. I...I don't know what I would have done if you hadn't helped me."

Mina tried not to blush with guilt. In truth, she had not been thinking of Hilda at all. She had been trying to show both the baron and Roger that she was now the mistress of the castle and expected to be treated with respect.

"And I wanted to tell you, my lady—" the conversation paused while Reginald used the bucket again "—that I won't cause any trouble. Not that I think I could, you understand. That is, he's your husband now, and I won't go near him. You won't send me away, will you, my lady?"

"Not unless you give me cause."

"Oh, thank you, my lady. I won't. I promise." Her expression was still worried, but her eyes grew determined. "I hope Sir Roger will let Lud stay the reeve."

"Who is Lud?"

"My brother."

Payment for services rendered, no doubt, Mina thought. "Is he a good reeve?"

Hilda smiled broadly. "Oh, yes, my lady. I say it truthfully, even if he is my brother. Keeps everybody in line, he does, but nice, so they don't get angry. It's a gift he's got, making everybody happy."

Mina didn't doubt that Hilda had something of a gift for keeping men happy, but she refrained from mentioning it. "If Lud is a good reeve, Sir Roger would not wish to have another, no doubt."

"I think so, and so would most everybody."

"Then you have nothing to fear from Sir Roger, or from me."

Hilda grinned broadly, then frowned when Reginald groaned as if he had demons in his belly. "You go ahead now, my lady. I'll take good care of him and get him up to his bed as soon as he's able to walk."

With a nod, Mina went outside. A brace of lymers and the smaller brachets strained at their leashes, held by a man she had not noticed before. The squat, grizzled fellow spoke to his charges as if they were soldiers under his command, cajoling some, berating others until the dogs grew quiet. In that time, she caught sight of squires and boys saddling horses in the stables, and several of the male wedding guests waiting with their hunting weapons. Mina suppressed a sigh that was both weary and disappointed, surmising that she would have to spend much of the morning with the men's wives sewing or in idle chatter.

She dreaded such a day, because she had so little in common with most noblewomen. Her life had been too difficult, her days so much like those of a servant, that she suspected she would have more to share with Hilda than any of the fine ladies currently visiting. Fortunately, she understood most of them were leaving later today, or early tomorrow, so she would not have to put up with them long.

"My lady!" said a friendly voice behind her. "May I present Edred, your husband's falconer."

Mina turned to see Sir Albert coming from the kitchen stores nearby, a piece of bread in his hands. At his side walked a slender man of middle years with a large, hooded gerfalcon on his wrist.

"Edred, that looks to be a fine falcon," Mina said.

"Sir Roger likes the best, my lady," Edred replied with a nervous smile. "Best wishes on your wedding."

Like Roger, Edred's brown hair was long and touched his narrow shoulders. He sported what should have been a beard, although the growth looked rather erratic because of several scars on his face. Still, he seemed a pleasant fellow, and even rather in awe of her. Because she was Sir Roger's wife? Mina fought to subdue a twinge of dissatisfaction. Wasn't that what she had wanted? Surely it was expecting too much to be respected for herself alone.

"Thank you." She turned to address Albert. A glance from the corner of her eye showed that Edred relaxed when she wasn't looking directly at him. "I take it Roger is not attending mass?"

Albert shook his head as Edred sidled off toward the horses. "He says not, and I don't suppose we'll be back in time for the noon meal, either, so I decided to help myself to some food. Forgive my rudeness."

She gave Albert a genuinely warm smile. *He* treated her with respect. He also asked for forgiveness and thanked her with sincere gratitude. She moved a little closer to Albert and said, "Edred seems a nervous fellow for a falconer. Does he not upset the birds?"

Albert chuckled. "Edred is only nervous around women, my lady. Around the hawks, he is a veritable Titan. Why, I've seen one claw his face nearly to ribbons, and he stood there as calm as we are now."

"Albert!" Roger barked, and the friendly mood was shattered as they both faced Roger. He strode out of the stable, leading a magnificent black stallion. "What the hell are you doing? Get your horse."

"At once, Roger," Albert said, hesitating a moment to return Mina's smile. "I understand a groom who is grumpy on the morning after is a good sign," he whispered quickly.

Mina sighed as Albert walked briskly away and Roger mounted his high-spirited, prancing horse and headed toward the gate. There was no need for her to remain here, so she turned toward the chapel.

Whatever else Mina thought of Sir Roger de Montmorency as she slowly walked to the chapel to listen to Father Damien mumble the mass, she had to admit that he was the epitome of a Norman nobleman. He was arrogantly vain, but not without some cause, considering his looks and the magnificence of his muscular body. He was stern and harsh, yet he lacked that haunted look of permanent sadness she had observed in the baron. He must have a friendlier side, too, or why would a person like the kindly Sir Albert remain with him?

Roger had been truly dismayed to think he had hurt her. There could be no doubt of the anguish in his eyes, and for a moment she had been tempted to tell him the truth. Only her instinct for self-preservation had held her back, because she did not know what Sir Roger would do if he discovered she had lied to him.

He had mentioned a physical pain. She did not know losing her virginity would hurt, and she was glad to think she had avoided any further harm. Hadn't she already endured enough at men's hands?

As she knelt in the small chapel, Mina told herself she was relieved she was still a virgin and proud that she had outfoxed Sir Roger de Montmorency.

# Chapter Seven

Later that day, several peasants surreptitiously watched their lord riding home along the edge of his fields.

The men saw a tall, strong, handsome and very serious man whose piercing gaze seemed to exhort them to work even harder, and they quickly bent to their tasks. The unmarried women sighed furtively and blushed at their own lustful thoughts. They also thought it best to avoid his eyes, in case Sir Roger de Montmorency might somehow guess what was in their minds and—gracious God!—stop to speak to them. Still, more than one permitted herself a brief, improbable dream.

Roger, however, was oblivious to the scrutiny as he rode upon the remains of the old Roman road that skirted his lands. He was thinking that Edred had done a fine job of training the gerfalcon. The young bird had taken a crane in a fast, easy kill and had even successfully gotten some rabbits Bredon's dogs had roused. All in all, a fine day's catch hung from his saddle, as well as Albert's and some of the other noblemen.

His head felt much better, too, because of the fresh air, no doubt, and being away from that confusing, unsettling woman he was married to. He allowed himself to admit that he was also relieved to be free of the worry of offending the baron. Out here in the woods and the fields, he was his own master again, beholden to no one, in command of his own destiny.

Roger surveyed his domain. His fields looked well tended; the crops were growing as they should, and the outbuildings and houses of his tenants seemed in good repair. The cattle pastured on the common land were fat and contented. The herd of sheep had grown considerably. He could hear the blacksmith's forge ringing with the strokes of the smith's hammer at the farthest edge of the small village that had grown between the main road and the river.

Scattered around the village green were the houses of the local craftsmen, and close to the smithy was the alehouse, where the serving wenches occasionally offered a lonely man solace. Roger supposed that was the type of place Mina thought the baron should patronize, although the idea of the baron going to a peasant's alehouse was quite inconceivable.

Mina must have heard about Moll and her sister, although if she thought they were whores, she wouldn't be quite right. Moll and Poll weren't above taking gifts, as he well knew, but it was always their decision to accept both the gift and the giver. He might decide to go there again himself. He might have to.

The notion of the baron having to pay for a woman's services was also ludicrous. Why, Roger could recall several jealous quarrels among noblewomen who were vying for the honor of his favor, either secretly or with astonishing audaciousness. There had been plenty of quarrels about *him,* too, of course.

What would his bride make of that knowledge? Probably not much, he thought with a scowl. "What do you say to a horse race to the castle gate?" he proposed, coming out of his reverie to give Albert a very brief smile.

Albert reigned in his horse and stared with mock dismay. "You cannot be serious, my lord. My poor beast against that demon stallion? It would not be even close to fair."

"You make it sound as if your horse is an old nag," Roger complained. He wanted very much to feel the wind whistling past his face and the surge of the horse's muscles beneath him.

"I thought you were sick," Albert countered.

"I'm feeling much better now."

"Undoubtedly seeing your manor in such good condition has helped," Albert noted dryly.

"Indeed it has. Come, race me. Prize to the winner."

"Well . . ." Albert suddenly kicked his horse into a gallop, the motion taking Roger and his stallion by surprise. With a shout, Roger spurred his own mount and soon the other noblemen, Edred, Bredon and the lads who had helped with the hunt were left behind, splattered with the mud thrown up by the horses' hooves.

"Come on, Raven," Roger urged, pumping with his knees and whispering in his stallion's ear. As he had planned, the air rushed past, making his hair and clothing stream out behind him like banners in a stiff breeze. The game tied to his saddle bounced and jostled, but Roger ignored it. Indeed, he didn't care if it fell off, because Albert was still ahead, although not by much, and Raven was going to be beside Albert's horse in another moment—

Then Father Damien, his head bowed and his lips moving in silent prayer, stepped onto the road from one of the pathways leading out of the forest toward the village. With a cry, the old man jumped back, but by then Roger had already checked his horse and slowed until he saw that the priest, although surprised, was quite unharmed. Once more Roger dug his heels into Raven's side and urged him onward.

To no avail. Albert galloped into the ward first, albeit barely ahead of Raven.

Roger yanked his horse to a halt and jumped down, scowling darkly. "That wasn't fair!" he cried, stalking toward his friend.

Unperturbed, Albert dismounted and untied the game affixed to his saddle. "Your horse made it unfair to begin with," he replied calmly. "Now, what will I take for a prize, since you lost?"

"By God, I'll take your ears!" Roger snarled.

Albert grinned. "They are not my most attractive feature, but if you insist..."

"Oh, go to the devil!"

"Since I have sworn my allegiance to you, Roger, I always rather expected I might have to follow you there."

By now, Roger's scowl was merely for show, as they both knew. They turned toward the kitchen, by silent mutual consent deciding to get some ale. Suddenly Dudley erupted from the hall, looking as if he were about to burst into tears or fall into an angry fit.

"My lord!" the steward exclaimed, his tone one Roger had never heard him use before, "I must speak with you immediately!"

"What is it?" Roger asked, somewhat concerned, although he was quite used to Dudley's overwrought reactions to minor inconveniences. "Has the kitchen caught fire? Or a merchant cheated us?"

"My lord, I..." Dudley looked at Sir Albert and then the other huntsmen as they rode into the inner ward. "Come into the hall, if you please. I would rather speak to you alone." He grabbed Roger's arm and nearly dragged him inside.

This physical action was so unusual, Roger began to have a real sense of dread. He thrust the door closed and faced his steward. "What is it?" he demanded.

"It's her, your wife!" Dudley cried, looking about nervously as if he expected Mina to pop up from behind one of the benches. "She wants to run everything. I tried to explain I'm the steward, not a simple chamberlain or pantler, but she won't listen. She says the hall is her responsibility now, as well as the bedchambers and the food and the linens and God knows what else." He assumed a martyred air. "Apparently I am no longer necessary. If that is indeed so, my lord, I will gladly leave. I have been a steward here nearly my whole life, but perhaps that is of no account anymore. Perhaps you think me too old, too useless. If that is true, please have the mercy to say so at once. It isn't necessary, or kind, or honorable to have this woman do it, even if she is your wife!''

"Dudley, I don't know what you're talking about," Roger said firmly. "I gave my wife no such powers. She has acted without my knowledge or consent, and rest assured, I have absolutely no intention of turning the running of my estate over to anyone else, especially a woman. It would be ludicrous to let her try to do your job," he assured the agitated steward. "I quite understand that, and I will speak to her at once. Where is that...that...my wife?"

"She is in the kitchen, telling the cook what to do. He's going to leave us, I'm sure, and he's the best cook we've ever had. The look on his face when she started in on the cost of his ingredients! I sympathize with him, of course, but it would be terrible if he were to go."

Dudley kept up a continuous stream of similar complaints as he trotted after Roger, who headed toward the kitchen with a murderous expression on his face. For once, the usually softhearted Dudley felt as one with his tempestuous lord.

* * *

When Roger reached the entrance to the kitchen and saw the scene before him, he halted abruptly. What kind of merrymaking was this?

Thorbert, the cook, usually a morose fellow concerned only with culinary matters, was actually laughing out loud as he watched Mina rolling out some sort of pastry. Nearby, two scullery maids were giggling uncontrollably, their faces dusted with flour, and the spit boy was laughing so hard he could scarcely do his job.

Meanwhile, Roger's wife, the new mistress of Montmorency Castle, stood at the table with her cuffs rolled back, some kind of sack tied around her neck to protect her gown from flour and a decidedly ugly, manure-colored wimple covering her red hair.

Even more astonishing, the severe, cold bride he had left that very morning was laughing as loudly as any of them, her eyes sparkling with good humor.

Whatever problem Dudley had sensed before had obviously been overcome. "What is going on here?" Roger demanded, marching into the room.

The laughter stopped at once, and everybody stared at him, their faces flushed and guilty, as if he were accusing them of butchering the estate's best bull.

"We are preparing the evening meal," Mina said, and he noticed that she was neither flushed nor contrite. "I am showing Thorbert how to make a mince pie."

By now, Dudley had entered the kitchen. Roger heard his startled gasp but didn't look at him.

"I see," Roger remarked, going closer to the table. The aroma coming from the bowl of minced meat, fruit and spices certainly smelled delicious. "Reginald should have told me you had such skill," he said to Mina, who quickly moved away as if she dreaded touching him, even inadvertently.

"I don't suppose he knows," she replied.

"Do you think you can finish unassisted, Thorbert?" Roger inquired, fighting to keep his voice just as unemotional. "I need to speak with my wife and my steward."

"I believe so, my lord. There is only the pastry crust left to do, is there not, my lady?" Thorbert asked Mina respectfully.

"Yes, and let's hope it rises properly," she said. For some reason, this sent Thorbert, the scullery maids and the spit boy into renewed gales of laughter. Their reaction did nothing to lighten Roger's mood as he walked along the kitchen corridor toward the hall, trailed by Dudley and Mina.

The moment he reached the dais, Roger threw himself into his chair and glared at his wife. "What have you been up to?" he demanded.

"I have been helping the cook and teaching him a new recipe," she replied coolly, raising one brow very slightly.

Roger had never noticed how shapely her eyebrows were—and he shouldn't be noticing such things now. "Dudley tells me you are usurping his position. I won't allow that. He is my steward, not you."

Mina turned to the puffing, red-faced Dudley, her expression the very image of remorse. "Is that how you felt, Dudley?" she asked, her voice full of sincerity. "I didn't mean to upset you. I thought I was doing my duty as my lord's wife. I certainly didn't mean to offend you or anyone else. Perhaps in my desire to please my husband, I acted over-zealously. Please accept my apologies."

Roger's eyes narrowed. Was she truly sorry, or was this some clever display of regret? He honestly couldn't tell. Surely a more infuriating woman had never existed.

Mina smiled at Dudley. An incredibly warm, friendly smile that lit her whole face and made her beautiful.

She had given such a smile to his steward, not her own husband.

Dudley blushed and shifted, as uncomfortable as any lad facing a pretty girl. "To speak the truth, my lady," he said, "I was rather affronted. I have been steward here for many years, and I thought..." His voice trailed off shyly.

She went to him and took his two plump hands in hers. "Please accept my humble apologies, Dudley. I am counting on you to help me here. I may have been out of place, but I have never had the opportunity to run such a large household. As I said, I want only to please my husband—" she glanced at Roger, and he didn't know what to think "—and perhaps I was too anxious and abrupt. I beg your pardon."

"Oh, my lady, please!" Dudley cried. "I spoke too hastily, I'm sure. Ask me anything, anything at all."

God's wounds, was everyone here going mad? Or was this red-haired witch casting spells on them? Roger didn't know, and he told himself he didn't care. "Since this little misunderstanding seems to be over and all is forgiven and you two are such great friends," he snarled, "I'm going to the armory."

He strode from the hall, convinced that swinging a few swords would make him feel better.

* * *

Roger's notion that Mina's apology was not sincere was incorrect. In fact, she meant every word, and was genuinely distressed to think that she had upset the steward. She knew that she would need his cooperation in order to run the household, and she also believed that in her anxiety and zeal, she may have acted with unseemly haste and apparent rudeness.

There was another reason she did not want to alienate Dudley. Aside from Sir Albert, she suspected that Dudley knew Roger best, since he had served the family for so long. It was imperative that she learn how to please Roger—or at least keep his mood relatively pleasant, for everyone's sake. Dudley might be the best person to teach her how to gauge her husband's humors.

So, as she stood beside Dudley after Roger had marched away, she said, "I hope I haven't angered him too much."

Dudley grinned and patted her arm like a kindhearted relative. "Don't be too concerned, my lady. He can be ill-tempered, especially when he's tired. I learned long ago not to pay too much attention, although it doesn't do to ignore his orders and requests. His rebukes are not ones to take lightly, either, I can tell you."

"Does he often go to the armory when he's upset?"

"Well, there, or riding, or hunting. He goes, that's all. He's always been that way, even when he was a boy. Many's the time his father had to drag him out of some hiding place when he'd done something wrong or was distressed."

She gestured for Dudley to sit. He seemed in a talkative mood, and she wanted to know about the man she had married. "He was an unruly child? Or a troublesome one?"

Dudley chuckled, his rotund belly quivering like one of Thorbert's sauces. "Troublesome? Not often. Nor was he what you'd call unruly. He was a one for mischief, though. Not a bad boy, just heedless. And he liked to have his own way. Many's the argument he had with his sister. How they'd scream at each other! My heavens above, the noise!"

Mina could easily picture that.

"But he loves Madeline, for all that. Why, she tried to trick him with that Welshman of hers, and he still let her marry him. Still, the fellow was certainly as fine and noble as any man you'd ever hope to meet, even if he was a peasant."

This was a little more difficult for Mina to imagine. The proud, arrogant Sir Roger de Montmorency agreeing to let his only sister marry a peasant? Perhaps there was more to the story than that.

She also thought she would like to meet Madeline, her sister-in-law. She must be quite a woman to try to fool Roger. If *she* had known Roger well, as a sister would, she probably would not have had the gall to attempt it. Either Madeline de Montmorency was very brave, or else there was a compassionate part to Roger that Mina had yet to see.

"But he was never a sly one, him. Temper, yes, but once the storm blew over, it was over. Not a mean bone in his body. Spare me a sly child, my lady. And then he'd joke about it. Oh, God's blood, how he'd get me going! His sister, too. The tears would roll down our cheeks."

"He doesn't laugh much now," Mina noted pensively.

"No, no, he doesn't. He hasn't since he come back from living with Lord Gervais. I suppose it comes of growing up."

"Lord Gervais was . . . ?"

"His foster father. That's where he went after his parents died, to be trained until he came of age. His sister got taken to a convent. Strict place, I gather, but it couldn't be as rigorous as what Roger went through, training under Lord Gervais's man. He's got some knight there, I hear, who's about as tough and hard as they come. I kept things here for Sir Roger till then,'' the old man added with pride.

"You did your task excellently, too. I can tell,'' Mina said.

However, her thoughts were not on Dudley's good stewardship. She was envisioning a young, hot-tempered boy who knew how to laugh. What had happened to that boy and his laughter? Trained out of him, perhaps, by ruthless, brutal teachers. Or stolen away by the death of loving parents.

Laughter had been her salvation, the only thing that brightened her long, lonely days, rare though it had been. She could still laugh, despite everything.

She had spent a very pleasant time in the kitchen today, making jokes about flabby dough that would not rise which, coming from a bride, had scandalized everybody. They had struggled valiantly to suppress their laughter until she had winked at them. Then they had spluttered, giggled and guffawed helplessly, especially as she continued to make such remarks with a straight face, for the most part, finally laughing herself only moments before the enraged Roger had entered the room.

Dudley rose and bowed, a pleasant smile on his face. "If you will excuse me, my lady, I have other duties to attend to.''

"Yes, of course," Mina replied thoughtfully, wondering what it would take to make the curt, forbidding Sir Roger de Montmorency laugh now. And if it was worth the trouble to try.

# Chapter Eight

Roger's mood did not improve this time. He stayed angry all through the evening meal, especially when he noticed the way Dudley, Hilda and all the other servants regarded Mina with respect and approval. Somehow, and he wasn't sure exactly how she had accomplished this, she had wormed her way into their affection. To him, she was still cold and distant, but among the others, her icy reserve melted away.

Even the remainder of the noble company were obviously comfortable and quite content, and blissfully unaware that he considered their good humor as something of a personal affront. It was as if it didn't matter whether he was there or not.

Roger could almost hear Albert gently admonishing him for being childish again. However, Albert was too engrossed in listening to Mina detail how she had spent her afternoon to pay attention to him. It was as if Albert had never heard such a fascinating revelation of domestic trivia.

The food, including the most delicious mince pie Roger had ever tasted, was finally cleared away and people scattered for the evening. Some of the men began to play at chess and dice; some couples decided to dance to the music of the minstrel or listen to his songs, and the rest of the women retired to embroidery.

Roger took no notice of where Mina went or what she did. She was not the only one with resolve, and he was resolved not to pay any attention to her. Instead, he left the hall completely and went to the battlements, climbing up the steps to the wall-walk around the perimeter of the castle.

He surveyed his lands, spread out below his castle. From the hall below drifted sounds of merriment and music, muted and disembodied as though they came from some other world far, far away.

Down in the small village, a few dim lights showed. Smoke curled slowly upward from the wooden houses. The alehouse door opened and a man staggered outside, illuminated by the lights inside and clearly the worse for drink. Two others hurried after him to lend him their shoulders for support. A woman laughed, a short burst of joy that was at once mirthful and understanding. Somewhere farther away, a dog barked. The sky, darkening quickly, still shone purple and indigo on the horizon, with no clouds to make a pattern.

Roger idly wondered where Madeline was. Perhaps she had already reached her new home with her Welsh husband, and was looking at this same sky. Sometimes, during the years they had been separated, he had looked at the sky late at night or at dawn and thought of her, trying to have some link with the sister who had been taken away from him.

How well he remembered that terrible period after his parents had died of a fever within days of each other! He had begged Lord Gervais to take her, too, but Lord Gervais had said he could not, that she should be with the holy sisters, that they would take care of her. Roger had tried to believe it, but when the time actually came for Madeline to leave, Roger had to be forcefully restrained from running after her. It had taken the passing of years, as well as hard work and responsibility, to lessen the pain. If mere brotherly affection could cause such agony, he would very gladly do without any other kind of love.

Such a feeling was just a fantasy concocted by minstrels and lonely noblewomen, anyway. Something to lend excitement to their day, or make them feel important. He had no need for such fantasies. He had plenty of excitement. Nor had he ever lacked for female companionship, at least of one kind.

But perhaps, he admitted to himself as he stood alone, *only* one kind. His experience of the opposite sex had been limited to brief interludes of necessary physical release. Well, what more did a man need?

All he had expected from marriage was a wife to oversee his household and bear his children, with the additional compensation of having a woman available whenever he wanted one. He had simply not considered how his life might change once he was...domesticated.

God's wounds, he sounded like some kind of wild animal! But then, maybe he had acted like one. He still couldn't believe he had beaten Mina, not after Fitzroy had made it very clear to the squires that it was dishonorable to hurt a woman, who was by nature so much weaker than a man.

If only he could remember what had happened. He *must* have hurt Mina. In the kitchen, she had recoiled from him as if she loathed his slightest touch.

Frustrated by his inability to remember, Roger picked up a stone and threw it over the battlements with all his might. It hit the moat below, a small sound in the stillness.

A sentry gave a warning cry and hurried toward Roger, his mail jingling.

"It is no cause for alarm," Roger said to the startled soldier, who stiffened to ramrod straightness when he saw who he had challenged. "Indeed, I am pleased that you were so alert."

The sentry relaxed a little, but not too much. Evidently he had proper respect for his lord. "It looks to be a clear night," Roger said companionably.

The sentry nodded. "Aye, my lord."

"What's your name?"

"Egbert, my lord."

From somewhere beyond the moat, they both heard a woman's giggle, which quickly changed to a low moan with a distinctly pleasure filled characteristic. Peering below, Roger saw a couple embracing passionately. He glanced at Egbert and jerked his head. "Somebody else is celebrating, I think."

Egbert slid sideways toward the parapet, his back still absolutely straight, and leaned over sideways to see. "That's Ridley. He's gettin' married next week, my lord."

"Ah, yes. Ridley's the one with half a thumb?"

"Aye, my lord."

"Not very clever, cutting himself and a loaf of bread at the same time, was it?"

Egbert relaxed a little more and nearly smiled. "No, my lord. He hasn't touched wine since, neither."

Roger smiled, too, and thought with some satisfaction that Mina wasn't the only one who could have both respect and affection from underlings. He simply wasn't used to having to work for it, and he had not planned to do so when it came to his wife. Not that he thought he *should* have to earn her respect or affection. It was his wife's duty to please him, not his to please her. On the other hand, Mina might be worth an attempt at reconciliation, when he remembered the kiss they had shared.

After all, he wasn't a beast. He was a nobleman. He would just take care to be very gentle, and like Ridley, he would stay away from wine.

"Stay alert, Egbert," Roger said jovially as he turned on his heel and headed toward the hall, whistling tunelessly.

Mina decided she would not wait for Roger to return from wherever he had gone. He had said no word to anyone of his intentions when he had left the hall, or his destination, or when he would come back. He had simply stalked silently out, his face as grim as it had been for the entire meal, when he had sat beside her as if she were some kind of effigy in a tomb. Without the recovered Reginald and the ever-courteous Sir Albert to converse with, the meal would have been tedious in the extreme.

The whores of the alehouse in the village came to mind as a possible explanation for her husband's continuing absence. She had heard Reginald speak of two alewives when they had first approached Montmorency Castle. It seemed he had fond memories of them.

Trust a man like Sir Roger de Montmorency to corrupt a weak-willed fellow like Reginald!

As for Roger's patronage of such an establishment, it simply didn't matter. In fact, she was glad to be relieved of an onerous duty. As she had told Reginald on her wedding day, she knew what transpired between married couples to produce children, but it sounded disgusting. She could do very well without that intimacy.

With that in mind, Mina decided it would be better if she were already asleep, should Roger return with such activity in mind. She was, after all, his wife, and he would be within his rights to compel her to...

Suddenly Mina moved her wooden embroidery frame to the side of her chair and rose, addressing Hilda. "Put the sewing away, please. I am going to bed."

The other noblewomen who were sewing or talking quietly among themselves looked her way. "I bid you all good night," Mina said with somewhat forced affability as she turned to leave the comfort of the hearth.

Reginald, who was embroiled in a game of dice, didn't notice that she was nearby, so she didn't bother to say good-night to him. Nor did she wish to disturb Sir Albert, who was listening to the minstrel sing a mournful lay, obviously engrossed in the lyrics. His expression was so sorrowful that she was sure he would not welcome any interruption. As she passed by, it occurred to her that she couldn't imagine the gruff Roger listening to a minstrel with such an expression. For that matter, neither would she. She had little patience for the fantasies minstrels sang about.

Once alone in her bedchamber, she drew off her headdress and rotated her stiff neck. She would have to adjust the frame of her embroidery tomorrow, she thought as she went to her small chest and took out her hairbrush. She walked to the narrow window and looked outside at the dark night sky. How lovely it was, with the stars shining above like fireflies in heaven.

With slow, pensive motions, Mina began to brush her hair. The gentle tugging on her scalp relaxed her and provided a welcome relief from the confines of the headdress. Perhaps she should consider committing a shocking breach of decorum and go with her hair uncovered tomorrow. It would certainly be more comfortable.

Sighing, she turned around—and caught sight of Roger standing in the doorway, his hand on the latch, watching her with his dark, intense eyes. She stared at him for a long moment, startled at first, then determined to hide her surprise and confusion. She swallowed hard and realized her hand shook as she clutched her brush. She lowered it quickly. "Have you never seen a woman brush her hair before?" she asked defiantly when he still did not speak or look away.

"Not in a very long time," he answered, finally coming inside the room and closing the door, shutting them in alone together. "You have beautiful hair, despite its color."

She felt a twinge of anger at his semicompliment. "I brush it every night," she replied, trying to sound matter-of-fact. She put the brush on the chest and faced him.

He came farther into the room, then halted, his gaze still penetrating, the only sound that of their breathing, the only motion provided by the flickering flame of the candles. Did he feel the tension between them, too, as strong as the odor of the melting beeswax?

Wordlessly, still staring, he started to undo his tunic. Suddenly her courage abandoned her, and she quickly turned toward the wall, her heart pounding in her chest, her face warm, scarcely daring to breathe. Why had he come here? What was he doing?

*Coward!* she admonished herself. Face him!

She could not, nor could she see that Roger's hands were not quite steady. "Everyone seems quite taken with you," he remarked behind her.

Did he mean himself, as well? she wondered. What if he did? What if he didn't? She wasn't sure which would be worse. "I am trying to..." Her voice trailed off feebly. She wasn't sure anymore just what she was trying to do.

"Be a fine example of a nobleman's wife?"

He was close behind her now. She could scarcely think, remembering his first kiss the night before and the stirring sensation of his lips upon hers. Her legs felt curiously weak, her mouth dry.

He put his hands on her shoulders and turned her toward him. His touch was light. Gentle. Kind. She, so unused to tenderness, felt confused and powerless when he held her and scrutinized her face.

She could not bear to think that he would see her vulnerability and uncertainty which she feared she could no longer hide, so she fastened her gaze on his broad chest, which was rising and falling with a rapidity that nearly matched her own. A scattering of dark hairs covered the exposed flesh revealed by his unlaced tunic, power and virility lurking beneath that surface.

Was it so wrong for her to be weaker than he? Was it possible for her, with her woman's body, her woman's desire, to continue to resist him?

"You are doing very well, Mina," he said softly, his deep voice almost a caress. "All you need do to please me completely is obey me."

Mina stiffened and in that instant, new resolve and new strength filled her. "I am a thinking, feeling woman, not some beast for you to command," she answered, every word a reproach, "nor a dog for you to train!" With flashing eyes and an angry heart, she twisted away from him. "I do not need your approval, Sir Roger de Montmorency. I know that I am doing 'very well,' as I did 'very well' tending my father—much good it did me!"

"There is no need for you to speak this way. I meant my words as a compliment." His expression was shocked, incredulous, perhaps even disappointed, but she didn't care.

"I am not a simpleton, my lord. I know what you meant. You want obedience. You want a dull, unthinking creature who will run your household, not upsetting the steward or servants, of course. One who will lie in your bed, submit to your embraces and bear your children. A fool with no more intelligence than a brood mare. Very well."

With quick, furious movements, Mina undid the lacings of her gown and stepped out of it. She threw it over the chest and swiftly yanked off her shift. Naked and too indignant to be ashamed, she went to the bed and lay down, glaring at him. "So here I lie, Sir Roger. Do what you will, and if it pleases you to think you have married an obedient little wife, think it. For my part, I will do my duty and while you take your pleasure of me, I will ponder household matters."

Roger's face darkened into a scowl as he moved toward her, his motion like a cat about to spring as he circled the bed, his gaze riveted on her face. "Who is it you think you are speaking to? Reginald? Or some other dolt? You cannot mean to speak thus to me, Sir Roger de Montmorency, your lord and husband." He sat upon the bed and slid toward her, coming closer and closer with agonizing slowness. "Or perhaps I have been tricked. Perhaps you are not, in truth, Lady Mina de Montmorency, but some shrewish alewife brought here to play a jest upon me."

Mina sat up and inched away from him, very aware of her nakedness as he continued to stare at her.

"Is this what happened last night, Mina? Did you make me angry? Did you treat me like a recalcitrant child until I hit you?" He smiled, but it was a cruel, leering smile that chilled her to the marrow of her bones. "Is that the way you prefer to take your pleasure, with a little pain?"

Aghast at his depraved suggestion and frightened by the cold anger in his eyes, she lifted her hand to slap his face. Before she could, he caught it in his strong grip, his fingers like the talons of a hawk.

"Leave me alone!" she cried, twisting her arm to make him let go. When she was free, she scrambled away.

He was off the bed in an instant, his expression cold, his eyes pitiless. "I won't beat you, Mina. If I did before, you have my apologies, and my word that I will never do so again." He went to the door, then paused on the threshold. "Since you find my presence so distressing, I will go away, at least for a little while. I have a smaller estate to the north that I should visit, and that will be as good a place as any to go." He ran his impertinent gaze over her once more. "Perhaps I would have done better to let the baron have you, after all. Unfortunately, the marriage cannot be undone. We shall both have to make the best of it. Farewell, Mina." He swiftly left the room.

When Mina was quite certain he was gone, she drew in a great, shuddering breath and crawled under the nurturing warmth of the bedclothes, not bothering to blow out the candles. Shaking with suppressed emotion and the aftermath of her fear, she stared up at the wooden beams of the ceiling.

Oh, dear God, what was she going to do? She should be glad he was gone. He was so harsh, so stern, so impossible. The accusation he had made, that she would want pain to give her pleasure, was abominable. Unnatural. Unforgivable.

Yet he had been tender at first. And he had apologized, albeit angrily. How often did a man like Roger express any regret? To a man, probably rarely. To a woman, surely never. But he had apologized to her.

What had his last words about the baron meant? It was impossible that such a man as Baron De-Guerre would ever want her. Yet Roger thought he had. He had even looked . . . what? Could he have been *jealous?*

If that were so, his jealousy and his grudging apology, which had to denote some respect for her, were the greatest compliments she had ever had in her life.

Then he had said the marriage could not be undone. Was that what he truly wanted? Perhaps.

Was it what *she* wanted? Mina forced herself to examine her innermost feelings, and the answer they provided offered little comfort. If someone had ever bothered to ask her the kind of man she would have wanted for her husband, she suspected the answer would very nearly have described Sir Roger de Montmorency.

Yes, she wanted Roger—she wanted him to respect her, to treat her as an equal, even to love her, if such a feeling truly existed—but only on her terms.

Nonetheless, as the night wore wearily on, she began to wonder if by trying to prove that she was the cleverer person, she had made the biggest mistake of her life.

Outside in the inner ward, under the shadow of his hall, Roger leaned against the cold stone walls, sick at heart, now convinced he was not the fine nobleman he had believed himself to be. For years he had prided himself on his cool detachment, on his ability to think rationally before making a deliberate attack. He had always prided himself on being the rational lover, too, practicing his skills with women the way other men practiced jousting. Mina had torn away his confidence there, as well.

He ground his fist into his palm. Of all the women in the world, why did Mina have to be the one to show him how brutish he could be?

Here in the cold darkness, he knew that he wanted Mina more than he had ever wanted a woman. Even watching her performing the simple, intimate act of combing her fiery hair, the brush caressing her, moving in long slow strokes down her back, had excited him beyond his expectations. He almost wished she had never turned to see him watching her.

But she had, and when he had gone to her and touched her shoulders, making her face him, he had thought he glimpsed a charming vulnerability there, all the more thrilling because of her usual self-assured confidence. It had delighted him to think that he affected her in any way.

And then he had said he wanted her to obey. It was the truth, but he had not meant it the way she had taken it. He had meant that he wanted her to do as he asked, yes, but freely. He didn't expect her to obey unthinkingly, like a dog. God's wounds, she had not given him one moment to explain, but had lashed out immediately. Then she had offered herself to him defiantly, not with passion or even liking. She had thrown herself upon that bed with undisguised loathing, as if he were an ogre from a minstrel's tale and she the sacrificial maiden.

Well, he was no ogre, although he doubted he could convince her otherwise. Perhaps he *had* made some mistakes—but she was no saint in women's clothing, either.

Roger pushed himself away from the wall, his mouth set in a hard, grim line. He didn't need her, or her approval. He was Sir Roger de Montmorency, and she was nothing but his wife.

# *Chapter Nine*

Nearly a fortnight later, after mass and breaking the fast, Mina decided to walk to the orchard, which was outside the castle and across the moat. She could easily be seen through the trees by guards on the battlements, so it was a safe place for a solitary ramble on a cloudy summer's morning.

Roger still had not returned. He had left at first light after their disastrous confrontation, and taken Albert with him. She had made no comment to anyone on his departure, and if any of those in the castle thought Sir Roger's behavior odd, they wisely kept their opinions from his wife.

As for Mina, she was pleased that he was gone. It meant she had considerably less to worry about, and if she did think of him often, it was only to count her blessings at his absence. Or so she tried to convince herself.

Mina looked up at the fruit and vaguely noticed that it seemed to be growing well. A few bees, more alert in the coolness of the early hours, buzzed past her as if on important business.

She felt more like a bee overstuffed with nectar during the hottest part of the warmest day of the season, she thought as she strolled slowly through the grass cropped short by the sheep allowed to graze there. During Roger's absence, she had discovered that she had almost nothing to do. To be sure, she had taken over the business of running the household, but with the wedding guests gone, there were only the day-to-day tasks to oversee.

The hall servants had clearly been well trained, so they needed little immediate supervision. Dudley saw to every aspect of the management of the estate, and she had no need to interfere except to make sure she knew what was happening every day. Several times the steward had sought her opinion regarding a household matter, and she had given it. If she suspected he was saving the important decisions for Roger's return, she also knew there was little she could do to change that.

She helped with the meals, although she sensed that Thorbert didn't fully appreciate any assistance. Indeed, he was such a fine cook, she had no cause to interfere except to escape boredom.

She had tried to assist Father Damien and his almoner, a man nearly as ancient as the priest and all too similar in comprehension, as they distributed the alms to the poorer members of the village. She had been forced to give up when the two men consistently ignored her. It wasn't a purposeful neglect; they simply seemed to forget that she was with them.

She had gone riding with Reginald a few times; however, the pace he preferred was so leisurely, she rapidly grew impatient. Her mare was too old for long gallops, too, and she soon felt that it would be less frustrating to remain inside the castle walls.

To think, during the long years that had seemed almost like captivity, she had harbored such wonderful plans for when she married! She had lain awake at nights imagining how she would command her vast household, gather important people about her, lead the society of the land, be respected. Be listened to. Be important.

Instead, she was finding that while she had everyone's respect except her husband's, and was listened to by everybody, save the elderly priest and his almoner, she was not really very important. She suspected that the estate would continue to function with only a slight interruption if she disappeared in a cloud of smoke like a necromancer. To be sure, there would be some talk, which she could easily envision: "I knew she was strange all the time." "Aye, so did I." "Well, let's get back to work before Sir Roger sees us talkin'." "Aye." And that would be it.

Mina was allowing herself a few more moments to wallow in self-pity when she noticed a couple at the far end of the orchard. She thought it was Hilda and a man. If the maidservant was dallying with a lover when she should have been attending to her duties . . . !

Mina strode toward them. As she drew closer, she noticed a young child toddling near the couple. The little boy had been hidden by the trunk of a tree before. "Hilda?" she called out, puzzled by these unknown visitors.

Startled, Hilda turned to her and the servant's gaze quickly darted between the child and the man beside her, a big, stolid fellow with a shock of thick black hair above equally thick black brows. "My lady!" she cried, hurrying to take the child's hand.

The boy buried his face in Hilda's skirts, then peered shyly at Mina. He was an adorable child, in the bloom of health, with plump rosy cheeks and serious big blue eyes. A thumb progressed pensively to his cherry bow mouth. Mina smiled warmly at him as she knelt in front of them. "Now, who have we here? Is he come to be a page for my lord?"

Hilda flushed and one hand went around the boy protectively. "This is my son, Hollis. Bow to my lady, Hollis," she said softly.

The little boy bobbed his head, his thumb still in his mouth. Mina rose and looked at the man beside Hilda, wondering if this was the child's father and if so, why he hadn't married her.

"This is Lud, my brother, the reeve," Hilda said, answering the unspoken question. "He brings Hollis to see me when he has business at the castle." The last was said with some defiance, but there was fear in the serving woman's eyes.

"Where does Hollis live?" Mina inquired, her gaze searching the child's face. She stopped when she realized she was trying to detect some semblance of Roger.

"With Lud and his family. Dudley doesn't mind him visiting me here, my lady. Truly."

"And the boy's father?"

"Dead, my lady. Drowned in the river when I was with child. Afterward, Dudley was kind enough to offer me a place at the castle. I...I didn't want to burden anybody with Hollis, and Lud and Mary offered to take him for me, and they let me see him as often as I can."

"This must not continue," Mina said firmly, and Hilda blanched. "You must bring Hollis to stay with you at the castle." She crouched down again and looked at the boy. "If that is what he would like. Would you, Hollis?"

Hollis solemnly nodded his head.

"Oh, my lady, I thank you with all my heart, but my duties—"

"There are enough women in the castle to help you look after him, I think."

Hilda grinned and looked at her brother. "Mary won't mind, I'm sure, with the new baby on the way. You've both been so kind to look after him, but I've missed him so much!"

"You will come to play with me sometimes, won't you, Hollis?" Mina said, addressing the child who she now knew was not her husband's offspring.

"Yeth," he lisped, taking his thumb from his mouth for the brief time needed to respond, and then he smiled at her.

Mina longed to scoop the little fellow up into her arms and press his soft, satin cheek to hers. The yearning was so powerful, so overwhelming and shocking in its strength that she straightened abruptly. "Perhaps one day, Sir Roger will make you his page. And then a squire, and then a knight, eh?"

The boy nodded, Hilda beamed and Lud, who had not said a word or even registered much change of expression, nodded as slowly and solemnly as

Hollis. "We'll miss him," Lud said, his voice deep and slow, but not without true compassion. "He's a good boy, my lady."

"I can see that," she said. "Hilda, you may go with Lud and collect your son's things. Take as long as you like. Hollis might need some time to get used to his new home, too. I excuse you from your duties for the rest of the week."

"Oh, my lady, thank you!" Hilda cried. "I can't thank you enough!" She gathered her child into her arms, tears of happiness in her eyes, and hurried off, with Lud trailing behind like a big dog.

Mina sighed as she watched them leave.

"What was that all about?" Reginald called out from behind her. "Wasn't that Hilda?"

Mina glanced over her shoulder to see Reginald tiptoeing through the damp grass as if it were a freshly manured field. He wore an intricately embroidered red tunic with slashed sleeves over a purple shirt. She noted with hidden amusement that somebody had managed to get his painted boots clean. Perhaps that was why he was walking with such care. "Yes. And her son. And her brother."

"I say, really? She has a child?"

"Yes. The father is dead. I've told her to bring the boy to live at the castle."

"That's generous of you, Mina."

Mina shrugged in response.

"She's a pretty wench, isn't she? And very kind," Reginald said. "I don't know how I would have recovered without her."

Mina thought time would have been sufficient, but she didn't say so.

"You know, I've often envied the peasants," he remarked philosophically. "Their lives and obligations are so simple, so uncomplicated."

Mina forced herself to keep a straight face. "Their clothes are so plain, so rough."

"You're making fun of me," he complained, aggrieved.

"I'm trying to imagine you in a simple homespun tunic with a hoe over your shoulder. It isn't easy."

"Very well, I confess I wouldn't want to wear a peasant's filthy, flea-infested garments—but there is a simplicity to their lives that I do sincerely envy."

Mina heard the earnestness in his voice, and decided not to tease him anymore. "What are you doing here, Reginald? I thought you'd be playing another game of dice or hounds and hare."

"Dudley couldn't spare the time and there wasn't anybody else, so I decided to come along and see what you were up to," he said, turning back toward the castle. Mina fell into step beside him. She had to slow her usual pace to match his. "I must say I didn't expect to see you strolling through the orchard.''

"I came to see about the fruit.''

"Hmm. Not a lot to do around here, eh?''

"Enough," she lied.

"Any word when Roger will be back?''

"No.''

Reginald paused and gave her a look that was surprisingly studious. "I say, Mina, is everything all right?''

"Of course it is.''

"I was just wondering, that's all. I mean, your new husband suddenly decided to go to his other estate after only one day of married life. People are talking.''

"What are they saying?''

"That you had an argument or something. That he looked angry. I don't put much stock in that, I must say. Roger always looks angry to me. Always has. If somebody were to ask me, who's the surliest fellow you know? Well, the answer would be Sir Roger de Montmorency." He gave Mina a sidelong glance. "But even so, he's not like Father.''

"How do you know? You were in France.''

"I remember the days before I left with some clarity, Mina. He was never a kind man, but he was already becoming a bitter one, thinking he'd made a mistake marrying your mother. Yes, a bitter, mean-spirited fellow already given to drink. I say it even if he was my father. I'll also say that Roger de Montmorency isn't mean spirited, for all his surliness. Look how he let his sister marry who she wanted, despite his respect for the baron's wishes.''

"Yet you fear him.''

"Fear *and* admire. He scares me because he seems to be so much that I am not.''

Mina regarded Reginald thoughtfully, and with some pity as well as understanding. Roger de Montmorency was like all the power of Norman France combined in one person. So was the baron, in a way, but there was one very important difference. The baron had a hardened quality that Roger had yet to acquire. She hoped he never did.

"Does it surprise you to hear me speak this way?" Reginald asked, breaking the silence. "I know what I am, Mina. I could never be like Sir Roger, nor am I quite sure I would want to be. Such responsibility! Such fortitude! He never lets his guard down, not for a single moment.''

Mina thought of the first kiss they had shared, and of the look she'd seen again in his eyes when he had turned her toward him in the bedchamber. Unless she was very wrong, his guard had been down on both occasions, if only for a fleeting moment.

"Mina?''

"Yes ?"

"Are you sorry for the marriage? Do you wish I had stood up to the baron and refused?"

"No," she answered truthfully, looking at her half brother steadily and giving voice to her feelings in a way that she was not used to. "I wanted to be married."

"I'm relieved to hear it, I must say. Still, he's not an easy man to know."

"No." Mina gave him another sidelong glance. "I don't suppose I'm an easy woman to get to know, either."

"That's right!" he exclaimed. Reginald's expression of surprise and enlightenment was almost comical to behold. "You know, you're a lot like him, sometimes. Proud, sure of yourself—"

"I would stop before you flatter me too much, Reginald."

"You deserve the compliments! I should think you two would get along very well, now that I think about it. Why did he leave?"

"Because we're both proud and altogether too sure of ourselves. Besides, the rumors are true. We had an argument."

Mina tried to walk ahead, but Reginald's hand shot out and clutched her arm. "My God! You didn't! Whatever did you say to him?"

Reginald's hand held her firmly in place. Aware of the sentries on the battlements above, she didn't want to struggle, so she didn't move. "Let me go, Reginald."

"I can't believe you would do such a foolish thing! To argue with *him!* What would be worth that risk?"

She smiled wanly. Reginald could never understand her, or why it was so important for her to stand up to Roger or anyone else, so she said, "Perhaps it was only a lovers' spat, Reginald."

That startled him, too, but at least he let go. "A lovers' spat?"

"Yes, and I am not going to go into the details," she said, striding forward. "Now if you'll excuse me, I need to see how many eggs were gathered today."

"Certainly. Go ahead. I don't expect you to tell me anything," Reginald spluttered, watching her go and reflecting that of all the people he could least imagine having a lovers' spat, it was Mina and Sir Roger. A lovers' shouting match, perhaps, but not a simple spat. Still, if that was what Mina said it was, there was cause to hope, and definitely no cause to go sticking his nose into their business.

Much better to mind his own, especially when the lovely, well-endowed, kindhearted Hilda was not so far away.

* * *

Albert stamped his foot on the stone floor of the small manor house, setting the chess pieces rattling on the makeshift board.

Startled , Roger glared at his friend in the dim light provided by a single rush torch. "What the devil was that for?" he snarled.

"You've been staring at that queen for so long, I thought you were dead," Albert answered, a hint of impatience in his voice as he looked at Roger. "Are you going to move it or not?"

"Since you are so upset, I will," Roger replied, his musing interrupted. He kept his voice calm, but he was also surprised by his own lack of attention to the game. He really had to stop thinking about Mina and their last quarrel. It hadn't been his fault. It was hers, and if she didn't understand that—

"Move that godforsaken piece!" Albert growled again.

Roger shoved the playing piece over the board, his movement casting a large shadow over the walls of the two-roomed building.

"The poaching problem has been addressed, your steward given his orders for the harvest, the repairs to the outbuildings underway—why are we staying here?"

"Since when are you so anxious to get home?" he demanded, determined to keep his mind on the game.

"Since we have had nothing to do here for the past three days," Albert replied, his tone returning to its customary calm.

"I like it here."

"You've never liked it here before," Albert charged as he moved his bishop. "And that was before you had a wife waiting for your return."

Roger didn't say anything. Instead, he kept his gaze on the board as if fascinated by Albert's conventional move.

"What's really going on?" Albert asked. "Did you quarrel with her?"

"What makes you ask that?"

Albert leaned back in his chair and contemplated his friend. "I've known you a long time, Roger. When you act in such a manner, you've usually had an argument with someone. And you've usually lost."

"I don't know what you're talking about. What mysterious 'manner' are you alluding to?"

"You are as cantankerous as a wounded boar gone off to lick his wounds in peace, and you know it. *Did you quarrel?*"

"My relationship with my wife is none of your business."

"It is if you are making everyone around you miserable!"

"You're a fine one to offer advice about married life, Albert, when you've never been married and have had only one liaison in your whole life, which was a complete disaster!" Roger complained. A look of surprised distress passed over Albert's face. "Forgive me, Albert," Roger said, immediately contrite. "I shouldn't have said that. You're right. I am angry and upset, and I shouldn't be taking it out on you."

"You shouldn't be taking it out on your wife, either."

"It's her fault."

"Is it?"

"Yes!" Roger stood and began to pace. "She doesn't have the first notion of how a wife should behave toward her husband!"

"Such as?"

"Obedience, for one thing."

"Unquestioning obedience, I suppose you mean."

"What's wrong with that?"

Albert sighed heavily and gazed steadily at Roger. "That's a fine quality in a soldier or a knight who's sworn fealty to you. I think a wife should feel free to disagree with her husband."

"That's because you've never been married," Roger observed, this time without the harsh condemnation he had conveyed before.

"Roger," Albert said firmly, "even I can tell that Mina Chilcott is not some simple country girl who's going to be overwhelmed by your magnificence. She has a mind of her own, and obviously expects to use it. Given what I know of her background, I cannot say that I blame her."

"What do you know about her former circumstances?"

"You've heard about her father, surely."

"I know he beat her."

"Isn't that enough to make you want to be gentle with her?"

"Yes," he confessed. "I tried. But she makes me so angry—"

"When I once tried to pity you, do you remember what you did? You blackened my eye."

"I never did understand why you forgave me for that."

"Because I guessed that you considered pity a confirmation of weakness. Perhaps Mina thought you were pitying her, or condescending to her. She looks to have a temper that would not accept either graciously."

Roger threw himself in his chair. "Suppose you are right. Suppose I did everything wrong with her. Suppose I even . . . hurt her a little. What should I do now?"

Albert's eyes narrowed. "What do you mean, hurt her a little?"

Roger flushed with shame. "That's what she said I did. I hit her, I gather."

"Don't you know?"

"I don't remember," he confessed mournfully. "I can't recall a thing about my wedding night beyond one kiss."

"You didn't seem that drunk."

"I didn't think I was."

"Still," Albert said, avoiding his eyes in a manner that struck Roger to the heart, "she says you did. I confess I cannot believe it, but we must accept her word. You are going to have a harder time than I thought, Roger, regaining her trust. You do want to, I assume?"

"Perhaps," he said sulkily. He didn't like having his marriage and his emotions discussed this way, even by Albert, and he regretted confessing what he had done. Albert would never regard him in the same way again, and that pained him greatly. "I don't think she ever liked me to begin with."

"She respected you, at any rate. I think she could come to forgive you, provided you don't do anything like that again."

"I won't!"

"Good. She's a fine woman, Roger. Clever and strong, beautiful—"

"Beautiful?"

"Beautiful," Albert confirmed, giving him a look that seemed to question his intelligence. Albert would never have given him such a look before, and Roger was certain he had lost some of his friend's esteem. He told himself it didn't matter. Albert obviously didn't understand the situation at all. "She's also a lot like you."

"Now you're talking nonsense."

"You know she is, whether you care to acknowledge it or not. She's as proud as you are, at any rate, and you expect her to act like a servant. Or one of your men."

"No, I don't."

"Roger, I've watched you around women before, and you've never treated one like this."

"Like what?" he demanded.

"As if she were a man."

Roger couldn't imagine another woman in the world whose femininity meant more to him. "You've gone mad."

"It's you who isn't acting normal. Listen to me, Roger, and don't just stare at me that way. If you didn't care a whit about her, you'd be charming and ignore everything she said."

"You sound very sure about that, Albert."

"I am. And you can also be sure that I want you to be happy. Happier than me, anyway. So why don't you just allow yourself to like her and address her accordingly?''

Roger heard his friend's genuine concern, so he answered with truth. "I do find myself thinking about her too much.''

Albert nodded, apparently satisfied with even this lackluster admission. "You have had the great good fortune to find the perfect woman for yourself, Roger.''

Roger was not as convinced, but he was pleased to hear Albert say so, nonetheless.

"The only question is, how to begin anew?'' Albert mused aloud.

"Begin anew? What are you talking about? She's my wife, by God's blood.''

Albert's frown showed his annoyed displeasure. "Roger, she's a *woman,* not some inanimate thing. To begin with, a little kindness would not be amiss.''

"I won't apologize, if that's what you're going to propose,'' Roger said resolutely. "She was as much in the wrong as I was.''

"Since I don't know what you argued about—''

"And I'm not going to tell you, either.''

Albert sighed with exasperation. "Roger, you are going to be married for some time, I hope, so you had best think about making amends, if only to ensure some measure of domestic tranquillity. It really doesn't matter what you quarreled about, and no, the great Sir Roger de Montmorency doesn't have to humble himself if he doesn't want to."

"Good."

"As I was saying, since I don't know what exactly you quarreled about, I can only speak in generalities. Maybe you should take her a gift."

"I'm not some lovelorn page going to hand my lady a red, red rose!" Roger said scornfully. "I would look like a fool."

"Fine," Albert answered querulously. "Don't give her a flower. Can't you think of something else?"

Roger crossed his arms and tried to envision a gift that wouldn't seem like a capitulation or admission of guilt. "That horse of hers is a disgrace," he said at last. "Maybe I could buy the mare I looked at yesterday, and give it to her."

"It would be a start."

## Chapter Ten

**M**ina held out the sheep's bladder inflated with air and smiled at Hollis, who waited poised for her to throw the makeshift ball into his chubby little hands, a look of intense concentration on his face. "Catch it!" she cried, tossing it toward him.

From his place at the other end of the small garden on the grounds of the castle, Hollis darted forward as fast as his legs could go. He tripped over one of the winding footpath's newly laid cobblestones and nearly fell into a bed of lavender. Mina moved to catch him, but he didn't fall. He caught the ball, his face breaking into a huge, triumphant smile.

"Good boy!" Mina said, holding out her own hands in invitation and quickly stepping back to her former position lest her young friend take offense at her apparent lack of confidence. "Throw it back and see if *I* can catch it this time."

Hollis's dark brows lowered, and he hefted the ball with all his boyish might. It flew past Mina toward the wooden gate that kept out the chickens and geese who ranged over the ground outside. The birds started to make a boisterous racket, which was surprising considering the ball came nowhere near them. "Hollis, you're so strong!" Mina cried approvingly as she turned around to retrieve his missile and see what had upset the birds.

The ball was lying on the ground at Roger's booted feet. He had obviously recently opened the gate and now stood just inside it, one hand still on the top of the wooden door. Hollis ran toward her and grabbed onto her skirt, his thumb thrust in his mouth and his eyes wide.

Mina stood where she was, surprised by Roger's unexpected appearance, noting the slight smile on his handsome face. He seemed tired, too, she thought, as he looked around the garden she was creating.

Roger leaned over and picked up the toy. "What have we here?" he asked, raising one eyebrow and rotating the ball in his hands.

Mina put her arm around Hollis. "This is Sir Roger de Montmorency," she said in a soft and reassuring voice. "This is his castle." She glanced at Roger. "Sir Roger, may I present Hollis, Hilda's son."

"Ah," Roger exclaimed quietly and with more tenderness than she had suspected he possessed. He knelt on one knee and presented the ball to the boy. "He's got a very strong arm, has Hollis."

Hollis took his thumb out of his mouth and snatched the ball, then ran around to hide behind Mina's skirts. "It's all right," Mina crooned gently. "He looks fierce, but he's not annoyed with you. I promise."

Hollis peeked out and gave Roger such a long, steadfast, measuring stare so like his own that if Mina didn't believe Hilda's account of her son's parentage, she would have been sure Hollis was Roger's child. "Is he angry at *you?*"

"No, I'm not angry at her," Roger replied before Mina could say anything.

"He *looks* angry," Hollis noted timidly, obviously refusing to accept any evidence but that of his own big blue eyes. "He looks angry enough to *bite.*"

"He won't," Mina assured him.

"I'm not hungry right now," Roger said solemnly.

That was enough for Hollis. Holding tight to his ball and calling for his mother, he ran to the gate and disappeared.

"You frightened him," Mina charged as Roger straightened.

"I was making a joke."

"He's too little to know that," she countered. She drew a deep breath. Roger had been gone for over a fortnight, and she had had plenty of time to think about what she wanted from him and from her new life here, as well as consider her conversation with Reginald. Most of all, she wanted her relationship with Roger to be better. It might never be perfect, but surely they could live in some kind of harmony. Now was not the time to start another quarrel or cause more recriminations between them.

Roger crossed his arms. "I'm not good with children." The admission was rather defiant, but she thought the expression in his eyes was more melancholy, which surprised her. "I've never been around children," he said. "You seemed to be enjoying yourself."

Mina shrugged and struggled to find some neutral words. "He's a good boy. Did you know his father?"

Roger glanced at her sharply. "He's not mine."

"So Hilda told me. I meant no accusation. How long have you been home?" she said matter-of-factly. "When did you leave the other estate?"

"We departed this morning and only just arrived. I went to the hall looking for you, and Dudley said you were here." He looked at the flowers growing along the edge of the pathway. "This is very pretty. I meant to start something here, but I've never had time to worry about a garden."

"Dudley told me what you were planning for this space, so I decided I would start. It's not nearly finished, of course, and I'm sure you'll want to approve all the rest of the plants, but I thought I could begin."

"I don't care what you put here."

"Oh." Mina clasped her hands together and wondered what to say next. "You must be very tired. That's a fatiguing journey for one morning."

"I'm fine." He was standing equally still, his arms at his sides. "The hall looks better, too. You've had the tapestries cleaned."

"A simple enough task, once it was ordered."

"Oh." He cleared his throat. "Come with me to the inner ward. I have something to show you." He held out his arm expectantly. A little taken aback by this show of courtesy, Mina placed her hand lightly upon him. A simple enough act, yet the contact with his body thrilled her to her toes. She could feel the tension in his muscle, and wondered if he could hear the hammering of her heart as he led her out of the garden.

In the inner ward, Sir Albert was holding the lead to a lovely brown mare, who had a splash of white on her forehead and very dainty feet. "She's beautiful," Mina cried, barely resisting the urge to hurry forward because it wouldn't be seemly to run in the courtyard—and because she would have to let go of Roger's arm. "Good day, Sir Albert. I'm very happy to see you again."

Albert smiled warmly. "And I am very glad to be back, my lady," he replied. "We've missed you."

Mina didn't quite know how to take his words, but she realized she was hoping that Roger had missed her, too. Afraid she would see denial in her husband's face, she kept her gaze on the horse. "Is she yours?" she asked Albert, reluctantly leaving Roger to pet the beast's soft forehead. "How I envy you!"

"She's yours," Roger said flatly.

His announcement took Mina completely by surprise. Since she had encountered Roger with Hollis's ball at his feet, she had felt confused, disoriented and uncertain—but never more so than now. She put her hand to her breast and slowly turned to her husband, trying to read his dark eyes. "Mine?" she whispered.

She could decipher nothing from his expression, so she looked at Albert for confirmation. He nodded his head and handed her the lead before moving away.

She looked back at Roger. "Why?"

"Because you need a new horse," he replied gruffly. "That beast you arrived on is fit only for pasture."

She put her arms around the horse's neck and suddenly realized that she was going to cry. Which was ridiculous, especially given what Roger had just said. "She's lovely," she said softly when she was more in control of her emotions.

"You like her then?" Roger demanded.

"Very much indeed."

Then she saw that Sir Roger de Montmorency was blushing the bashful way Hollis did when she gave him a compliment. Roger's reaction charmed her as much as the gift itself. "I'm glad you came home," she said quietly.

Roger's eyes widened for the briefest of moments. "I...I have to see the sentries," he said hoarsely before he spun on his heel and marched away toward the gatehouse.

As she watched him go, Mina rubbed the mare's nose gently. "Come, girl," she whispered, turning toward the stable when her handsome husband disappeared from view. "I shall have to give you a name, won't I?"

But Mina's mind was less on a suitable name for the lovely mare than the thrilling, hopeful yearning she had seen in Roger's eyes before he turned away.

* * *

Roger gave a luxurious sigh and slid lower into the wooden tub filled with hot water. He had ordered Dudley to have a bath prepared, partly because his muscles ached from the morning's long ride, and partly because he was afraid that he smelled. The manor at his smaller estate was primitive, and when he stayed there he didn't take much time to bother with personal cleanliness. Now that he was back home, however, he thought he would be wise to wash before the evening meal.

As he felt the tension flee his muscles, he recalled the sight of Mina with Hilda's little boy, and how it had suddenly filled him with an incredible desire to see *their* child clinging to her skirts. She would make a fine mother to his sons, as brave and bold as any man, and yet womanly, too, in her wisdom. A man would never have had the sense to act cowed that first night, and although her attempts to shame him had made him angry, he saw now that he would have been enraged had she responded as...well, as *he* might have, with harsh recriminations. It took wisdom to guess at his probable reaction when she had not even met him.

He envisioned Mina with their child again, a rosy-hued picture of a madonna with her cherublike youngster. A soft-spoken, gentle madonna whose child would not run away in panic, afraid of him. Nor would the happy smile on their child's face and laughter in his eyes dissipate into dread and a stiff manner as Mina's had when she saw him.

Until he had given her the horse. Albert had been right to suggest a gift, and Roger had been a fool not to think of it himself. How very pleased she was! And how beautiful, with her hair unbound and wild in the sunlight and her simple dark green gown. Indeed, his pleased reaction to her happiness had been so intense, he had fled the inner ward in case he said something ridiculous, something only a minstrel or a man like Albert might say. Something about love.

It was true that he cared about Mina, he admitted, splashing the heated, scented water over his chest. He admired and respected her. He wanted very much to carry her to his bed and make passionate love with her. She was more than worthy to bear his children. Was that love? He had no idea.

There was a soft knock on the bedchamber door, which disrupted his thoughtful reverie. "What?" he bellowed, sitting up straighter. He didn't need to have an attendant while he bathed, but sometimes Dudley forgot on purpose, thinking an attendant more proper for a man of his station.

The door opened a crack. "May I enter?" Mina asked.

Roger felt himself blush hotly, although his mind told him he was being absurd. She was his wife. They had been intimate.

Nevertheless, he quickly climbed out of the tub and grabbed a large square of linen, which he wrapped around his waist. "Yes," he answered when he was ready.

She came into the room and looked at the tub, then at him. Her face reddened and she turned away as if she were the most bashful maiden in the kingdom.

The ludicrous nature of their behavior struck Roger. Here they were, husband and wife, as embarrassed as if they were total strangers. Nevertheless, he found her sudden shyness captivating. "Hand me my chausses, will you?" he asked, attempting to sound perfectly at ease.

She did so, averting her eyes. He tossed the linen aside and for a brief instant had a nearly uncontrollable desire to pull her into his arms, naked though he was. Not sure how she would respond, however, he pulled on his chausses instead.

"I want to thank you for the present," she said quietly. "I've...nobody has ever given me a gift like that before," she said in an earnest rush, still not looking at him. "Reginald gave me some clothes for the wedding, I suppose because he was afraid I would embarrass him otherwise and I truly had no suitable gowns, but the mare is so...she's lovely, and—" Mina looked at him over her shoulder "—I thank you."

Roger realized at once, and to his dismay, that he did not know how to respond to her heartfelt gratitude. "It was Albert's idea," he mumbled, turning away to hide his blushing face.

"But it was *your* doing," she said, moving one small step closer.

He risked a glance at her. God's blood, she was beautiful, even in the plainest gown. How her luminous blue-green eyes glowed, surrounded by the halo of her glorious hair! Her half-parted lips helped to kindle incredible passion, filling him with a burning desire to kiss her.

Her breasts rose and fell rapidly, as if she felt the unspoken hunger, too. He went toward her and drew her to him. She did not resist, which sent the banked flames within him roaring into fiery life. He kissed her fiercely, with a possessiveness and need that he had never felt before.

She did nothing for the briefest of moments— and then it was as if she felt not the heat of passion, but a veritable conflagration of desire and need and lust as strong as anything he had ever felt, and more.

There was no need for him to subdue his want, either, or to hide his yearning for her. He sensed that there was no plan to follow, steps to take, games to play. She clung to him almost desperately, between them an equal, blazing craving.

With a low moan, he thrust his tongue into her mouth. A scant heartbeat later, her tongue reversed the action, plunging between his lips as if she must—and would—partake of every delight.

God's wounds, she was like no other woman, and she was his wife. His hands pressed her to him, his hard arousal against her softness as she leaned into him, her breasts against his chest.

"My God!"

They sprang apart to see Dudley standing on the threshold, his face as red as one of Reginald's tunics. "My lord!" he said, his voice an octave higher than normal. "Forgive my intrusion! The evening meal is ready, and I..." His words trailed off into an embarrassed silence.

Never had Roger resented an interruption more. "We'll be there in a moment," he growled.

"Yes, Dudley," Mina replied, her tone a marvel of self-control that Roger found himself envying. There could be no doubt that she had been as engrossed in that kiss as he, but one would never guess it from her calm exterior. Only the ripe fullness of her lips and two bright spots of brilliant red upon each cheek gave any sign that she was embarrassed, too. "I am well aware that Sir Roger does not like to wait for his meals."

Still flustered, Dudley merely nodded and ran away.

Roger grabbed Mina's arm and yanked her back to him, bringing her breasts and hardened nipples once more into delightful contact with his naked chest. "They can all starve as far as I'm concerned. I want to stay here with you." His lips wandered down the slope of her cheek and along her neck.

"I . . . they . . ." she murmured. "It would not be seemly."

"I don't give a damn." His hands found the laces of her gown.

"Roger!" she chided, pulling away with conspicuous reluctance, her face flushed and wearing a smile that did nothing to cool his ardor. "They are waiting."

"So am I," he said, following her with a lascivious leer as she hurried to the door.

"Get dressed and come to the hall," she commanded. Her lips curved up even more enticingly. "We can finish this . . . conversation . . . later."

She left the room, and only when he was belting his tunic did it occur to Roger that she had given him a direct order.

So what of that? Her final words made that a very minor point.

Mina had never eaten a meal so swiftly in her life. She took no note of the food's taste or texture, or if it had been well prepared or properly presented. Conversation whirled about her, making no impact on her own thoughts, tumultuous emotions or burning desire. She didn't care what anybody said to her, didn't want to reply. All that mattered was concluding this social necessity as quickly as possible so that she could be alone with Roger, his lean, hard body against her, promising untold delights to come.

There were two things she did notice as she sat beside her husband during the meal—Roger was also eating in some haste, and his hand kept straying to fondle her leg. More than once she almost choked as his fingers stroked her thigh. At first, terrified that someone would see what he was doing, she tried to shift enough to make it clear that he should stop.

He did not, and eventually, she gave up her subtle protests. Indeed, what he was doing was simply too unbelievably arousing. Short of actually telling him to stop inflaming her desire, she was helpless to resist.

Finally, enough time had elapsed that they could retire, and they both stood at nearly the same instant. Roger said a good-night to the assembly, she nodded hers, and together, they walked decorously, if rather quickly, toward the stairs. As soon as they were out of sight, Roger halted and pulled her into his arms.

He pushed her back against the wall as he gave her a long, heated kiss. She returned his kiss ardently, letting the force of her passion sweep her along like a twig caught in a river's rushing current until, with a low growl, he lifted her into his strong arms and carried her to their bedchamber, kicking the door shut before setting her down.

Mina said nothing. There were no words for what she felt, no means to express her emotions. Only actions. Immediate actions, with no more hesitation. She knew what she wanted, and she wanted Roger. She went to him and hastily started to undo the lacings at the neck of his tunic. She said no soft words, made no tender whispers, uttered no mild entreaties.

Passion took command of them both, making them nearly frantic in their need. In minutes their clothes lay in a pile on the floor, and they were in the bed, naked and unashamed, aware only of each other and the longing that could no longer be denied.

As they explored each other's bodies, Mina vaguely realized she had never felt this way. Her body was hers, yet not hers. She was clay in Roger's hands, molded to his desire. Not *just* by his hands. His lips, his tongue, his fingertips—everything combined to provide the delightful sensation of his touch.

But he belonged to her, too. As he caressed her, she caressed him, letting him teach her. Soon, very soon, the pupil had mastered enough to mold the teacher. His gasps of pleasure were her reward, the fervent want in his face the sign of her newfound skill.

His knee pressed between her legs and willingly, like the flower seeking the sun, she opened for him. Grasping his powerful shoulders, she kissed him again, letting all the raw potency of her released emotions guide her to him.

He thrust inside her, pausing a moment when she uttered a sharp cry at a brief pain. Then she drove her hips against him, forgetting the pain as she sought to bring him nearer to feel every inch of his naked flesh against her. She wrapped her legs around him, clutched at him, held him tight.

With soft cries, Mina undulated beneath Roger, instinctively, almost thrashing, in a dance of such incredible animal sensuality that Roger felt as if he were a virgin again, experiencing the delight of being in a woman's arms for the first time. Never had he felt anything like this, never had he known such freedom to give rein to his passion and his need.

The crescendo came quickly, for both of them. Her fingers gripped him as she suddenly arched, rigid, when the overpowering tension burst into an astounding release for them both.

Panting, spent, enraptured, Roger rolled onto his back, taking her with him so that he was still enveloped by her, letting her lay her head on his chest, holding her gently there. It was a moment of tenderness such as he had never known. His heart swelled to think that she was responsible, this woman, his wife. He could have this experience again and again, and he was quite sure that the joy of the compassion...the *love*...he felt for her would never diminish.

Yes, love. There could be no other word, no other explanation.

Mina sighed softly, her breasts rising against his chest. He marveled at her perfect form and pale silky skin as she lay enfolded in his arms. She was no weak vessel, no fragile creature. She was strong, powerful, desirable as no woman had ever been to him before. And to think she was his wife!

"I am sorry I was so rude to you before," she whispered, raising her head to look at him. "I wouldn't have been, if I had known the sacrifice I was making."

He chuckled and brushed back a lock of her hair, tucking it behind her ear as gently as a mother tucks a blanket around a sleeping infant. "And I must be sure to give you more presents, if this is how you thank me."

Her brow furrowed slightly. "You make me sound—"

"Forgive me, Mina," he said at once, guessing her supposition. "I didn't mean it that way at all." He raised himself on his elbows to press a kiss between her eyes.

When he lay back, he saw that she was smiling. "You would not have apologized before," she noted.

He grinned and ran his hands over her back. This time it was his brow that furrowed. "These scars, Mina. You must have had a terrible life."

She nestled against him. "Some parts of it. My father was not an easy man, especially after my mother died. He became convinced that his other children were right, that he had debased the family by marrying a Saxon. There I was, the evidence, always before his eyes."

"He should not have beaten you."

"It doesn't matter now. He is dead, and I have you."

Her words made him more proud than any prize he had won or honors he had been given. "Mina, Mina," he whispered, cradling her in his arms, pleased beyond words.

She rose slightly. "I am so happy, Roger!" she said, a delightful giggle breaking from her lips. "After how I have tormented you, surely I don't deserve it!"

His deep laughter joined hers. "I was so uncivil, I don't deserve it, either!"

After a moment, when they had little breath left, they both sighed and smiled. "I must say, Mina," Roger said pensively, touching her cheek, "I don't know how you can have any sense of humor left."

Her expression grew serious, and she bent close to whisper in his ear, her voice like a caress. "It was laugh or die, Roger. Some days, my sense of humor was all I had."

"You will never feel that way again, Mina. I promise you," he replied, equally serious.

Mina lay back down upon his chest, content for the first time in years, happy to the core of her soul. She had never, in her most secret dreams, guessed that being with a man could be so intoxicating, so wonderful, so exciting. He was no lovelorn youth, nor afraid that she would find his caresses too much for a mere woman. He had loved her fully, without restraint, with passion and a flagrant need. Somehow, by a fluke of fate or perhaps the intervention of an unknown saint, she had been given the best husband in the world. A man she could honor and respect. A man she could trust.

A man she could love.

Yes, love. There could be no other word, no other explanation. A soft sigh of happiness turned into a yawn of tired serenity.

"We should sleep," Roger mumbled, his lips against her forehead.

"Yes." She shifted, lifting herself from him, and gasped.

"What is it?" he murmured.

"I'm a little sore," she said softly, grimacing as he withdrew.

"I was too hasty, perhaps."

"Perhaps."

"I didn't mean to hurt you," he said solemnly, lying beside her and running his finger along her chin, his deep voice intimately tender. "I'll be more careful next time. And every time. I will never hurt you again. You have my word."

She looked at him gravely, knowing it was time for the truth. "You didn't before."

He blinked and his hand became still. "What?"

"You didn't hurt me before, not the way you think."

His eyes narrowed and his mouth hardened as he abruptly sat up. "Mina, you had best tell me exactly what I *did* do."

## Chapter Eleven

Frightened by the harsh anger in Roger's midnight dark eyes, Mina reached for the coverings and wrapped them around her as a sort of shield. "You fell asleep."

"I fell asleep? *When* did I fall asleep?"

Her desperate though necessary words came awkwardly, but she would not be a coward. She would tell him everything. "I was angry with you. I heard you talking to the baron the day before our wedding, and your words...hurt me. I know I am not a beautiful woman. You were marrying me only to please the baron. But to hear your arrogant dismissal of me...I wanted to hurt you, the great, powerful Sir Roger de Montmorency. So I tricked you. I put some sleeping potion in the wine in the bedchamber. You kissed me and went to the bed...and then you fell asleep."

Still he stared at her. "You lied to me."

His words were as cold and unforgiving as his expression.

"You talked of me as if I were your property," she replied, a tinge of desperation in her voice.

"My wife *is* my property," he said scornfully, rising from the bed like an angry god of ancient lore roused by the follies of mortals. "What other tricks have you played on me? Were you still a virgin when I married you, or was that another lie? Is that how you had the skill to inflame my desire for you?"

"I was a virgin until a moment ago, when you took my maidenhead. Here is the proof." She pulled back the coverlet to reveal a small stain of fresh blood.

"There was blood before," he noted with an unbelieving sneer.

"From my finger. Can you doubt you took my virginity tonight? Can you honestly believe that what I did with you was only art? That I have been taught by some other, unknown man?"

He yanked on his hastily discarded chausses. "I can believe almost anything of you, my lady."

Horrified by his accusations, dismayed by his words, she could only stare at him, too speechless to respond.

Straightening, he said, "Two things I prize above all else, Mina. Honesty and loyalty. I see that I cannot trust your honesty. You had better not give me *any* reason to question your loyalty.'' He grabbed his tunic and strode toward the door.

''Roger, I am being honest with you now!'' she exclaimed, drawing on all her strength to protest the fierce, completely unjustified condemnation she had seen in his eyes.

His hand paused on the latch of the door.

''Are you?'' Roger demanded, his eyes inscrutable once more. ''How can I ever be sure?''

''Because I give you my word!''

He stared at her for one long, unbearable moment before he yanked open the door and was gone.

Mina sat motionless on the bed. How could he have so quickly and so completely changed toward her? How could he not believe her? Would he prefer to think that he had beaten her?

What had she done that was so very terrible, anyway? She had only tried to retain her dignity in the one way she could. She *had* tricked him—but was his rigorous judgment of her fair?

Who was he to act so wounded? Her slight fraud had been a secret one. She had not exposed him to the jeers of others. She had not shamed him before his men.

She racked her mind trying to see a reason for his extreme reaction and remembered that first morning, when it had dawned on him that he had apparently injured her. He had been very upset, she realized now, certainly far more than others who had truly laid a hand on her. Afterward, those others had barely noticed her cuts and bruises, and carried on as if nothing at all existed to impede her in the continuation of her tasks.

But Roger—Roger had looked horrified. She knew him well enough now to understand that any expression of his innermost reaction revealed its strength. Then had come his angry defensiveness, calling forth a similar response from her.

Yes, *now* she knew how to gauge his responses, but she hadn't then, and she didn't think it was right that he should have expected her to. She was no mind reader. What was she supposed to do, judge his moods from that throbbing vein in his temple or the way he tilted his head?

Why should she, when he was not prepared to make the same effort for her? *She* had put her thoughts into words, and still he would not hear, not even after what they had shared.

She was who she was, and there was nothing so very wrong in that. Regrets would not help. They were a weakness, and she prized strength, just as he prized honesty and loyalty.

If he could not understand her, if he would not listen to her or hear her words, it did not matter. If he acted like a willful child, she would treat him like one. She would ignore him. Certainly she was getting used to that.

And as for her stupid notion of loving him...

Mina turned her head into the pillow, which still held the scent of Roger's hair, determined to forget everything that had so recently happened here. Instead, she burst into stormy, anguished tears, and raged against the weakness that brought them.

The next morning, Roger strode into the stables.

"My lord!" one of the stable hands cried, snapping to an attentive position and pulling his forelock. Roger could tell from the worried frown on Neslin's face that he was afraid some mistake had been discovered in his work.

"I've come to saddle my horse," Roger snarled, in no mood to lighten an underling's worries. He had enough of his own.

Neslin hurried to fetch his saddle while Roger went to Raven. The horse snorted a greeting, lifted his head and pranced in anticipation of exercise.

Raven's objectives were simple and understandable, Roger thought fretfully as he rubbed the animal's snout. Not like Mina's. She was as inscrutable as a cat and clever as a fox. What other tricks had she played on him? What other schemes were running through that head of hers?

He was a fool to think he could care for her. He had been an idiot to even consider this notion of love. He had been right to hold himself aloof and apart.

He sighed heavily. For a brief time, he had forgotten that lesson, and as his punishment he had to endure this terrible ache in his heart.

Raven nuzzled his hand, seeking an apple, and Roger wished he had thought to bring one. A simple thing it was to give Raven a gift!

"Where are you going?" Albert asked, appearing at the stable door. "And where have you been? I didn't see you in the chapel."

"I have been busy commanding my castle," Roger replied brusquely. "I'm going hunting, or we shall have no meat on the table tonight."

"Oh? Well, I'll fetch Bredon, shall I? And do you want Edred, too?"

"They've already got their orders," Roger snapped before surveying his friend's fine attire scornfully. "If you want to come along, you'd better get out of those fancy clothes. You're starting to dress like that conceited fool Reginald."

Albert looked taken aback and slightly hurt, but Roger didn't care. It was true, and the sooner Albert quit dressing like some stupid youth and remembered who and what he was, the better!

"I believe I shall *not* go with you, Roger," Albert said solemnly. "In your present mood, you shall surely do yourself, or somebody else, harm."

"Fine. Stay here with the women!"

Albert didn't reply, but spun on his heel and marched into the inner ward. Roger told himself it didn't matter. Albert was too full of reproaches these days, treating him as a master treated a dull pupil. Well, he *wasn't* stupid and he wasn't a fool, and Albert didn't know anything about this business with Mina, and he never would!

The stable boy returned, holding Roger's saddle as if it were made of the finest crystal. "Give it to me!" Roger ordered, yanking it out of the lad's hands. "What are you staring at?" he bellowed when Neslin didn't move away.

"No...nothing, my lord," Neslin stammered, reddening and wringing his hands.

"Then get out of my sight!"

Albert approached Lord Chilcott, who was always the last to leave the table at any given meal. This morning, Reginald was attired in a tunic of such bright green it was almost too much for the eyes to look at. He was busily sampling some pears when Albert sat beside him.

"Lovely meal, eh?" Reginald said, wiping the juice that was running down his chin.

"Excellent, as always," Albert agreed. He cleared his throat deferentially, hoping to alert the not-very-astute Reginald that he was about to speak of serious matters. "How do you think your sister and Roger are getting along?"

Reginald gave him a startled look. "Well enough, for a newly wedded couple. I confess I had some doubts about this marriage, considering Mina's . . . strength of character. But everything seems all right."

*At least it did last night,* Albert thought, remembering the couple's behavior at the evening meal. He had seen Roger anxious to bed a woman before, but never had his urgent desire been more blatant. Albert had half expected him to grab Mina and take her right there on the high table.

And perhaps even more surprising, judging from the way Mina had acted, Albert had little doubt she would have let him.

Unfortunately, something seemed to have gone very wrong in the interim. Mina had not left the bedchamber this morning, and Roger looked as angry and impatient as Albert had ever seen him.

Albert rubbed his chin thoughtfully. "Relations look a little strained to me," he observed.

"Oh, I say, really? I suppose you're right," Reginald replied, biting into another piece of fruit. "They hardly said a word during the evening meal.

Well—'' he paused in his chewing to sigh wearily "—they probably quarreled again. I don't attach too much importance to that. Any man would undoubtedly argue with Mina. She's too outspoken sometimes. And her temper! It goes with her hair, though. Surely Sir Roger knows that and can overlook it.''

"I am not so certain," Albert said slowly.

"She liked his present, didn't she? She was a long time in the stable, getting the mare seen to properly. I've never seen her so pleased. She's named it Jeanette.''

"Yes, I thought she was delighted, too. Why do you suppose she hasn't come down yet? Do you think she's upset because of Roger's foul humor this morning?''

Reginald, having finished all the fruit, stopped eating and wiped his fingers delicately on a clean napkin. "With Mina, who knows? Maybe. Maybe she's upset because she's not sure *what* he's feeling. It's certainly hard for me to tell whether Sir Roger is annoyed, or extremely angry or just his usual self.''

"I saw the vein in his temple throbbing. That's usually a sign of agitation.''

"Indeed? Maybe somebody ought to tell Mina that. I mean, she might be enraging him without even knowing it. You know, she could be staying in the bedchamber for one of those mysterious female reasons. An ache in her head, or some such thing. It could have nothing to do with Roger at all.''

''True,'' Albert conceded doubtfully. ''Do you think she might be angry at *him?*''

Reginald waved his hand in an airily dismissive gesture. ''Who knows? She gets angry over so many things, and at nothing. Perhaps Roger said he didn't like her headdress, or her gown, or something, and she's up there sulking.''

Albert didn't think Mina was nearly as vain as that, nor could he envision her sulking. ''Maybe someone should speak to them. Offer a word of advice.''

Reginald pushed back his chair abruptly. ''If you think so, you are welcome to do it. For my part, I intend to stay well out of the way. Now, if you will excuse me, I'm going to see if I can get somebody to wash my hose.''

Albert sighed heavily as Reginald scurried from the hall as if he thought Albert intended to drag him before Roger that very moment.

Was it his place to interfere, either? Albert pondered as he slowly walked from the hall out into the warm morning sun. After all, who was he to offer any man advice on marriage or love?

Roger was a stubborn, arrogant man, and intruding in his marriage might cost Albert a valued friendship, but if he spared Roger any of the heartache that was his daily lot, it would be worth it. With that thought in mind, Albert strode toward the stables and entered. He squinted as his eyes grew accustomed to the dimness.

"Can I help you, Sir Albert?" a stable boy asked nervously, tugging his forelock and then clasping his hands behind his slim back.

"Ah, Neslin, yes. Have you seen Sir Roger hereabouts?"

"He's gone out on Raven. Left just a bit ago, Sir Albert."

"Did he say where he was going?"

"No, sir, he didn't." Neslin shifted and said quietly, "He was in a pretty foul humor, Sir Albert. Angry, like."

"Ah. Well, saddle up my horse, will you?"

In a very short time, Albert was riding after his friend.

A little later that morning, Reginald hesitated outside the door of his bedchamber and gazed down the hall toward the stairs leading upward to Mina's chamber.

Perhaps he should speak to her. If she was unhappily married, he was responsible. Or rather, partly. After all, it had been the baron's doing. *He* could not have refused the powerful Baron De-Guerre. Besides, Mina had agreed. He had given her the opportunity to refuse, but she had wisely realized that it was something of an elevation for her to be married to one of the baron's favored knights.

Probably she would only snap at him and tell him her marriage was none of his concern, at least not anymore. Truly, it wasn't his duty to interfere in the affairs of husband and wife, despite Albert's obviously heartfelt words. Albert might do better to find himself a wife rather than stick his nose into Sir Roger's business.

Yes, Reginald decided, it was not their place to offer advice or even a sympathetic ear. Better for the newly wedded couple to solve their problems without interference. Feeling much better now that he had talked himself out of any responsibility or obligation toward his half sister, Reginald entered his bedchamber.

There was somebody inside, and he quickly realized it was Hilda standing in the middle of the room, her expression eager and excited.

"What...what do you want?" he asked awkwardly.

Before she could answer, it occurred to him that this could be the answer to his prayers, and he quickly closed the door.

"Forgive my intrusion, my lord," she said nervously.

"Think nothing of it," Reginald replied, tugging on his tunic and trying to act as if he frequently discovered pretty, buxom serving wenches who had filled his dreams night after night standing in his bedchamber. He knew he should go closer to her. Or smile seductively. Or say something else. Instead, he stood like a training dummy, hands at his side, his only movement the trickle of sweat running down his back.

Her lovely brows knit with concern, Hilda came closer until she was almost touching him. She leaned forward. Reginald felt faint. "It's about your sister, Lady Mina," she whispered.

"M . . . Mina?" he squeaked, confused. At the moment, he couldn't remember who Mina was.

"She's not treating Sir Roger right."

"Oh." The mention of his brother-in-law returned Reginald to disappointing reality with startling speed. "She's not?"

"No," Hilda said, shaking her head so that her thick, wavy brown hair brushed her breasts.

Reginald didn't dare look at her, not if he was expected to think coherently, and he didn't want to seem a fool to her. "And what do you think should be done?"

"I was hoping you could speak with her. I know Sir Roger well—"

"Just how well?" Reginald demanded.

"Intimately well," Hilda admitted. "But that's over now. Has been since before the wedding ceremony." She gave him a searching look. "I thought if I told you about him, you could tell her. It would be better coming from you, my lord."

"I see," Reginald replied, trying to appear wise. "What advice do you have for her?"

"She should never talk back to Sir Roger, for one thing."

"What happens if you do?" Reginald asked sternly. "Does he punish you?"

"Oh, no! No, my lord," she answered quickly and sincerely. "I... I don't know what he'd do. I never tried. I never had the gumption. I thought maybe she had, you see, and that was the trouble."

"I see your point. Anything else?"

"If she wants to give orders, she should ask him first. He's used to giving all the orders."

"Yes. That makes good sense."

Hilda came close again. "And she might try..." She whispered something that made Reginald blush as scarlet as his hose.

"I'm not going to say anything of the kind to her!" he protested, backing away. "I've never heard of such base, evil, disgusting, unnatural—"

"It's perfectly natural," Hilda said, taken aback by his repelled reaction to her revelation that Sir Roger often enjoyed making love in places other than a bed. "Haven't *you?*"

"Certainly not! I would never demean myself in such a manner! It's too...too...peculiar!"

His indignation was so extreme and so charmingly blustery that Hilda was quite sure she was addressing a virgin, as well as an adorable if somewhat affected young man who might lose some of his more outrageous vanities with the love of a good woman. Such as herself.

"Perhaps you should find out firsthand, my lord," she proposed coyly, sauntering toward him with an enticing smile.

"I don't know...."

But soon he did. Indeed, Reginald was shortly convinced that there was nothing so very sinful in Hilda's suggestion, and he quite forgot Mina, Roger and everything except the delights he found in Hilda's arms.

Unfortunately, Albert's attempt to help his friend did not meet with such fascinating results.

## Chapter Twelve

Albert couldn't find Roger, at least not before his horse threw a shoe and he had to return to the castle. With rare bad luck, this happened when he was quite far away, and it was going to be a long, hot journey back, leading his lame gelding. With a weary sigh, Albert started walking, reflecting on the thankless task of trying to help a stubborn man. Maybe this was a sign from God not to interfere.

"Sir Albert!"

Albert halted when he heard his name, and with great relief spied a mounted patrol riding toward him.

"Sir, are you all right?" the leader asked anxiously. Albert recognized the young soldier, whose name was Egbert: Roger had spoken highly of him recently, and this position of leadership indicated that Roger had acted upon his opinion.

"My horse has thrown a shoe," Albert replied, holding it up.

"Ralf, give Sir Albert your horse," Egbert ordered. "You and Gerrald can bring Sir Albert's horse home."

With a nod, Ralf dismounted, and soon Albert was again riding back to Montmorency Castle. "Why is there a patrol out?" Albert asked Egbert. "Is Sir Roger expecting trouble?"

"No, sir," Egbert replied. "He sent us to look for you."

"He's come back, then."

"Aye, sir."

"Did he say where he was?"

Egbert darted his questioner a surprised look. "Not to me, Sir Albert."

"No, no, I suppose he wouldn't." After that, Albert lapsed into silence for the rest of the journey home.

Unfortunately, by the time the patrol reached Montmorency Castle, the sun had set, and they had missed the evening meal, as was obvious when Albert entered the hall. Dudley bustled up to him immediately and pressed him to take a seat and eat. Albert complied, scanning the room. "Where is Sir Roger?"

"He's gone," Dudley responded unproductively. "He stayed until the watchmen saw you on the road. Then he went off on his own." Dudley inclined toward him conspiratorially. "Sulking, if you ask me," he whispered.

"And Lady Mina?"

"She ate her supper and retired. *She* looks to be moping, too," he added knowingly. He sighed wistfully. "A good shouting match is what we need around here."

Albert grinned a little at Dudley's proposed remedy, but not too much. Some kind of communication between the couple might be just what was necessary. "Do you have any idea where Roger went?"

"No, sir. He didn't tell me."

Albert tried not to feel frustrated, but Roger couldn't have been harder to locate if he was purposefully trying to avoid him.

Nevertheless, Albert would not be dissuaded from his helpful mission, so as soon as he had eaten, he set about conducting his own search for Roger in and about the castle and village. He examined the stables and armory; he went to the kitchen, and he even peered into the servants' quarters. There was no sign of him anywhere in the castle.

Tired and disgruntled, Albert could think of only one other place Roger might take himself, and that was the alehouse in the village. Roger had frequented the company of one of the serving wenches until Hilda had arrived at the castle after the death of her husband. With weary steps, Albert went into the darkened town. Occasionally a child cried or a dog barked, but for the most part, all was silent.

Until Albert got closer to the alehouse. Then he could hear loud and heated voices arguing about something. Albert strained to make out some of the speakers, but could only be certain of one, who sounded more reasonable and calm than the rest. That was Lud and he seemed to be trying to settle the excited men.

Albert shoved open the door of the alehouse and immediately a silence descended. Standing, Lud had clearly been in the midst of trying to placate his fellows, and he was the first to recover. "Good even, my lord!" he called out rather warily, since Sir Albert was a stranger to this particular building.

The rest of the crowd, all men save for the serving wench, who was a florid-faced, robust young woman clearly at ease among the masculine gathering, shouted out similar greetings, for Albert was not one to inspire fear. He was known as a good-hearted fellow of limited power. Harmless, in fact, unlike most other Norman noblemen.

"What brings you here, sir?" Lud asked politely.

Before Albert could answer, Lud shouted, "Moll, an ale for his lordship!"

Albert decided it might not be prudent to admit that the lord of Montmorency Castle had taken himself off like a disgruntled child, so he accepted the offered ale with good grace, all the while wondering if Roger was in a back room or a loft over the stairs with Moll's sister, whom he had heard about, though never met. She was, so Roger said, a voluptuous, generous young woman of very hearty appetite for all manner of things.

Albert sipped the proffered potent concoction. "Pray go on with your discussion," he said when he realized his presence was continuing to cast a pall over the proceedings.

"We're deciding on the northern boundary for a foot ball game," Lud explained. "The village of Barstead-on-Meadow has challenged us to a match. Some think the bell tower of St. Ninian's over by the river, some the oak by the fallow land. What do *you* think, Sir Albert?"

"I'm sure I have no idea," Albert prevaricated. He had witnessed a few such matches in the past, when men from two villages would meet and try to get an air-filled pig's bladder from one point to another. Whichever village succeeded was declared the winner, and the losers would have to pay for ale for everybody. Or rather, provide free ale for whoever was left standing, for the only rules agreed upon were the boundaries and that the ball had to stay on the ground in the open. Other than that, anything was permitted. "When is this event to take place?"

"Two Sundays hence, after mass," Lud said. "Care to join in?"

"No, thank you. I don't want somebody to mistake my head for the ball. Good luck, though, to you all!" Albert replied, raising his ale. He took another drink, noting how warm his throat felt when he gulped the golden liquid. When he had finished his first, Moll appeared with a second. Albert decided it might be taken as a discourtesy if he got up and left, and he was by now rather interested in the decision regarding boundaries, so he sat and listened.

Besides, he thought as he reached the end of the second ale and accepted the third mug Moll offered, if Roger had gone someplace to sulk, he wouldn't be in a suitable frame of mind to listen to advice anyway. Sometimes it took days for him to calm down.

Albert found himself nodding in agreement as each group loudly and forcefully offered reasons for their particular choice. The bell tower was more uphill than the oak, but the ground around the oak was more uneven. Either one would make it difficult for the opposition.

This ale was certainly delicious, Albert thought as he reached for a fourth mug. And how delightful it was to be thinking of nothing more serious than a foot ball match. It had been too long since he had appreciated the simpler life of the Saxon peasants, and since he had tasted such a delightful beverage.

By the time the discussion ended, the bell tower had been noisily proclaimed the northern boundary, and Albert was too drunk to see straight or stand without staggering. For his part, he felt in rare good humor, the friend of all mankind and the potential savior of Roger's marriage.

"Here, let's give you a hand," Moll said cheerfully, putting her shoulder under the nobleman's arm when Lud realized it was time Sir Albert was safely tucked in bed.

"That's...thank...you're marvelous," Albert slurred, bestowing what he thought was a gracious smile upon Moll.

Moll had seen many men drunk and recognized the lopsided grin for what Albert meant it to be. "Do you think you'll be able to get to the castle all right?" she asked kindly as she opened the door.

"Shertainly," Albert said. He took a large step in the wrong direction. Moll put her hands on his shoulders and gently faced him the right way. "I thank you, kind lady!'' Albert said, bending to bow and almost tipping over.

"God's teeth, what is this sight before my eyes!" Sir Roger exclaimed, coming out of the darkness like an avenging angel.

"It's only me,'' Albert said with another ridiculous grin.

"I see you were not lost, after all,'' Roger remarked sardonically. "Were you hiding in the alehouse all day?"

"No. I was trying to find *you*. I thought you might be here. But you *weren't*,'' Albert said, his tone between accusation and satisfaction. He started to weave precariously.

"He's a bit...'' Moll began apologetically.

"So I see,'' Roger remarked, raising one eyebrow, his mouth grim.

"Now don't look like that, you grumpy old bear!'' Albert cried, weaving even more as Moll withdrew her support. "The ale's marvelous, and Moll's marvelous and I feel marvelous! Everything's marvelous!'' He wrapped his arms around his body as if embracing somebody, or anybody. "Mina's marvelous, too!''

Then Albert frowned deeply and jabbed his finger at Roger. "And you're not, you knave!''

"Really?'' Roger crossed his arms and frowned just as critically.

"If you'll excuse me, my lord, I've got things to do," Moll said, hurriedly decamping. If Sir Roger was going to start shouting—and judging by his face, that seemed not unlikely—she wanted to get far away.

In reality, Roger wasn't angry. At least, not at Sir Albert, the sight of whom struck Roger as rather harmlessly comical and reminded him of the first time they had met. Albert had been lying in a gutter, his hand clutching a mug. Even then, there had been a serene dignity in his demeanor that Roger had found interesting. He had carried Albert back to the barracks of the castle he was visiting and waited for the fellow to sober up. On this rather unusual basis, their long friendship had begun.

However, right at the moment Roger wasn't pleased to hear his wife's name spoken so loudly in the streets of the village, even if Albert was making a compliment. "Come on, Albert, time for bed," he said, going to help his staggering friend.

Albert dashed Roger's hand away and glared, the effect hampered by his obvious inability to focus. "I don't want your help! You're a fool! A slimp...shrimp...fool!"

"You're talking like a fool yourself," Roger observed patiently. He grabbed Albert's arm and put it over his shoulder. "You're going to fall on your face in the mud in another moment."

"So what of that?" Albert cried, pulling away and stumbling. He managed to right himself. "What do you care? You only care about yourself, Roger, like a babe. A child. A bully!" He flung his arm wildly toward the castle. "You've got a beautiful wife who's better than you deserve up there, and you're down here with some wench in the alehouse!"

"No, I wasn't and that's quite enough, Albert," Roger said firmly. "Let's go."

"Oh, no! I'm not goin' with you. Not till you tell Mina you're sorry. I don't know what you argued about, but I'm sure it's all *your* fault."

"She's not here to apologize to, is she?" Roger said, getting more desperate to get Albert out of sight and into bed where he could sleep off the effects of the ale. And where he would be quiet.

"Oh," Albert said, slightly befuddled. "She isn't?" He looked around. "She isn't." He straightened, and as with the first time Roger had seen him intoxicated, there was a certain semblance of dignity to his disheveled appearance. "Very well then, my lord. Let us depart." He took a step forward and fell flat on his face.

Roger bent down and rolled him over, examining his friend's muddy countenance. "Are you hurt?" he demanded.

Albert blinked bloodshot eyes. "You know what the trouble with you two is?" he asked thickly. "You're exactly alike! Two slub...shub... studd—" he took a deep breath, "—thickheaded fools who can't see that they're perfect for each other! Like Winifred and me." Albert blinked, then moaned and covered his face with his filthy hands. "Oh, Winifred, where are you now?" He pulled away from Roger and curled up in the mud, his chest heaving and his sobs heart wrenching to hear.

Not sure what to do but not willing to leave his friend, Roger patted him on the back. "Come on, Albert," he said softly. "Let me help you home."

"I don't have a home," Albert groaned disconsolately.

"As long as I live, you have a home with me," Roger said. With compassionate care, he assisted his friend to his feet. Albert grew quiet and Roger realized he was nearly unconscious.

Gently Roger hoisted Albert over his shoulder and carried him to a quiet place in the castle stables where no one would disturb him. He set him down in a pile of straw and tucked a blanket around him. Then, sure that Mina would not welcome his company, Roger lay down a short distance from Albert and tried to sleep.

Without much success, although his legs ached from exhaustion. He had been walking over the fields and about the village ever since he had returned from the hunt and discovered that Albert had gone out searching for him as if he were a child needing tending. He was glad Albert was unharmed, of course, and in truth had almost welcomed worrying about his friend instead of his wife.

Now that Albert was here, however, his thoughts returned to Mina's deception.

The shame she had caused him had been completely unfounded and unnecessary. She had made him feel like a savage brute, and then an easily duped fool. Her lie was completely inexcusable and unforgivable.

And despite Albert's observations on their respective characters, they were not alike at all. He could never deceive anyone as she had deceived him.

Albert would never understand. His experience of love had been chaste and pure, and if he had been disappointed, it was because of the woman's sense of honor. Not a lack of it.

When Albert awoke the next morning, the first thing he saw, once he could force his eyes open, was Roger sitting with his back to the wooden slats of the stable walls, the sunlight streaming in around him so that he looked like one of the sterner disciples in a stained glass window.

"What did I do?" Albert moaned, sitting up very slowly.

"You got drunk," Roger replied evenly.

"God's holy heaven, I did?"

"Yes."

"I was looking for you, and I went to the alehouse . . . were you there, after all?"

"No." Roger stood up, brushing stray wisps of straw from his clothes. "It's a good thing I happened by, or I might have had to drag you from the gutter again."

Albert looked at his soiled clothes ruefully. "I take it I was in just such a location? God save me, my head aches!"

"Only for a short time, and the sore head serves you right. You were making enough noise to rouse the entire village."

"I was?"

"You were. Why were you looking for me? There was no alarm at the castle. Everything was quiet when we got back."

"I wanted to talk to you about Mina."

"Again?" Roger asked skeptically. "Spare yourself. You said enough about her last night."

Albert's eyes narrowed suspiciously. "Something else *has* happened between you. What is it this time?"

"I think that is between my wife and me."

"She's a lot like you, you know," Albert said pensively, rubbing his temples.

"So you announced to the whole world."

"I did?"

"You did."

"Well, it's true."

"No, it isn't."

"Roger, I suspect she doesn't talk about what's troubling her, either. That's what you two need to do, talk."

"God's wounds, Albert!" Roger cried, releasing some of his pent-up frustration, "we *have* talked! That's the whole bloody problem—what she *told* me! Since you seem unwilling to let me keep some matters to myself despite my best efforts, I will tell you—but once and only once. Mina lied to me. I never touched her on our wedding night, except for one kiss!"

"One kiss?" Albert said incredulously.

"One kiss. She doctored my wine. I passed out. I never hit her."

"Thank God for that!" Albert said fervently. "I didn't want to believe you capable of such a thing."

"But now you see what *she* is capable of."

"Why did she do it? Was she afraid?"

Roger looked away. He had said enough; there was no need for Albert to know about his conversation with the baron, since Mina was in the wrong. "It doesn't matter why. She told a base, evil lie, and for that I will not forgive her."

Albert's brow furrowed with doubt and his eyes were sorrowful. "That's a harsh judgment, Roger, and it sounds final. Perhaps if you let her explain—"

"No! We've *talked* more than enough! There can be no justification for what she did." Compelled by Albert's compassionate face, Roger finally revealed the true cause of his distress. "For what she made me believe about myself."

Albert slowly nodded. "What are you going to do?" he inquired despondently, and Roger was relieved that Albert at last understood. "Annul the marriage? Surely if you slept alone on your wedding night, the marriage wasn't consummated. And then we went to your other estate—"

"The marriage has been consummated since then."

"Oh."

"So she is my lawful wife, for the rest of my life."

"I'm so sorry, Roger." They sat in sympathetic silence together, then Albert spoke. "Roger, I have to confess that I don't see why Mina would do that to you. There must be some kind of explanation, if only—"

"Albert, is your loyalty to her, or to me?" Roger demanded, dismayed to think that even after all he had divulged, Albert was still willing to exonerate Mina.

"To you, of course, Roger," Albert replied staunchly. "First and always, to you."

"Then you will please have the goodness to stop talking about Mina. I don't want to discuss my marriage with you, or anyone else, ever again."

Before Albert could respond, they heard a loud cry from the battlements. Without saying a word, the two men rushed to the door of the stable just as the enormous gate to the inner ward swung open.

# Chapter Thirteen

As Roger and Albert stepped out into the bright light of midmorning, they saw a beautiful young woman dressed in extraordinary finery enter the yard, mounted on a pure white horse. She was followed by a woman—obviously her servant—riding a mule, and by a troop of well-armed men.

"Who is *that?*" Albert asked, instinctively straightening his garments and running his hand through his disheveled hair.

"I don't know," Roger replied, automatically brushing the last of the bits of straw from his clothes. "But she's not a pauper, by the looks of it." He strode forward, a welcoming smile on his face. "Welcome to Montmorency Castle," he called out.

When he was closer, Roger halted and looked up at the stranger, noting her pale, smooth skin, long slender neck and gleaming blue eyes. In many respects, he realized, this woman represented the epitome of female beauty combined with the trappings of rank and wealth. Yet her attributes left him curiously unmoved, especially when the persistent image of Mina, her hair spread over the pillows, her face filled with blatant desire, intruded upon his thoughts.

Where was that sense of challenge a beautiful woman used to inspire? Before he was married, he would have been determined to get this lovely creature into his bed. Now, he simply wondered who she was and what she was doing here.

The young woman gave him a smile as beautiful as the rest of her delicate features. "I must beg your pardon, Sir Roger," she said in a soft, breathy voice. "And your indulgence for this intrusion. Perhaps you will not be angry when I tell you Baron DeGuerre has sent me."

"Baron DeGuerre has let such an exquisite woman escape his castle without marrying her?" Roger asked, smiling.

The young woman emitted a fluttery little laugh. "Oh, you flatter me, Sir Roger!" Then she looked around, her finely shaped eyebrows knitted into a slightly worried expression. He caught her unspoken message and quickly offered his hand to help her dismount, all the while keeping a knowing grin from his face. Roger had been the object of many a lady's wiles and he knew them well. This calculated, affected inability to get off her horse without assistance was one example.

Dudley came bustling out of the kitchen and halted in midstep, his mouth falling open at the sight of the stranger and her entourage. "We have a visitor," Roger announced somewhat unnecessarily. "Please tell my wife." Dudley nodded and wordlessly trotted into the hall.

Roger turned back to his unexpected guest, offering his arm to escort her to his hall. "It isn't fair, my lady, that you know my name, and I do not know yours," he said, noting that the hand she placed upon his forearm was rather reminiscent of a limp fish.

"Oh, pray forgive my forgetfulness, too!" she cried with an alarmed little squeak. "I am Lady Joselynd de Beautette. My father is Sir Ranulf de Beautette, cousin to the baron."

Roger introduced Lady Joselynd to Albert, who had waited silently. The knight nodded in response, but his greeting was definitely lackluster, probably because he was still feeling the aftereffects of his nocturnal activity.

Roger looked at his guest with a warm smile and a renewed resolve to act as he always had as he led her to the hall. "To what do we owe the honor of your visit?"

Lady Joselynd didn't have time to answer before Mina came hurrying out.

His wife halted awkwardly, made a swift survey of their guest and her cortege, then glanced down at her own garment in a gesture that was both self-conscious and startling for its unexpectedness before she clasped her hands behind her back.

Roger had never seen Mina concerned with her garments before. She always seemed above vanity, as if her appearance was of little import, quite a contrast to Reginald, and to this woman.

Perhaps the comparison would do her good, Roger thought spontaneously making his own. This Joselynd was like pale moonshine compared to Mina's fiery sun.

But a fiery temper was not a good attribute, he reminded himself.

Mina's shrewd gaze scanned the entire crowded yard, then came to rest on Lady Joselynd's hand upon her husband's arm. It was at that moment she again became the strong-willed, confident woman he knew. The infuriating, fraudulent woman he knew. "Lady Joselynd de Beautette, may I present Mina," he said with a touch of defiant grandeur. "My wife," he added after an appropriately inso-lent pause.

Mina did not look directly at him. She knew what he was trying to do. He was attempting to humiliate her by acting as if she were not nearly so important as this pale, overdressed, simpering noblewoman who had probably been coddled and cozened all her life.

Mina smiled a satisfied smile, one with more than a little superiority. A person like Lady Joselynd probably would never have survived Mina's upbringing, and that knowledge strengthened her.

She needed that strength, because despite all her vows and resolutions, the sight of Roger brought back a flood of memories that threatened to weaken her again, just as the sight of that woman's hand upon him filled her with rage. She struggled to control her emotions, and when she spoke, her voice was as sweet as honey. "Do tell us how we come to be so honored with your presence."

"Well, it's a bit embarrassing," Lady Joselynd said with an adroit show of shame complete with stutter and suitably lowered eyelids that didn't fool Mina for one moment. She doubted there was very much at all that would embarrass this vain, artful young woman who was holding on to Roger's arm too tightly, and at whom Roger was smiling with more friendliness than he had ever bestowed on her. "I would rather tell you about it inside."

"Please enjoy the hospitality of my home," Roger said kindly. They swept past Mina so that she had to follow them like a servant, or a dog.

Dudley, looking worried, appeared at Mina's elbow inside the entrance to the hall. "Should I instruct the maids to prepare a chamber for her?" he whispered anxiously as he gestured at Lady Joselynd.

"Yes," Mina snapped with more anger than she had intended to show. She forced herself to be calm, to be in control. This was *her* home, too, after all, and she was mistress here.

Roger escorted Lady Joselynd to a chair beside the hearth. "Now, what has brought you to my castle?" he inquired gallantly.

A strange, uncomfortable feeling stole over Mina. With her father, she had learned to bear her sufferings without flinching. Reginald she had learned to coerce or ignore. Toward her other half siblings, she had maintained a composed, stony silence.

But what could she do to protect herself from this beautiful woman? Despite her attempts not to make a comparison, there was no denying Lady Joselynd's pale blond beauty, the expensive quality of her blue overgown with gold embroidery, the bejeweled band about her slender head, the thin silk fabric of her wimple, the embroidered kid gloves and the delicate shift that peeped beneath her dress, everything combining to heighten the young woman's outward perfection. Compared to her, Mina felt poorly dressed and ugly and as awkward as a bull standing beside a doe.

"I understand Lord Reginald Chilcott is still here?" Lady Joselynd inquired with another feigned blush.

"Yes," Roger replied, leaning closer to hear the breathy voice. Mina was quite sure that if the lady were among other women, her voice would dominate the conversation.

Out of the corner of her eye, she saw Dudley hustling Hilda and Aldys toward the stairs, their arms full of fresh linen, a basin and a ewer. The two servants stared at Lady Joselynd with frank curiosity as they went up the stairs to prepare another chamber.

"The baron thought...that is, the baron hopes..." Lady Joselynd spluttered in a masterful performance of confused femininity.

"What? What does the baron hope?" Mina demanded as she approached the hearth, her bluntness earning her a condemning glance from Roger, but she didn't care. She couldn't tolerate this woman's artificial manner another moment.

"He thinks Lord Chilcott and I should marry," Lady Joselynd said, batting the lashes of her big, blue and extremely cowlike eyes at Roger.

The basin came clattering down the stairs, and a red-faced Hilda rushed after it. She bobbed a curtsy. "Please forgive me," she said hurriedly as she grabbed it and rushed back up the stairs.

"Is Reginald to have any say in this?" Mina asked offhandedly, at the same time wondering where Reginald was.

Lady Joselynd's gaze turned to her, and the innocence disappeared from her shrewd eyes, although her voice retained its breathy childlike quality. "Yes, of course. He is still here, is he not?"

At that moment, Reginald appeared on the stairs, nearly stumbling down them in his haste as he fastened his belt buckle. As further evidence of the speed with which he had dressed, the brooch on the left shoulder of his tunic was hanging crookedly, and he hadn't had time to curl his hair. He skittered to a stop halfway between the stairs and Lady Joselynd's chair and bowed with flourish.

"Reginald Chilcott, may I present Lady Joselynd de Beautette," Roger said solemnly. "Your future wife, or so I understand."

Reginald started to make another bow, but halted in his half-bent position and raised his widened eyes. "My...my *what?*"

"Oh, please, Sir Roger, you...oh dear, how truly disconcerting! I didn't mean it to sound like that!" Lady Joselynd demurred immediately, and Mina was hard-pressed not to smile with enjoyment at her discomfort. If that was what the baron had truly planned, why not be forthcoming and say so, unless you were the type of person who shrouded everything in empty courtesies and pleasant distortions?

"Whatever the reason for her arrival," Roger said magnanimously, "we are pleased to welcome her, for however long she is able to stay. Isn't that right, Mina?" He shot his wife a glance, its meaning very clear. She would be rude at her peril.

Mina smiled and said very, very sweetly, "We are completely delighted. Would you care for some wine? Have you journeyed far?"

"That would be most welcome. And if your steward could show Brunhilde, my servant, to our quarters, that would be most kind."

"Of course I shall see to that at once. Please excuse me." Mina hurried to the stairs and found Dudley in the room that had been hers when she had first arrived at the castle. Lady Joselynd's accommodations were already well in hand, so she simply asked him to have wine, cheeses and bread prepared for Lady Joselynd's refreshment. Dudley, with a harried nod of his head, scurried out of the room, leaving the maidservants to complete the preparations.

Mina was in no hurry to return below, where her husband was being so completely charming to a total stranger. She moved the basin a fraction of an inch more to the center of the table and straightened one of the candles in its holder. Hilda brought a ewer of fresh water to the table and set it down with trembling hands.

"Aldys," Mina said at once, "go to the kitchen and help with the refreshments. Hilda and I will finish here."

Aldys nodded and scampered away. The moment she was gone, Mina turned to Hilda. "What is it?" she asked worriedly. "Is Hollis all right?"

"He's fine, my lady," Hilda replied, biting her lip. "It's . . . it's nothing."

"You dropped that basin on the stairs," Mina noted.

"It's a little dented, but easily fixed, I'm sure!" Hilda protested, an edge of hysteria to her tone that belied her assurances that nothing was the matter.

"Is it Lady Joselynd? Have you met her before?"

"No, my lady, never. What could Lady Joselynd have to do with me?"

"She may be visiting us for some time."

"Oh, really?"

"You can go now," Mina said, sensing that whatever was troubling Hilda, she was not going to reveal it. "The chamber is quite ready."

"Thank you," Hilda said with relief before she bolted from the room.

Mina followed her out in a more leisurely fashion. Obviously she was not the only person less than delighted with Lady Joselynd's sudden arrival. But why should Hilda care? Lady Joselynd was merely another guest, and only that.

It should be Reginald who was the most upset. Mina guessed that Lady Joselynd was a very crafty young woman who had set her sights on someone called Lord Chilcott, with his title and ancient family name, rather than the simple, vain but well-meaning Reginald.

Then Mina thought of the ridiculous picture Reginald made when he had halted in midbow. Maybe Lady Joselynd would not find Reginald Chilcott to her taste, but perhaps there was another man she *would*.

Mina suddenly recognized the emotion she had been feeling from the moment she had seen Lady Joselynd standing beside Roger, an emotion she had felt often in her childhood and only rarely since she had arrived at Montmorency Castle.

She was afraid.

Afraid that Roger would want Lady Joselynd. Afraid that even now, he was finding his own wife lacking. Afraid that he would share his incredible, powerful passion with another woman.

The way he was treating Lady Joselynd would seem to provide some justification for her fears.

What of his talk of loyalty and honesty? He had sworn to be faithful to her before the people and the church, and by God, she would ensure that he abided by that oath!

"I am going riding today," Mina announced a few days later after she broke the fast. The hall was nearly empty. The soldiers and lesser knights had finished their meal, and most had gone to prepare for the business of the day. It had been raining off and on since Lady Joselynd's arrival, and the men were anxious to get to outdoor tasks, just as Mina was anxious to get out of the confines of the castle, away from the affected Lady Joselynd and away from Roger, too.

She had been watching the two of them whenever they were together, as if she were one of Edred's hawks on a hunt. The continuous surveillance was exhausting, as well as demeaning and, she feared, ultimately useless. If Roger wanted to seduce a woman, Mina did not doubt as to his eventual success, or his ability to keep an illicit relationship concealed, if he wanted it to be. Few women would be able to resist his potent combination of physical attraction and gallant charm.

Surely Lady Joselynd would not.

However, she also presumed that Joselynd would not be clever enough to hide an immoral liaison, and so far Mina had no evidence that there was anything improper between Roger and their guest. She continued to hope that he intended to honor his marriage vows, although she could not completely allay her apprehensions and insecurity.

"It's going to rain," Roger said bluntly from his place on Mina's right. He reached out to take hold of his goblet, but quickly pulled his hand back when there seemed to be a danger of coming into physical contact with her.

Mina flushed and condemned her failure to overlook his actions. She should be used to his aversion now.

"I would dearly love to ride out myself," Lady Joselynd murmured deferentially. She was seated to Roger's right as a token of her special status as a relative of the baron and their guest. "But not if it looks to rain. What do *you* think, my lord?" she asked Reginald, who sat beside her.

"Rain would ruin that gown," he remarked. "I had a tunic in a similar fabric once. One drop and it was marked forever."

"Oh, my! Well, I suppose I could change. Has that woman—Hilda, is it?—mended my green brocade?"

"I believe so," Mina replied uninterestedly.

"I must caution you against risking the weather," Roger said to Lady Joselynd. "I'm sure

the baron would not be pleased if you were to fall
ill while you were in my care."

"Oh, you are so kind to fear for me," Lady Joselynd said with a simpering smile. "I would not
wish to make any mischief, my lord, although I am
quite sure the baron thinks you incapable of doing
wrong. However, I shall obey your wishes and stay
inside the castle walls today."

Mina wiped her lips and rose. Her emotions felt
as batted about as Hollis's ball. One minute she was
determined to ride, the next she was determined to
stay if Joselynd was planning on joining her, then
she was eager to leave, but only if she could ride
*alone.* "If you will excuse me, I shall return
shortly."

"Where are you going?" Roger asked sternly,
finally looking at her and not at the company, or
Lady Joselynd.

"A little rain does not frighten me, nor will it
damage my clothes, and I am sure the baron does
not particularly care if I am sick or not," she answered evenly. "I bid you all good morning."

Roger ground his teeth in frustration as his wife
left the hall. He was used to unquestioning obedience to his orders. He had discovered, though, that
he did not particularly enjoy unquestioning obedience to his every suggestion, as demonstrated by
Lady Joselynd. He kept wanting to shout to the

pale, lackluster creature to make up her own damn mind. As for arguing, he almost wished Mina would. Her dispassionate refusal to obey or even cooperate and the ease with which she ignored him was completely outside his experience, and he had no idea how to deal with it.

"I must say I think she's quite wrong," Lady Joselynd said, leaning toward Roger with sympathetic eyes and placing her hand over his. "I'm sure Baron DeGuerre would be most distressed if anything were to happen to your wife."

Roger turned his dark, inscrutable eyes onto this vain, tiresome young woman he rarely listened to and said, "As would I, Lady Joselynd."

Fully convinced of her abilities to beguile men, Lady Joselynd saw only the smile on Sir Roger's extremely handsome face and surmised that the bold Sir Roger de Montmorency was answering as he did because of the foolish young man beside her, who was the bride's relative.

It was really too bad that Sir Roger de Montmorency had slipped through her fingers, she thought, letting her hand remain on Sir Roger's strong one for a moment longer than necessary, enjoying the physical sensations the touch aroused within her. Sir Roger was everything she had heard, and more. Nobody could possibly describe the irresistible physical presence of the man. Or the lust he could induce. Why, even she, well aware of her virginal value as a potential wife, was tempted to let him seduce her.

The great mystery was how his wife could be so immune to him. She acted as if she barely noticed him. She had to be a fool, for all her arrogant, superior ways. It might be good for her to realize that others appreciated her husband's merits, if she did not.

The woman was homely, with her outrageous red hair and stern temperament, and surely Sir Roger more than welcomed having a demure, womanly companion.

Still, Joselynd realized, it would probably not be wise to alienate Mina completely, or she would never be welcomed back, even if she became Reginald Chilcott's wife. Lord Chilcott would be quite a catch, considering his family's social position and wealth. And Sir Roger *was* married, so she placed her hand on her lap. "Perhaps, my lord, if the weather clears, we may enjoy a ride together," she said innocently.

"I do believe, now that I think on it, that the clouds were thinning as we left the chapel. What do you say to a hunt, Albert?" Sir Roger said. His friend agreed, and then Sir Roger faced her with one of his attentive smiles that proved he found her tempting. "Would you care to join us? Your company would be most welcome."

The warmth of Lady Joselynd's smile was very genuine, as was the triumph in her eyes. "I will be more than happy to accept any invitation you extend, my lord."

## Chapter Fourteen

From her place on the ridge, Mina watched Roger, Lady Joselynd and Sir Albert ride along the main road at a leisurely pace. The sun had broken out shortly after she had taken Jeanette from the stables, and the morning had turned warm and bright, allowing Mina to see the sight before her all too clearly.

Behind the mounted nobility came Bredon and the dogs. Edred carried both the merlin and the falcon. Another servant carried a blood-soaked bundle. The hunt must have been successful.

Mina's gaze returned to the nobles. So, it looked to rain, did it? And the poor dear creature might take cold, might she?

Roger had probably tried to stop his wife from riding out because he knew it would give her pleasure. Maybe he had guessed she would insist upon going if he tried to stop her, and had only protested to ensure that she would go—that was assuming, of course, that he had taken the trouble to ponder his wife's method of arriving at her decisions. Whatever his thoughts, he did not have his wife's troublesome presence to interfere with his conversation with the beautiful Lady Joselynd. True, Sir Albert and the servants were with them, but Roger could find plenty of ways to elude them if he wanted to.

Imagine his annoyance if his wife joined them.

That was all the prompting Mina needed to act. She gritted her teeth and spurred Jeanette into a gallop, riding down the slope at a breakneck speed that didn't scare her. Instead, it increased Mina's excitement as she rode to a flourishing halt in front of the threesome.

"That was a reckless thing to do," Roger declared. "You might have broken that mare's leg."

"Or my head, I suppose, but I didn't," Mina replied with a condescending smile. "Lady Joselynd, what a pleasure to meet again—and you in your easily spotted gown, too! Pray forgive the mud. It was the rain. Greetings, Sir Albert."

Albert inclined his head in a silent response.

"The weather cleared," Joselynd said softly, looking uneasily from Roger to Mina with a show of distressed helplessness. "Your husband suggested I join the hunt."

"I'm sure he did," Mina remarked, and Roger gave her yet another condemning look. She ignored him, and turned to Sir Albert. "Have you recovered from your illness?" she asked solicitously.

"Yes," he replied, blushing like a boy. "It was only the effects of too much ale," he confessed. "Combined with a touch of ague. I am quite well now."

"It is nice to know that some men will admit to a weakness," Mina said.

Roger didn't make any comment, but she saw the vein in his temple begin to throb. Thinking she had done enough for one day, she allowed Jeanette to fall back beside Lady Joselynd while Roger and Albert led the way home.

"So, Lady Joselynd, did you enjoy the killing?" she asked lightly. "I can tell you are an expert when it comes to prey."

"Your husband has wonderful hawks," Joselynd replied. "Exceptionally well trained."

"Speaking of prey, what do you think of Reginald?"

"I'm sure I don't see the connection," Joselynd replied coldly, so Mina was absolutely certain she did. "He is a fine fellow."

"He'll make a good husband, you think?"

"Yes, my lady, I do."

"For you?"

Lady Joselynd gave her a confused and suspicious look. "Has someone else proposed a wife for him?"

"Not lately. It has been Reginald's unfortunate experience to be rejected by his one and only betrothed."

"Oh, that."

"You heard about Madeline de Montmorency?"

"Yes. I think she must be a fool."

This time Mina was rather taken aback by the uncharitable condemnation uttered in Joselynd's dulcet tones. However, she also sensed she was getting close to Joselynd's true personality beneath the lovely, helpless mask. "Apparently she fell in love with another man," Mina remarked.

Lady Joselynd actually smirked. "He's a peasant, or so I understand."

"You doubt the power of love?"

Joselynd gave Mina a shrewd look. "You and I, my lady, know better, I think." How cold she sounded, how unfeeling—and yet she was uttering Mina's own opinion of love, wasn't she?

Joselynd's expression returned to its usual bland pleasantness. "But you should not be asking me, my lady, not when you have someone who has suffered so much for love in your midst."

"Who?" Mina demanded, and for a horrible moment she thought Joselynd was going to say Roger.

"Sir Albert."

"Sir Albert?"

"Yes. Do you not know the tragic story of his past?" Joselynd asked with patronizing superiority.

Mina glanced ahead, then decided she would have to put up with Joselynd's condescending manner if she was going to learn about her husband's friend, so she shook her head.

"Well," Joselynd began eagerly, obviously more anxious to reveal what she knew than to exasperate Mina, "he was a great champion at tournaments not so many years ago. He comes from a noble family, although not a great one, and was making quite a name for himself when he met a woman. She was the wife of a wool merchant who had come to live near the castle of the lord to whom Albert had sworn fealty at that time, Lord Gervais. Anyway, she was said to be quite beautiful—a *merchant's* wife, if you can imagine—but whether she was or not, she managed to captivate Albert completely.

"Unfortunately, as I said, she was married, and her husband was a horrible brute. Albert asked her to run away with him. She wouldn't. She claimed it would be dishonorable. Really, a peasant concerned about honor. It's *too* ridiculous. *I* think she was afraid Albert was too poor, even if he was a knight, and then where would she be?''

Mina did not share Joselynd's opinion of the impossibility of a peasant's ability to possess a sense of personal honor, but she remained silent. She was feeling both sorrow and pity for Albert, and wanted to hear the rest of his story. Maybe if she knew it, she could help him somehow.

''Albert kept begging her to go with him,'' Joselynd continued, ''especially after the lout of a husband beat her terribly one day. I gather he just about *killed* her. Nevertheless, she continued to refuse, despite all Albert's entreaties.

''Then Albert discovered why the husband had been so savage. The woman was with child, and her husband accused her of an adulterous relationship. He said he wasn't going to raise another man's bastard. Apparently this was not the truth. Albert had never made love to her. Maybe if he had...but she was clearly a clever thing, denying him to ensure that he wanted her even more.''

''Perhaps she did not wish to commit adultery.''

''Didn't you hear what I said? She was nothing but a merchant's wife,'' Joselynd said with a dismissive sniff. ''At any rate, when Albert managed to get the woman to tell him everything, he went berserk. He found the merchant and in his anger, killed him.

"He was more than justified, according to everyone in Bridgeford Wells, but incredibly, the woman took a different view. She told Albert what he had done was murder, because her husband couldn't win against a trained knight. She said she was guilty, too, of committing adultery in her heart if not in fact, and although she had certainly wanted to leave her husband, she didn't want him dead because of her.

"Albert implored her to marry him. Pleaded on his knees. Just think! A nobleman on his knees to a merchant's pregnant widow! Anyway, she still refused, because of the baby. She was afraid that Albert would hate her child, or resent it.

"Albert tried to convince her otherwise, to no avail. The woman disappeared. Nobody knew where she went, and he never saw her again. Afterward, he went to Europe and fought in a few tournaments, but never with the same zeal as before. He was barely earning enough to keep himself and didn't seem to care very much whether he lived or died when Sir Roger became his friend and offered him a home."

"Did Albert ever try to find her?" Mina asked softly.

"Yes, but it was as if the ground had opened up and swallowed her," Joselynd answered.

"How is it you know so much about him?"

"Oh, it's common knowledge. A minstrel made up a ballad about it all. He used a different name for the knight, yet everyone who knew anything about Sir Albert Lacourt recognized him in it. It all sounds rather ridiculous, doesn't it? A knight getting so worked up over a merchant's wife?"

"I think it's very sad and very wonderful," Mina replied, looking ahead at the gray-haired knight.

"Well, love certainly didn't do him any good," Joselynd said with another sniff.

Mina thought of Albert's gentle goodness, his concern for his friend's well-being, the respectful way he treated her and all the other women of the castle, whether noble or not. "Didn't it?" she murmured before nudging her horse forward and leaving a confused and dumbfounded Joselynd behind.

On the dawn of an August day as Mina sat on a stone bench recently added to her garden, she disconsolately created a pattern in the dirt with a stick. It was quiet here, save for the low, contented clucking of the chickens and the occasional squawk of the geese. Here she could be alone and think.

For the past few days, she had had ample opportunity to observe her husband being charming toward another woman and to think about Albert's story. Like Albert, Roger was unfailingly polite, extremely pleasant and consistently concerned for Lady Joselynd's well-being. The only thing Mina could not be sure about was how Roger actually felt about the woman.

Toward her, his wife, he was coldly courteous and invariably brusque, as if *she* were a guest—and not a welcome one. She didn't even know where he spent his nights. She was afraid to guess and more afraid to find out.

So she had endeavored to ignore him, and sometimes succeeded when she was busy in the hall or in the kitchen. Then her mind would not recall the passionate moments they had shared in their bedchamber. Unfortunately, a thing as simple as the sight of Roger's discarded tunic would bring back the uncontrollable memory of his caresses.

Sometimes, too, especially while she was here, she remembered Roger talking kindly and tenderly to Hollis. How easy it was to imagine him speaking so to a son of his own. A son who would be her child, too. A son who would be like his father, strong, resolute...and charming to beautiful women while being obnoxious to his wife.

With angry swipes, Mina destroyed the pattern she had made in the dirt.

There was one other thing of which she was certain, and which added to her misery. Sir Albert's manner toward her had definitely changed. He was as kind and gracious as ever, and yet there was a coldness in his eyes when he spoke to her that upset her.

The explanation had to be that Roger had told his friend what she had done on their wedding night, and Albert thought she was in the wrong. Albert's reaction was not at all surprising, really, considering he was her husband's friend first, nor did it alter her opinion concerning her original act, but she regretted the loss of his good regard and wished Roger had not exposed her deception.

Now more than ever she wanted Albert's friendship. There were things she wanted to ask, and he was the only one who might have the answers. Things about love, because it had slowly dawned on her that perhaps the reason she could not rid her mind of Roger was that he was too firmly in her heart. After all, if she cared nothing for him, he could be easily dismissed.

So she had to admit, to herself at least, that she did care about Roger, very much. Was that love? Was it love that made her so jealous of Roger's attentions to Joselynd that she wanted to scream?

Was it love that made her weaken in his presence, to the point that it took every particle of her self-control to appear otherwise? Or was it fear that her husband's respect was lost forever?

Was it love that she could remember so clearly the time they had spent in each other's arms and that she so desperately wanted to repeat? Or was it merely lust? A desire of the flesh?

The garden gate squeaked open. Startled, Mina half rose, wondering who had come to interrupt her peace and for a moment fearing it might be Roger.

It was Reginald, who usually slept very late. He was wearing a plain tunic and chausses, and his hair was uncurled, brushing his narrow shoulders as if he were trying to imitate Roger or the baron. The expression on his face was one of unfamiliar determination, until he saw her. "Mina!" he gasped, surprised.

"Yes," she replied. "What has brought you here so early?"

"I . . . I . . . uh . . ." he muttered, glancing over his shoulder before coming inside and shutting the gate. "I wanted to speak with you."

She didn't think that was strictly true, nor did it explain his early rising. "About what?"

"About Lady Joselynd," he said nervously.

"Yes?"

"I hate her!" he snarled with a sudden vehemence that was all the more shocking considering it was coming from the usually mild Reginald.

In truth, however, Mina couldn't think of anyone who liked Lady Joselynd, except Roger. She was forever fussing about the way her chamber was prepared, or the food that might upset her sensitive stomach, or her clothing that required such special care, always using that childlike, breathy tone of voice. Many a time in the past few days, Mina had wanted to shout at her to be quiet and go away.

But that Reginald should feel so! Joselynd had gone out of her way to be nice to him. She had seemed fascinated by whatever he uttered, which was a feat that had actually come close to making Mina have some grudging respect for her. She had deferred to his wishes whenever possible. She had spoken for hours with him about his clothes and showered him with so many compliments, Mina had been ashamed for her. Yet never once had Reginald so much as hinted that he had found her company onerous. She said as much now.

"I was just being nice," her half brother protested. "I mean, I didn't want to hurt the poor girl's feelings. It's not her fault that the baron thinks she should marry me. And she's nice enough, in a boring way. I mean, all she wants to talk about is clothes!''

Mina had to stifle a smile at that, since clothing had been Reginald's major preoccupation prior to coming to Montmorency Castle. "So I presume this means you are not willing to obey the baron's wishes regarding a marriage?''

Reginald got up and paced agitatedly. "That's the problem. No, I do not want to marry her, although she's very pretty and certainly understands fabric.'' He halted and looked at Mina with his pleading, sorrowful eyes as if he were a puppy begging for a bone. "How can I tell the baron I don't agree?'' he pleaded. His expression grew more hopeful. "Do you think Roger would tell him if I asked?''

"I don't know what Roger would do. However, if you don't want to marry Joselynd, you should tell her right away, before she goes on making a fool of herself.''

Reginald cleared his throat awkwardly as he sat beside her. "That was the other thing I wanted to talk to you about. I don't have the heart to disappoint her. Could you, would you, *please?* You're a woman, you'll know better what to say. Please, Mina?''

Mina didn't relish the idea of being related to Lady Joselynd in any way, so she was truly delighted to think that Reginald had not been persuaded by the young woman's artful campaign. She was also quite certain that the sooner Joselynd knew the futility of her situation, the sooner she would leave and take her breathy, pouting demands elsewhere.

Yet should it not be Reginald who spoke to her? And should it not be Reginald who made his feelings known to the baron?

That was the honorable way, but as she looked at Reginald with his desperately pleading eyes, she realized that the clever Lady Joselynd might cry or somehow manage to upset Reginald so much that he would overlook his objections and find himself betrothed. Nor could she imagine Reginald standing up to the baron. "Reginald," she said slowly, "this is what I propose. I will speak to Lady Joselynd, if you will go to Roger with your request that he intercede for you with the baron."

"But you're Roger's wife, and he might listen to you."

*I would not be so sure,* she thought. She said, "He knows the baron better than you, so he would know best how to express your reservations about the match. Don't forget that you are a nobleman from a fine family, Reginald, and don't let Roger bully you. You don't have to marry anybody you don't want to, and I'm sure Lady Joselynd will have plenty of other prospects."

"Yes, yes, you're quite right. About Roger and Lady Joselynd both. But you promise you'll talk to her for me?"

"I promise."

Reginald gave her a swift, hearty embrace that caught her off guard. "Thank you so much, Mina! I mean, this is so kind of you, and it's such a weight from my shoulders! I didn't know what I was going to do!"

The garden gate creaked again. "What is it, Hilda?" Mina asked the maidservant who stood on the threshold.

"Oh, here you are, my lady. Good morning, my lord," she said with a pleasant, if somewhat flustered, smile. "I came to tell you that the cook says we can't have the dumplings Lady Joselynd asked for today. He hasn't got the right kind of flour."

Mina muttered an expletive that made Reginald blush. "I'm sorry," she said sheepishly. "I am so tired of worrying about Lady Joselynd's tender stomach and wondering what she will and won't eat. I'm sure Thorbert has aged ten years since she's arrived."

Hilda smothered an amicable giggle. "And I'm sure Aldys and I never want to see those gowns of hers again, either. I've never had to take such care of clothes before."

"You've done an excellent job," Reginald said kindly.

"Only because you told us what to do," Hilda answered with a warm smile.

"She's made everybody work much too hard," Reginald said, walking toward Hilda. "The earlier she leaves, the happier we'll all be."

Mina suddenly had the distinct feeling that she was completely superfluous here, and that Reginald and Hilda wanted to be alone, or perhaps had been planning to be alone before she was discovered there.

Reginald and Hilda? No, she couldn't believe it.

Then Mina looked again at Reginald and at Hilda, and believed it.

Not sure quite what to do or think about this unexpected dalliance—and wondering if that was all it was, or something more—she cleared her throat loudly. "I should be about my duties, and I thank you for telling me of Thorbert's difficulty, Hilda," she said. "Now you should be helping Aldys with the rushes, shouldn't you?"

Hilda gave a guilty start and bobbed a hasty curtsy before hurrying away.

"Reginald, I want to ride later," Mina said, noticing that Reginald's gaze did not stop following

Hilda as she scurried away. "Would you like to join me?"

"No, thank you, Mina," he said with a heavy sigh. "You go too fast for me."

"I don't want you to be bored."

"Never mind about me, Mina. I'll be fine."

"Reginald?"

"Yes?"

"I like Hilda," she said, "and I don't want her to be hurt, but she is only a serving wench."

"I know what she is. Why should anybody hurt her? Has she done something wrong? Does she have to be punished?"

"No, no, it's nothing like that," Mina assured him quickly. "I just couldn't help noticing..."

"That I care for her?" Reginald demanded, and once again her usually mild relative surprised her with his blunt, resolute tone. "I love her. I intend to marry her."

"Reginald!"

"Don't try to talk me out of it, Mina," he said gravely. "I know you married because you very reasonably wanted to better your lot. However, I have no such needs. I love Hilda, and she loves me, and there's no more to be said."

"But how can you be so positive?" Mina protested halfheartedly, more confused than ever about the emotion of which he spoke. "She is nothing but a serving woman. She already has a child. You barely know her! I can see that the baron would forgive your refusal to marry Lady Joselynd for another noblewoman of equal or higher wealth or position, but to refuse his own relative for Hilda? And I think Roger would refuse to be involved in such a scheme, too.''

Reginald looked at her doubtfully, then straightened, grim resolution appearing on his youthful face. ''Then I shall have to go to the baron myself.''

''You would do that for Hilda?''

''Yes.''

Mina stared at Reginald, overwhelmed by the change in him. Could love be this transforming, this powerful? ''Reginald, tell me . . .'' she began, and then she stopped, unsure how to proceed and unsure if she should reveal her curiosity to the young man before her who was, despite the apparent change, still Reginald. He could yet prove to be a foolish boy, and love nothing but a delusion. ''You have only known her a short time to risk the displeasure of one so influential,'' she warned.

''You didn't know Roger at all before you married him.''

''Reginald,'' she said gently, taking his hand. ''Reginald, do you think I have a marriage to emulate?''

This time it was Reginald who looked startled. "Why, yes, of course."

Mina shook her head. "No, I most certainly do not. Roger barely speaks to me. He pays more attention to Joselynd than he does to me."

"He doesn't like Joselynd. He's just being polite."

"You sound very sure of that. I wish I could be."

"Albert's fairly certain of it. You can trust his opinion, can't you?"

"How do you know what Albert thinks?" she asked, a note of hope creeping into her voice.

"I asked him." He flushed a pale pink. "I . . . I was worried about you," he confessed. "I mean, Roger can be fairly rude, and I thought I might have to speak to him about the way he talked to you. Fortunately, Albert explained to me that Roger is usually the most civil to the people he likes least."

"That doesn't make sense," Mina said.

"The way Albert put it, he said that Roger's courtesy is like putting on your best garment for a guest. You are your true self when you're wearing your most comfortable garments, not in your occasional finery."

"What you're saying is, if Roger is rude to me, it's because he likes me?"

"It's because you upset him, and if you upset him, he cares about what you think or do. If he didn't, you wouldn't. Do you follow?"

"I actually believe I do," Mina said, the seed of hope she had tried to destroy blossoming in her heart, although she still wasn't certain what she felt for Roger was love. All she could be sure of was that she was happy beyond belief to think that he didn't hate her.

"I'm going to marry Hilda," Reginald repeated, his expression solemn, "and nothing you, or Roger, or the baron says will change that."

Mina gave him a tender smile. "What does Hilda think of this? Have you told her?"

"I asked her to marry me. She thought as you do, that I didn't mean it or that I could be persuaded to change my mind."

"What about Hollis?"

Reginald's eyes lit with joy. "He's a fine little fellow, isn't he? We've had some jolly times, I can tell you."

"Doesn't playing with him spoil your clothes?"

"Yes, but I don't mind. I have plenty."

This was the final confirmation Mina needed to gauge Reginald's sincerity. If his feelings for Hilda could overpower his vanity, they must run deep indeed.

She was tempted to ask him to describe the emotion, but it seemed rather embarrassing to think that Reginald might actually know more than she did on any given subject. Nevertheless, she was about to when she heard Albert's voice across the courtyard and a better idea presented itself to her. She would go to Sir Albert with two objectives: to explain to him why she had done what she had on her wedding night, and to get him to describe love somehow without confessing her humiliating ignorance.

## Chapter Fifteen

"Excuse me for interrupting," Mina said softly as she drew near Albert and the minstrel who were strolling across the inner ward deep in conversation. "I would like to speak with you, Sir Albert."

Albert gave her a brief, distant smile and nodded his assent. Gerheart, the minstrel, smiled more warmly and said, "We were finished discussing the song anyway, my lady. A good day to you." And with that, he strode off toward the hall.

"I must say I am surprised that you wish to spend so much time in a minstrel's company," Mina said as she led Albert toward the garden.

"Why is that, my lady?"

"Because...because of what they've done with you...with your..." She hesitated, not sure of the right words.

Albert paused and regarded her steadily. "You know my story then, and the song a minstrel made of it?"

"Lady Joselynd told me," Mina confessed, feeling that she would have done better not to raise the subject.

Albert, however, smiled indulgently and continued toward the garden. "It doesn't mortify me to have my tale so widely told. Not anymore. I'm used to it."

It amazed Mina to think that he could become accustomed to the reminder of his failure, and yet it was very clear that he did. "I would not be so tranquil. Doesn't it pain you to hear it?"

By now they were in the garden, and Mina sat on the stone bench. She gestured for Albert to sit.

"It pleases me to think that our love will be remembered for a long, long time, perhaps even when we are dead," he answered with a wistful smile. "I confess I live in hope that Winifred will hear it and know that I will always love her. I continue to hope she might return to me someday." He regarded Mina solemnly. "Now, how may I help you, my lady?"

The sun was hot and bright in the garden, but that was not why Mina began to perspire. She hesitated a moment, then took a deep breath and spoke. "I need your help, Sir Albert."

"*My* help?" he asked, his expression puzzled. "Of course, you have but to ask."

"First, I have noticed a change in your behavior toward me. Oh, nothing to fault, let me assure you," she hastened to add when she saw his reaction. "However, that leads me to assume that Roger has told you something of our wedding night?"

"He told me about it, my lady."

"That I tricked him?"

"Yes, my lady."

"Did he tell you why?"

Albert gave her a frankly curious look. "No, he did not."

"I overheard him talking to the baron about his lascivious prowess, the implication being that although he considered me unattractive, he would do his husbandly duty. And, furthermore, with very little effort on his part, I would experience complete bliss."

Albert blushed and shifted uncomfortably. "Roger sometimes speaks unwisely."

"Needless to say, I was not pleased."

"His words hurt you, and so you sought some revenge," Albert said with an understanding nod.

She stiffened a little at the implication that anything Roger or anyone did could hurt her—and then decided that this was not the time for defensiveness. She was here to learn, not to dissemble.

"Yes," she admitted. "I know I am no beauty, but to hear my betrothed say that..."

"A perfectly natural reaction," Albert said sympathetically. "I can see where you were driven to teach him a lesson."

"Unfortunately, I didn't realize how my suggestion that he had physically hurt me would upset him so. I... my experience had not prepared me to believe a man would be so ashamed of such a thing."

Albert took her hand in his and patted it with brotherly comfort. "You could not know about Roger's training. He was taught by a man who drilled it into his pupils' heads that it was a base and utterly despicable thing to hurt a woman." Albert cleared his throat and the ghost of a smile appeared on his face. "I must also say that Roger has always considered himself a masterful lover. Although I am his friend, I think it might not be so bad that his arrogant vanity was called into question. He could use a dose of humility."

"Nevertheless," Mina said, comforted by Albert's words, "had I known how my confession would anger him, I would have kept silent."

"Honesty is never a mistake. The mistake was in Roger's rather unreasonable reaction. He can be impetuous at times, my lady. You must be patient with him. He has not had an easy life, despite his wealth and power and personal attributes. The early deaths of his parents, his separation from his sister, the years spent in the exclusive company of soldiers . . . all these things do not make a man who reveals his feelings easily.''

''How old was he when his parents died?''

''Ten, or thereabouts. He never speaks of it, but others have told me they died of a fever within three days of each other. It was decided that Roger should be fostered by Lord Gervais, and his sister sent to a convent. It was another ten years before they saw each other again.'' Albert paused, then went on. ''I heard that they had to forcibly restrain him from going after his sister when she was first taken from him.''

Mina didn't say anything, yet Albert's words affected her deeply. She could so easily remember her mother's death and the pain of the loss. Roger had lost his entire family in so short a time! Might it not cause him to withdraw into himself and believe himself better off alone, without love?

Just as she had come to believe. ''I thought he hated me for what I had done,'' she murmured, ''until Reginald told me what you had said to him, about Roger's rudeness toward me.''

''Ah, yes, the contrary nature of Sir Roger de Montmorency. I meant it quite sincerely. His courtesy toward Lady Joselynd is absolutely meaningless. I should also tell you that he argued a great deal with his sister Madeline, and not quietly, yet there is no doubt that he loves her very much.''

''And his incivility toward me?''

''Means you affect him, and I would venture to say he cares a great deal more about you than he would ever dare to show or say.''

''I am glad to hear that you think so,'' Mina said fervently, then she straightened her shoulders and looked Albert directly in the eye. ''He affects me, too, very much. I was thinking...wondering...'' She took another deep breath. ''Sir Albert, how does a person know when they're in love?''

Albert's smile lit his whole face. ''You think you are in love with Roger?''

''I don't know,'' she confessed wistfully.

''The very fact that you are confused is a good beginning,'' Albert said, his tone pleased and blessedly not patronizing. ''However, I regret there are no specific symptoms. All I can tell you is that if you are in love, you will come to know it.''

''What was it like, for you?'' she asked softly. ''Pray forgive my meddling, but you are the only person I feel I can ask about such a matter.''

''I am honored by your confidence, my lady.''

''Did it happen slowly?''

He shrugged his shoulders. ''I cannot say for certain when I began to love. Was it at first sight when I felt as I never had before, or later when suddenly every graceful gesture of Winifred's touched my heart and inflamed my desire?''

"But to be so smitten, so weak, so vulnerable..."

"Love is worth anything," Albert said firmly. "Any danger, any risk. It is wild and glorious beyond belief, though it can lead to despair greater than death when it is thwarted." He spoke so quietly and so sorrowfully that she took his callused hand and pressed a tender kiss to it, to show him that she cared and that he did not have to bear his pain alone.

Then she made a silent promise to do anything she could to try to find the woman Albert had adored, and obviously still did. It would be difficult, but a woman from her mother's family had also been a foster child of Lord Gervais, the lord of Bridgeford Wells. She had met Fritha Kendrick only once, but for Albert's sake, she would send a message asking for any information at all about the lost Winifred.

She rose and held out her hand. "Thank you, Albert, for all your help."

Albert stood beside her. "Roger needs love, my lady. He may not know it yet, but he does."

Mina nodded, even as she wondered what she should do next. She was still too unsure of her own feelings to tell Roger; it had taken more courage than she had guessed to speak to Albert.

And there was still the matter of the seductive Lady Joselynd, whom Reginald did not want. The question haunting Mina now was, if Roger needed love, would he come looking for it from his wife?

Roger did not hear Albert's final words, or Mina's response. By then he had left the shadow of the garden gate, more distraught than he had been since Madeline's departure all those years ago. He hurried away, struck to the very center of his soul by this duplicity.

He had heard the words about love being worth any danger or risk; he had seen her kiss Albert's hand. To think he had been about to ask his traitorous friend for advice about his marriage.

He stumbled and righted himself, glancing around to make sure nobody saw him. They would surely think him drunk. He *was* intoxicated—but with dismay. Oh, God, how could Mina betray him like this? He hadn't been so very horrible to her, had he? And why did it have to be with Albert, his trusted friend? His only friend.

Roger halted at the door of the hall and slumped against the frame, trying to gather strength. Trying to think.

Perhaps he had been wrong. Perhaps he had misinterpreted what he had seen. After all, what exactly had he witnessed? His best friend and his wife sitting alone in her garden, very close together, talking softly and earnestly.

That looked bad. However, the gate had been open. If it had been their intention to have a secret assignation, would they not have closed it?

She had kissed Albert's hand. Not his lips. His hand. What did that signify? Nothing—or the beginning of something that would end in stifled, ecstatic cries?

There was only one way to find out. With strange reluctance, Roger turned and resolutely returned to the garden.

Which was completely empty.

Surely he had been mistaken.

Please, God, let him be mistaken!

A few nights later, Roger stood again on the battlements, lost in thought. He was no more sure about the state of the relationship between Albert and his wife than when he had seen them in the garden. They spoke together often, but with no more intimacy than Mina displayed with Dudley, Hilda or anybody else in the castle. Indeed, Albert and Mina seemed to treat each other with less affection than he showed to Lady Joselynd.

Then Reginald came sidling along the wall-walk.

"Reginald, what brings you up here?" Roger asked, disgruntled that his solitude had been invaded.

"I, um, that is, I was admiring the view."

"Oh."

"Yes." Reginald moved a little closer, and it occurred to Roger that the fellow was not so outrageously dressed as usual. His garments actually looked . . . subdued. "I also thought this might be a good time to speak to you."

"What about?" Roger inquired, trying not to sound bored, although he could not imagine that Reginald would say anything remotely interesting.

"Lady Joselynd and the baron."

"Joselynd and the baron?" Roger asked, wondering what Reginald meant linking those two together.

Reginald waved his hand. "Oh, God, no! That didn't come out right. I mean, I was hoping . . . that is, I was wondering if I could get you to speak to the baron for me *about* Lady Joselynd."

Roger didn't bother to hide his amusement from his brother-in-law. "What about her?"

"I don't want to marry her."

"May I ask why not?"

"I'm going to marry Hilda."

Roger straightened abruptly. *"What?"*

"I'm going to marry Hilda," Reginald repeated with unexpected boldness.

"She's a *peasant!*"

"I know her social station. I don't care."

"Don't be stupid, Reginald."

"I don't think it's stupid to marry the woman I love," Reginald replied defiantly. "I think I would be stupid if I didn't."

"You'll regret it!"

"I don't think so."

"The baron won't want to hear this," Roger declared in a slightly angry tone.

"That's why I came to *you*. He respects you. He'll listen to you, and—"

"I'm not going to interfere in this. If you want to ruin your life, that's your business. Don't ask me to help."

"I tell you, I won't be ruining my life."

"You're deluded! There is no such thing as love."

Reginald's eyes widened, then softened into sadness. "I am very sorry to hear Mina's husband say so."

Roger turned on his heel and marched away. He didn't want to hear anything else Reginald had to say. The man was more of a fool than he had suspected. To have the audacity to sound as if he pitied *him!* The very notion of marrying a woman like

Hilda was simply ridiculous! Completely unacceptable! Hilda was a fine woman, of course, and would make some man a good wife, but not a nobleman.

And then to think that *he* would intercede with the baron on his behalf. Reginald was a stupid, blundering, gullible dupe who had listened to too many minstrels!

Roger's anger propelled him across the inner ward. This idea of a marriage had to be stopped. He glanced up at the tower and saw the pale beam of light from his bedchamber window. He and Mina didn't agree on much, but surely she would have to agree with him about this.

"What is this nonsense about Reginald and Hilda?" Roger demanded as he marched into his bedchamber. He nearly marched right back out again when he realized Mina was wearing only a thin—*very* thin—shift and brushing her curling, luxurious hair.

Before he could get away, Mina swiveled on her stool, her hairbrush still in her hand. "It's not nonsense. He's quite determined to marry her."

He stalked over and grabbed her brush, putting it down with a bang on the table. "Is he mad?"

She picked up the brush and began to run it through her hair again, looking straight at him. "He claims to be in love."

"That's utterly ridiculous!"

She merely shrugged her shoulders as if Roger's declaration were not worthy of a vocal response.

"Put that damned thing down and answer me!"

"What was your question?"

"What are you going to do about Reginald?"

"Nothing at all. He is quite adamant. He says he's in love."

"He'll make a greater fool of himself!"

"I take it then, Sir Roger, that you do not believe in the power of love?" she asked evenly, slowly putting down the brush.

"No, I do not."

She looked at him with her gray-green eyes and her full lips in a small, probably meaningless smile. "Reginald does, and he is of legal age to do as he likes."

"And you? What do you think of this 'love' nonsense?" Roger blurted, cursing his own weakness. He should not care what she thought about anything other than the running of his household, and he had tried to avoid any discussion of that. Indeed, he had tried not to notice her at all, unless she was talking to Albert. Then he was drawn to watch them like one of his hawks sighting a rabbit.

Her gaze faltered for an instant, but only for an instant. "Since I have little experience of the emotion, I have tended to doubt its validity," she replied calmly. "However, there seem to be plenty of other people who are not only quite convinced it exists, but claim to have suffered it themselves."

"They're fools."

"Would you call Sir Albert Lacourt a fool?"

"Where love is concerned, yes, I would."

"A ruthless judgment, my lord," she remarked, rising and turning toward him, presenting him with the nearly overwhelming view of her virtually naked body.

The sight of her rosy nipples straining against the transparent fabric of her shift was nearly enough to make him forget his jealous anger and risk a rebuff by taking her in his arms. She went toward the bed and absently ran her hand over the coverlet in a gesture that was almost a caress, and he wondered if she was intentionally trying to divert his attention. Based on her past deception, it would be just like her to try such a diabolical scheme, and it was nearly working. "Will you please cover yourself? Have you no sense of shame?"

"I am covered, and you are my husband, so I have nothing to be ashamed of."

God's wounds, how arrogant she sounded! If she were properly dressed, he would make her understand that he was in command here. However, she was driving him to distraction and making him remember with excruciating exactness the pleasure he had felt in her arms.

He reminded himself forcefully that the more important issue was this outlandish business of Reginald's alleged intention to marry Hilda.

"So, you believe I will be able to succeed where you have failed," she remarked, moving away from the bed.

"I want you to talk some sense into your mutton-headed brother, that's all," he said, steeling himself against her wiles. "And what about Joselynd? She doesn't know about this yet, does she?"

"I would think you should be more aware of what Lady Joselynd knows than I, since you have spent more time in her presence. However, the answer to your question is, she has not yet been informed of Reginald's feelings."

"Why the devil not?"

"Because he's reluctant to tell her. He doesn't want to upset her."

"He'll have to. *I* won't."

"*I* will. I have already told Reginald so."

"Then why haven't you?"

"I have not yet found an appropriate time."

"Well, you had better—and soon. And you can tell that idiot brother of yours I have no intention of going to the baron on his behalf. If he wants to make a fool of himself, he can do so without my assistance!''

''Is it my 'idiot brother's' apparent predicament that has upset you, or the fact that your clever plan has floundered?'' she inquired.

''What clever plan?'' he demanded.

''Didn't the baron want Reginald to marry your sister to ensure his obedience? To put him under your control, and therefore his?''

''The baron does not control me.''

Her skeptically raised eyebrow infuriated him. ''Now you want me to exert some influence over poor, confused Reginald? Do you honestly think *I* will encourage him to obey?''

''Perhaps my request is not overwise. It's probably your fault that he disagrees with me now.''

Mina sighed sorrowfully. ''To think, the great Sir Roger thwarted by a mere woman's influence. How very sad for you.''

''Mina...'' he warned, not sure what he intended to say.

''I should think you would want the best for Hilda, though,'' she observed, at last crossing her arms and hiding the pink hint of her nipples, to Roger's relief. ''Or is it that Reginald has stolen her affections away from you? Has Hilda refused to sleep with you anymore?''

"I haven't slept with Hilda since before you arrived," he declared defensively, then once more cursed himself for letting her prod him into that admission. In truth, he had been spending his nights in a variety of locations, either alone in her garden when the nights were warm and cloudless, or with his soldiers, hoping that no one would notice he never slept with his wife. He walked toward the window and feigned great interest in the evening sky.

"So what does it matter to you if another man wants Hilda for his wife?"

Out of the corner of his eye, Roger saw her finally put on a velvet robe he had never seen before. The fabric was a thick, rich indigo blue that made her skin appear almost translucent.

He faced her again, noting immediately how her eyes had darkened to a deeper blue, a shade like the western sky at dusk. "It matters to me if the man in question is a Norman nobleman who has sworn fealty to my overlord."

"Reginald has not sworn fealty to any man."

"I don't believe you."

Mina's lips twitched, yet she didn't actually frown, and he was reluctantly impressed by her self-control. "He only arrived here from France a few months ago," she explained impartially, pulling the robe tight and once again disclosing her exquisite shape, "and I see I must remind you that the baron is of lesser rank than Reginald. If Reginald swears fealty to anyone, it will be to the king himself or to the baron's overlord, Lord Trevelyan, whose own daughter married a man not nobly born."

Her cool, calm argument stunned Roger. It had simply never occurred to him that Reginald was not the baron's liege man. If that were so—and he could certainly confirm this startling news—then it didn't matter what the baron wanted. "Why did he agree to the baron's proposal of a marriage between himself and my sister then?" he charged.

"Knowing Reginald, you should be able to guess. The baron is a powerful, persuasive man, and Reginald values his friendship and the alliance between them. At the time the baron proposed the match, it probably only mattered that it was the baron's idea, and Reginald saw no reason to disagree. That has obviously changed."

"Obviously," Roger echoed scornfully. "I was forgetting the power of love."

Mina gave him a hostile look that distressed him more than he cared to acknowledge. "Or could it be that Reginald has finally grown up enough to make a decision for himself and not blindly *obey?*"

Her emphasis on the last word had all the force of an insult. She made it both a condemnation and an intimation of absurdity that he should expect anyone to obey him. God's teeth, he was *never* going to understand her! He didn't want to, and he shouldn't have to.

Grinding his teeth in agitated frustration, Roger marched from the room without another word, slamming the door, now determined to leave Reginald to his fate.

He halted at the bottom of the steps. A quick survey of the hall proved that Reginald was not there. Several of the soldiers were drinking ale and talking among themselves before retiring to their barracks. Some played dice or chess, and Albert and the minstrel were sitting together, singing softly.

Roger nodded briefly to those who acknowledged his presence, then continued on into the inner ward. He kept going until he had left the castle. Once outside and away from the sentries' view, he went to the river and sank onto the grassy bank.

He never should have gone to his bedchamber and tried to talk to Mina. He had been certain that whatever she thought about marriage in general, she would not approve of the alliance of her half brother with a woman who was, although kind and good, a servant. He had convinced himself that she would agree Reginald's talk of love was the foolishness of a dull-witted simpleton. He had never imagined she would disagree.

Nor had he wanted to be alone with her. It was necessary that they keep this matter a secret as long as possible, that was all. It was not that he half hoped, in the secret recesses of his heart and in the intimacy of their bedchamber, that she might say she could love...someone.

Even if he had voiced his imprudent thoughts, that antagonistic look on her face demonstrated all too plainly that she had no understanding or sympathy for lovesick blockheads—like him.

He lay on the ground and stared up at the night sky and the twinkling stars, trying to decipher his discordant emotions.

Reginald might be a fool, and a deluded one at that, with all his talk of love. And Albert might be a pitiful man who had let his affection for a married woman destroy his prospects.

But what did that make *him?* He wanted to be with Mina all the time, to listen to her voice, watch the play of emotions in her luminous, beautiful eyes, to feel her arms around him. He wanted her to bear his children, and live with him all the days of his life. He wanted her to desire and need him with equal fervor.

And yet he did not risk even touching her. He did not dare let her know how she had reached the vulnerable core of his heart, because he was terrified that she did not care for him at all.

Perhaps this was God's vengeance for his arrogant belief that he alone had no need for another person.

If so, he was regretting that arrogance now. Now that he was in love.

When the door banged shut, Mina slumped down onto the stool with a shaky sigh. Her encounter with Roger left her feeling weak and spent from the effort of maintaining her composure while inwardly she was filled with a confused battery of emotions, each one trying to take precedence.

Ever since the night they had consummated their marriage, her first reaction to the sight of her husband or the sound of his voice was a rapid increase in the beating of her heart and the memory of the myriad sensations of pleasure she had felt in his arms.

For so long she had hoped he would come to her, to speak with her, to share his feelings. Instead, he had barged into their bedchamber like some kind of righteously indignant potentate, overwrought about Reginald, of all things. Reginald was well able to make his own decisions, whether Roger de Montmorency wanted to believe it or not.

She sighed heavily. That was not what really disturbed her. What was more dismaying was his reaction to *her*. Wanting to know if he cared for her at all, and feeling like some kind of lust-crazed wench, she had deliberately tried to entice him.

And what had happened? He had told her to cover herself and accused her of having no shame!

She had felt totally embarrassed, even ridiculous, and so had striven to pay attention to the business at hand, as well as sustaining an aura of calm indifference, which was getting harder all the time. It was all too easy for her mask to slip, at least inwardly, and when that happened, it took all her fortitude not to weaken and show him that his words, his expressions, his requests *did* affect her. There was not another man in all the world it would be so difficult to disregard.

She was a fool. A weak, lovesick fool.

## Chapter Sixteen

Three nights later, Roger crept up the steps to his bedchamber. He had gone to his other estate, leaving Albert behind this time. Tonight he had returned secretly, hoping to find...nothing. Fearing that he would discover Mina in their bed, but not alone.

If he did catch her in bed with Albert, there could be no question that he would be completely justified in whatever punishment he meted out, and if they were guilty, he was quite determined that they would be punished.

If Mina was alone, he hoped his constant anxiety would be alleviated.

Despite his determination, his steps faltered and his hand hesitated as he reached out to lift the latch.

He reminded himself that he was in the right. This was his castle and his wife. There could be no excuse for adultery, none whatsoever. No matter how he had treated her before, or what he had said to the baron. *He* would never betray his oath of marriage, no more than he would betray the fealty he had sworn to the baron. And certainly Albert, his trusted liege man, should never have broken his oath of loyalty. There could be no pardon for him, either.

So at last he quietly lifted the latch and stepped into the darkened room, his footfalls muffled by the carpet.

Mina was sleeping in the bed, and, as he could clearly observe in the moonlight, alone. Relief, mixed with hope, flooded through him.

How peaceful and how vulnerable she looked, so different from her appearance during the day. Then she seemed so aloof, so remote...so alone. And what had he done to alleviate that loneliness? Nothing. But it was her fault for having lied to him. Wasn't it?

If he had been born a woman and heard such an assessment of his characteristics, might he not have considered some kind of revenge, too? If he was unkind to her, was it any wonder she might seek solace in another man's arms?

Perhaps they were too clever for him. Maybe they had been warned of his return somehow. With drooping shoulders and the sickening realization that he might never be free of his suspicions, Roger went to leave the room. Before he could do so,

Mina sat up and asked sleepily, "Who is there? What is it?"

Her tousled hair curled around her pale, soft face. She held the coverings to her chest, although she wore that same thin shift.

His body responded instantly to the enticing vision, and it took only another instant for his mind to formulate a plan. He would test her. If she were truly unfaithful to him, she would not welcome his embrace. If she felt a duty to do so, she would surely not respond with the same enthusiasm she had when they had consummated the marriage.

"It is I. Roger. Your husband," he answered softly, closing the door quietly.

"Why have you come back?" she asked, obviously confused and rather alarmed. "Is something amiss?"

"I wanted to be home," he answered, stepping closer.

She shifted and brushed back a stray curl in a delicate feminine gesture that inflamed his desire. "Why... why are you here?"

"A husband surely need not explain his presence in his own bedchamber," he replied before he pulled off his tunic.

Mina didn't move. Indeed, she could barely believe the evidence before her eyes. Roger here, instead of miles away? And using an inviting, sensual tone of voice that sent the blood thrilling through her body even before he took off his tunic and revealed his muscular chest and strong, broad shoulders?

She held her breath as he walked toward the bed and sat on the edge, uncertain why he had come back, and if she should ask the question again. Then he reached out to move back another loose curl, and his fingers brushed her cheek. Who would have guessed such a simple gesture could have such a devastating, intense effect on her? Every limb turned to liquid, every thought disappeared, leaving only the burning need to have him touch her again.

Was it lust or love? Did she care? Did he? "Roger, why are you here?"

He leaned forward to press a gentle kiss on her cheek, his lips moving slowly toward her neck as he seized her shoulders. "To be with you," he whispered.

"Why?" she asked, her voice more a low moan as he pressed her back onto the pillows.

*Say you want me,* she thought fervently. *Say you need me. Say you love me!* His body slowly moved over hers, his leg draped across her thigh.

"Does it matter?" As he moved between her legs, he used his tongue to tease the hardened peaks of her nipples through her shift, the sensation nearly overpowering.

But not quite. The horrible notion that perhaps it was only his intention to use her to satisfy a physical need struck her. Why else would he come here? Why now, after all these days? Maybe Joselynd had refused his advances, so he went where he could not legally be denied.

"Why are you here?" she demanded again, using her elbows to shove herself up and away from him. Oh, God's blood, to think that she weakened so easily in his arms.

"This is my bed," he said, one hand snaking up her leg. "You are my wife. What other reasons do I need?"

"Where have you been all these other nights?"

"That doesn't matter. I am here now, and I want you."

"For what?"

His expression hardened and he moved back a little. It was then she saw what could only be dismay in his eyes. "I see you have no desire for my company, my lady," he said with a trace of bitterness, then, rising, added, "so I will rid you of it."

She did not know what to make of his troubled look or the agitated tone of his voice. "Roger—"

The look he gave her was full of scorn. "What is this? Are you changing your mind? Have you thought better of refusing me?"

She climbed out of the bed and faced him, confused but determined not to be vanquished even in the bedchamber. "Are you thinking of forcing me?"

"Of course not!" He yanked on his tunic.

She couldn't stand the uncertainty any longer. "Roger, we must talk," she said decisively and with true desperation.

"You have made it very clear that you wish me to leave, so I will take myself away. Nor will I trouble you with my conversation. Good night, my lady."

"Roger!"

Out he went, leaving her alone once more.

As she stared helplessly at the back of the door, Mina did not feel the burning, cleansing anger she needed. Instead, she thought of a forlorn little boy trying so desperately to stay with his sister. She had seen a wisp of that child in Roger's eyes, and she knew exactly how he must have felt on that long-ago day: abandoned and completely alone, watching the one person he loved going away.

The Sabbath dawned fair and fine, with a hint of the cooler days of autumn to come. Roger went to mass and afterward broke the fast as if this were any other Sabbath. Mina sat in the hall at the high table to his left; Lady Joselynd, who apparently remained ignorant of Reginald's foolish notion regarding Hilda, sat on his right. Albert sat to Lady Joselynd's right, and Reginald on Mina's left, as far away from Joselynd as he could get. Hilda wisely made herself scarce, performing her duties swiftly and silently before seeking refuge in the kitchen.

Roger noted that Albert accepted his place at the table without a qualm. But he was a clever man, and his apparent acceptance of not being beside Mina might merely be a way to avert suspicion.

As always, Mina avoided speaking to him, her husband. On the other hand, she didn't speak much to anybody.

This state of living was slowly becoming impossible. Unfortunately, Roger could not decide how to deal with it—astonishing in itself, he knew. He had always been decisive, but perhaps the stakes had never been so high.

As he sat in his hall, he went through his choices one more time.

He could accuse Mina and Albert right here and now, in his hall and before the assembly. However, he had no real proof of their adultery. He had seen nothing definite himself, and no one had come to him with tales of illicit meetings or overheard conversations of an intimate nature. The case would have to go before a higher authority, too, and that meant the baron. At one time, Roger would have been absolutely sure the baron would pass a judgment favorable to him; however, after seeing the way Baron DeGuerre admired Mina, he could not be so certain now. If the baron decided against him, it would be completely humiliating.

He could confide in Dudley, and perhaps one or two others among his men, and enlist their aid in finding evidence of wrongdoing. That would mean revealing his shame to others, though, and admitting that he had failed as a husband.

He could ask Mina and Albert outright. Yet he could no longer be certain that he would believe their words and, indeed, his mistrust proved the complete opposite, so that would surely be futile.

There was one final course of action, and although it seemed the least likely to give him any peace, it appeared to be the only one that would not cause him public dishonor: he would allow things to continue as they were at Montmorency Castle, at least until he found indisputable evidence against Mina and her possible lover.

"Didn't you hear me, Roger?" Albert said loudly, interrupting Roger's melancholy ruminations. "It looks to be a fine day for hunting."

Roger realized he had been staring at the table in the vicinity of Lady Joselynd's trencher and quickly looked at Albert. "A fine suggestion," he said, wondering what other parts of the conversation or what other glances and smiles he had missed.

Obviously under the mistaken impression that Roger's attention had been focused on her, Lady Joselynd smiled her bright, empty smile and said excitedly, "Oh, how delightful! It is such a pleasure to watch you."

"Have you not forgotten the game?" Mina asked.

Roger turned to look at his wife. God's wounds, why could he not see her as he had at first, a thin, homely creature with overbright hair? When had she turned into the pale, green-eyed enchantress who made every other woman's beauty commonplace in comparison? "Game?" he asked vaguely.

"The foot ball game, between our village and Barstead-on-Meadow, after the noon hour. The villagers are expecting you to be there, at least to watch."

Roger was hard-pressed to keep a scowl from his face at the way she said "to watch," as if he were incapable of participating. "Ah, yes. The game. I have been asked to lead our village. And you, Albert?" he asked, facing him. "Do you intend to play?"

"It was *my* intention to be nothing more than a spectator, given my age."

"Oh, come now! You are not much older than I. Isn't that right, Mina?"

"If Sir Albert declines to participate, we should respect his wishes."

*So you two can be alone together?* Roger thought contemptuously. "We wouldn't want the villagers to think you are a helpless, feeble old man, would we?" he chided. "They might question your ability as my knight. All you need do is take care. I'm certain you'll be able to stay out of the thick of things."

Albert smiled good-naturedly, and it was like a needle under Roger's skin. Was he truly as innocent as he looked, or was his deception only that much greater? "If you insist, Roger, I shall play. However, I must warn you, I have no lightness of foot. I shall surely shame us with my clumsiness."

"You underestimate yourself!" Mina cried. "I'm sure you'll do very well, indeed. After all, you have the honor of the Normans to uphold."

Roger, thinking of Mina's Saxon mother, shot her a quizzical glance, but she was already rising from her chair and did not see it. "If you will excuse me, I've offered to supply some cheese and mead from our stores for the participants. I should ensure that Dudley has matters well in hand, although I'm quite certain he has."

When Mina had gone into the kitchen corridor, Lady Joselynd's hand touched Roger's arm. "I look forward to seeing this game," she said softly, batting her long, dusky eyelashes at him. "I have only heard of such riotous sport. I have never witnessed it."

Roger glanced down at the pale, soft, slender hand on his sleeve and wondered if Lady Joselynd was deliberately trying to entice him.

He gave his guest a provocative smile. "I promise you it will not be dull."

She blushed at his scrutiny and looked away, but her hand slid from his arm with what could well be deliberate slowness. "And you, Lord Chilcott? Will I have the pleasure of watching you, as well?"

"God's holy rood, no!" Reginald said firmly. "I have no desire to go traipsing about after an inflated bladder!"

"I think we can uphold the honor of the Normans without you," Roger said, standing up. Albert did likewise. "I am going to have to change my clothes," Roger remarked, thinking of the mud that would be churned up by the players' feet, especially in the meadow and riverbank. "Shouldn't you, Albert?"

"Yes," his former friend replied. "The game is to start just after the noon, at the crossroads."

"We shall meet the villagers on the green before that," Roger said, heading for his chamber.

When he got there, the room was empty, as he had expected, and he quickly donned an old tunic and chausses whose ruin would not matter. In the bottom of his chest, he also found an ancient pair of boots. They might be slippery in the mud, but he wasn't about to destroy a better pair. It was as he was pulling them on that he noted the writing materials on Mina's table.

What did Mina have to write about?

He went to the table and scrutinized the pot of ink, the quill, the small piece of unmarked parchment and the red sealing wax. The sealing wax would indicate a message rather than a simple household document such as a list.

To whom was Mina writing? If he understood things, the only relative she had anything to do with was Reginald, and he was right here.

Did she have some friend or other relation she wished to communicate with? And if so, why? It couldn't be to relate her happiness in her married life.

Another thought momentarily took his breath away. If she was planning to leave him, it could be that she was trying to find a refuge for herself and her lover with someone who could offer them sanctuary.

The idea made a terrible kind of sense to him, and suddenly he felt tears spring to his eyes.

Just as quickly, he swiped them away. He was Sir Roger de Montmorency, and she was his wife, and he would be damned before he would let her shame him in front of anyone!

The bedchamber door opened and he spun around, filled with murderous rage, expecting to see Mina and instead finding Lady Joselynd. Her eyes widened and she took a step back, until he smiled. "You startled me," he said by way of explanation.

"I...um...I came to see if Lady Mina could suggest the best situation from which to watch the game."

"The battlements, over the main gate," Roger said, moving toward her. "Dudley will see that there are chairs and refreshments for you."

*Yes, he was Sir Roger de Montmorency and most women wanted to be in his arms.* "I hope you will save your loudest cheers for me," he said quietly.

Joselynd lowered her eyes with charming bashfulness. "You are a married man," she whispered.

"And you are a very beautiful woman," he murmured.

"Sir Roger, this is most improper," Joselynd demurred, although she leaned closer to him and ran one hand up his arm with practiced ease.

Roger gazed down into her blue eyes and saw the cold calculation there. No fires of passion, no heat of desire, no underlying hopeful yearning. "You're quite right," he said, suddenly disgusted with her, and with himself. He moved away from her. "I can only say that your beauty must have intoxicated me, and like a drunken man, I forgot myself. Please forgive me."

Her expression was a masterpiece of wounded pride, confusion and frustrated lust.

"You had best be on your way," he said, not really caring if his words sounded like a dismissal or not.

"Yes, I should," she responded coldly, her tone no longer dulcet but hard as granite. "I should hate the baron to hear that you made improper advances toward me."

"Is that a threat, my lady?" Roger asked calmly. The baron's wrath meant very little to him compared to the heartache of his wife's infidelity.

"Perhaps." Joselynd smiled again and pushed the door shut, closing them inside. "It need not be."

He was tired of this game. Tired of speculation. Tired of everything. "I have to go."

With a grim face, Roger marched past her and headed for the inner ward, there to meet Albert prior to participating in an event that had led to several serious injuries in the past.

Mina sat in one of the chairs so thoughtfully provided by Dudley on the wall-walk. From this vantage point, she and Lady Joselynd could watch the game in comfort. If Roger and his men were successful, they would move the ball over the common land, across the wood and through the meadow toward the church of St. Ninian's at Barstead. She had a clear view of the men of Montmorency mustering on the green, including several villagers led by Lud, and the soldiers from the castle led by Roger.

Dudley had also ordered a small table set out, on which was placed some wine and fruit. The day was warm and clear, the breeze refreshing. Had everything in her life been well, Mina thought, she would have enjoyed this immensely. As it was, it was nothing but a distraction, and not a very effective one.

Her gaze kept straying to her husband as he spoke quietly to the foot soldiers from the castle. How strong he looked, how fully in command. She could make out his stern expression and guessed that he was approaching this competition over the procurement of an inflated pig's bladder as if it were a major battle.

Albert, looking not nearly as confident, wandered over to join Lud and the villagers. Mina wondered why Roger had wanted Albert to participate so vociferously. It was clear he did, however, and like so many others, Albert did not contravene his lord's orders.

"Lady Mina, here you are!" Joselynd exclaimed, sliding into the chair next to her. "I have been searching for you everywhere—and for Lord Chilcott, too. He is nowhere to be found."

"Reginald is otherwise occupied," she explained. She had her suspicions as to Reginald's exact location, but she wasn't about to tell Joselynd.

"I have not seen much of him these past few days," Joselynd said wistfully, and Mina almost felt sorry for the woman. After all, if Joselynd thought Reginald was her way to greater status or wealth, it would be disappointing for her to discover that he had no desire to marry her.

The men moved off toward the crossroads, the white marker clearly visible. It was on the closest side of the wood, where the main road to Montmorency Castle joined the road to London and branched onto the northern road, which led to Barstead-on-Meadow.

"There are so many of them!" Joselynd noted. "And some of them are so huge. Just look at that fellow there!"

"That's Lud, our village reeve," Mina said.

"How many men does Barstead have?"

"The lord of Barstead Hall generally allows most of his tenants to participate, or so Dudley tells me, and it is a large estate. Sir George also sends a fair number of soldiers. I believe they outnumber our men by nearly two to one."

"Oh, blessed Mary!" Joselynd exclaimed. "No wonder Lord Chilcott declined to take part. It would not be safe for one of his gentle goodness. Some of those men look very vicious."

"Oh, you needn't worry," Hilda said jovially, arriving with some fresh rolls, which smelled delicious. "Sir Roger's men are well trained. Usually nobody gets hurt, except for a broken bone or two."

"I'm sure Sir Roger's men are well trained for fighting, but not for this peasant's sport," Joselynd replied, her tone making it very clear that she resented a servant's remarks, however pertinent.

"They play this all the time, and other games, too. Sir Roger says it keeps 'em nimble," Hilda said, undeterred.

"You may go," Joselynd said dismissively to the maidservant.

Mina was still not completely certain that the marriage between her half brother and Hilda would take place. Judging by Hilda's manner, though, it seemed *she* was. However, Hilda was intelligent as well as confident, so she did not linger where she was so obviously unwelcome.

"Is that quite true?" Joselynd demanded of Mina after Hilda had sauntered away.

"Oh, yes," she replied. "Roger has many interesting ideas about training."

Not that she had heard them from Roger. She had spent several pleasant minutes one recent morning watching Roger's soldiers play such a game. At first she had been rather taken aback by their display of frivolity, until Albert had taken the time to explain its apparent usefulness for keeping the soldiers fit and fast on their feet.

Mina noticed that the sentries were watching the villagers and mumbling what she took to be wagers on the outcome; no one else was nearby.

Mina had told Reginald she would help him, and this might be a good time to disillusion Joselynd as to her prospects regarding a marriage. She had put off the task, certain that Joselynd's reaction was likely to be emotional, and because a distrustful impulse forced her to continue to watch for signs of her husband's possible infidelity. However, if she didn't speak to Joselynd soon, the lady might discover the state of the relationship between Reginald and Hilda for herself and cause a tremendous furor that might involve the baron.

"Lady Joselynd," she began not unkindly, "there is something I must tell you."

The young woman gave her a puzzled look. "You sound very serious."

"I am. I think you should know that Reginald does not plan to marry you."

Lady Joselynd blinked once, twice and a third time before she opened her mouth, then closed it, then opened it again. "Are you saying he has refused me?"

"It was my understanding that nothing definite had been arranged by the baron. I thought you had simply come to meet Reginald and see if a match might be amenable to you both. There has been no formal betrothal."

"The baron expects it," Lady Joselynd snapped, her winsome frailty nowhere to be seen. "He told me so."

"The baron is not the potential groom," Mina observed. "Despite Reginald's decision, you are quite welcome to extend your visit." It would be a sacrifice to endure the woman's company any longer, Mina thought, but one she would make for Reginald's sake.

"*He* does not want *me?*" Joselynd reiterated in disbelief.

"Apparently," Mina said. "I would not take it as a personal affront—"

"I consider it an insult that such a creature as that overdressed popinjay brother of yours has the gall to refuse my hand in marriage," the lady growled in a most unladylike manner, leaping to her feet. "However, I shall take this as a blessing in disguise. I have no desire to be wed to *him* and was only acting polite, for courtesy's sake. Nor do I have any desire to be allied to your family, either to your brother, you or your lustful husband." Her eyes narrowed, she pushed her face uncomfortably close to Mina's and whispered, "Oh, yes, my lady, I would watch Sir Roger de Montmorency very carefully, indeed, if you value your family's honor. Just this very day he tried to *seduce* me."

To Joselynd's surprise, Lady Mina didn't move, nor did her expression change. She knew Sir Roger's wife was a cold, unfeeling creature, but she would not have believed any woman could remain so completely unmoved by an accusation of infidelity.

"I think you had better leave. Today," Mina said softly.

"Oh, I will and with pleasure! And I hope I never see you or your husband or your idiotic brother again! Just wait until Baron DeGuerre hears how you have treated me!''

Mina eyed Joselynd coolly. "I would suggest that you remember Sir Roger is a favorite of the baron's, and unless you are very sure of your place within his affections, you might do better not to force him to choose who he regards more. I might also point out that the baron is not married, either.''

For an instant, Joselynd looked taken aback, then she majestically swept past Mina.

Mina remained absolutely still, alone in her thoughts, isolated in her anguish, her horrible suspicions confirmed.

Roger didn't want her.

She felt paralyzed, as if the whole castle had come crumbling down around her ears and buried her under tons of stone.

What was it Albert had said? Love could lead to despair greater than death. Oh, God in heaven, that she should discover the terrible truth of his words! Mina covered her face with her hands and tried desperately not to howl in pain like a wounded animal.

"It's all right, my lady," one of the sentries called out. "He's not hurt. He's gettin' up, see?"

Mina slowly removed her hands and followed the direction of the soldier's gesture. Roger was climbing to his feet and in another moment was rapidly running after the gang of men chasing one stout fellow who lightly kicked the ball ahead of the pack.

Look at him, she thought bitterly. Sir Roger de Montmorency, with all his talk of loyalty and honesty.

All his lies.

# *Chapter Seventeen*

"What, winded already?" Roger demanded as he trotted up to Albert, who was bent over, his hands on his knees and his breathing labored. "I haven't been working you hard enough, obviously."

"Obviously," Albert gasped. "Nor am I a young man."

A great cry went up from the Montmorency men as the ball hurtled past Roger and Albert. "Come on!" Roger cried, dashing after it. He caught it nimbly with one foot and managed to kick it behind, back in the direction of Barstead. His men surged past him.

"Catch it!" Roger shouted at Albert, who obediently ran forward.

"God's wounds, Roger, it's only a game," he muttered breathlessly as he paused to catch his breath again and see where the ball was.

"Giving up?" Roger challenged, halting with his hands on his hips. "Maybe you should go and lie down in the gutter to rest."

Albert gave him a searching, angry look. "What are you driving at?" he demanded.

"Maybe your fighting days are over, and I have been too preoccupied to notice."

Suffering with his angry jealousy, Roger was dismayed to see Albert's beatific smile. "Ah, this is your way of testing me, is it?" Albert asked merrily. "Well, hurry up, then, Sir Roger!" Albert dashed off with renewed vigor, leaving Roger to chase after him, as well as the ball.

Albert caught the ball and for several minutes was a master of footwork, parrying the ball between his nimble feet and advancing it many yards toward St. Ninian's. Roger, well aware that Mina was watching from the battlements, finally managed to get the ball away from Albert and sprinted ahead, only to be met by a surly mob of sweaty opponents from Barstead.

Not to be outdone, Albert ran toward the ball and got it away from his lord. With amazing dexterity, he wove through the line of opposition, followed by Roger and his men. Roger gritted his teeth, determined that Albert should not have the glory of achieving this victory. When he drew near to him, Roger suddenly elbowed Albert viciously, sending him sprawling into the mud.

Lud and a group of ten fellows, slow but nearly equal in size to the reeve, had caught up to Roger by then. Forming a guard, they surrounded Roger, neatly intercepting any challengers. In that manner, Roger was able to get the ball the final few yards to the church.

When the ball touched the wall, a great cheer went up from Roger, Lud and the others.

It was only after the cheering and shouting had died down that Roger realized Albert had not gotten up.

"You've done another fine job," Mina said to Dudley as she surveyed the inner ward. In preparation for the end of the game, trestle tables had been brought out of the hall and set up there. Great barrels of ale stood ready to be tapped, for Mina had decided that win or lose, the Montmorency participants would be thirsty men and should be rewarded for their efforts. If they won, the townspeople were ready to haul more barrels inside the yard.

An air of expectation had descended on the castle when the ball moved out of sight from the battlements. Those who had wagered against Montmorency, a small minority, had already deserted their posts and gone to console themselves at the alehouse. Those who had placed bets on their comrades had quieted into hopeful silence.

Hilda was nowhere to be seen, having been hastily and angrily pressed into the service of Lady Joselynd, who was making noisy preparations to depart. Her obvious displeasure didn't bother Mina. She would be happy to have the woman gone.

There was a sudden delighted shout. The minstrel, who had taken Mina's place on the battlements, called out, "We've won!"

All over the castle, excited babble broke out. Even Dudley, whose main concern was for the celebratory preparations, joined in the cheering.

Mina drifted away from the inner ward toward the relative silence of her garden. Soon Roger and the others would be here, laughing and talking and drinking. They would not notice her absence.

Sinking down onto the stone bench, she laid her head in her hand and stared at the blooming flowers. She had come into this marriage without a lot of girlish hopes or foolish delusions, and, indeed, if Roger had made it clear he intended to bed other women right at the start, she probably would have accepted that as part of the marriage contract.

However, he had not. If anything, she had been rather sure that he would remain true to his vows of faithfulness. In hindsight, that might have been stupid. Nevertheless, she had, and now the pain of knowing he had tried to seduce the insipid Joselynd was horrible, especially after his reproaches about loyalty and honesty. He was a dishonorable, deceitful scoundrel.

But there was nothing she could do. The marriage was consummated, and she had nowhere else to go.

Worst of all, she wanted the fortitude of hatred, and felt only the frailty of her hopeless love.

"My lady!" Dudley suddenly exclaimed from the inner ward, his voice filled with distress.

Mina lifted her head and rose apprehensively as the garden gate burst open. "What is it?" she demanded fearfully, thinking of some of the tumbles she had seen the men take. "Roger...?"

"No. Sir Albert."

That revelation provided some small relief as Mina ran toward Dudley and looked at the crowd jostling their way through the gates. At the front of the subdued mob came Roger, carrying an unconscious Albert in his arms.

"What happened?" she cried, hurrying to her husband and walking rapidly beside him.

"He fell and struck his head."

Albert moaned softly, and to Roger's surprise, Mina smiled. "A good sign. Take him to the hall," she ordered. "Dudley, I need warm water and clean cloths. Is there an apothecary in the village?"

"No, my lady," Dudley replied weakly as he caught sight of the blood trickling down Albert's forehead. "He visits regularly, but—"

"Get the water and cloths."

"Yes, my lady." Dudley bustled off toward the kitchen.

"Carefully, now!" Mina adjured as Roger turned sideways to make his way through the entrance to the hall with his burden.

Hilda saw them and gasped. "Help Dudley," Mina ordered. "He's in the kitchen." Hilda nodded and disappeared.

Roger bent down to lower a groaning Albert onto one of the benches.

"No, not here," Mina said decisively. "Take him to our bedchamber."

Roger glanced at her sharply.

"It will be quieter there, and the bed is softer."

Without a word, Roger lifted his friend and followed her. He laid Albert in his bed and stepped back as Mina pushed him out of the way. With her gentle hands she carefully brushed back the blood-dampened hair on Albert's scalp. "A rock?" she asked as if Roger were no more than a servant.

"Yes," he replied, too concerned for Albert to take much offense. This was his fault. He had shoved his friend, pushed him down, made him strike his head.

"Albert, can you hear me?" Mina asked.

Mina heard a whispered yes, and nodded. "If he is conscious, the injury might not be very severe. Unfortunately, I have little knowledge of such wounds. My experience has been cuts from a switch or bruises. A head wound will be beyond my skill. Is there no one who has a knowledge of medicine here?"

"Bredon," Roger replied immediately.

"The huntsman?" she asked, turning from her ministrations and eyeing him skeptically.

"He will know how to stop the bleeding and prevent infection. For the rest..."

Mina frowned, then muttered, "Where's Dudley with that water?"

"Here, my lady," Dudley called from the corridor.

Mina returned her attention to Albert, Roger seemingly forgotten.

Father Damien shuffled into the room and at once fell to his knees near the bed, his hands clasped and his eyes pressed tightly shut. He began to mumble in Latin, obviously praying with his whole heart.

Roger brightened suddenly. "Father Gabriel! The abbot at the monastery of St. Christopher. He tended me when I was similarly wounded. He will know what to do.''

''But that is far away,'' Mina protested. ''It will take too long.''

''Not if I go at once on Raven, with another swift mount for Father Gabriel. He is a good, kind fellow who knows Albert. I'm sure he'll come.''

''Then waste no more time here.''

Roger anxiously watched as Father Gabriel, whose gray eyes were as mild as Mina's could be severe, carefully examined the wound on Albert's head, which he had unbandaged. Mina stood near the head of the bed, chewing her lip with more show of concern than Roger had ever seen her display before.

She looked exhausted, too. Dudley had reported that she had rarely left Albert's bedside.

He didn't fault her for that. He would have stayed there, too, had he not been certain that it was more important to fetch Father Gabriel from the monastery some miles to the south.

During his frantic journey, he had contemplated the state of his emotions. After the accident, he had been horrified by his own cold-blooded viciousness. Albert had been his best and dearest friend for many years, and he had behaved in a cowardly, despicable manner. He did not excuse Albert for the adultery any more than he excused Mina, if indeed it had happened, yet he had come very close to doing murder and with no real proof of any wrongdoing.

"A most competent job," Father Gabriel muttered. He bent down closer and sniffed. "No sign of infection at all, although I must confess I am not familiar with this poultice."

"I made it up myself," Bredon said from his place in the corner. As always, there was a dog nearby, sitting quietly at his feet. "I tried it on Daisy here when she got caught in some brambles," he explained, pointing to the large hound who looked rather fierce for such a floral name. "Worked like a charm, it did."

"You must describe the ingredients for me later," the priest said. He smiled at Mina as he rose from the bedside. "A severe wound, but not life threatening," he said quietly. "He has regained consciousness several times?"

"Yes, and answered my questions correctly."

"Good. Keep waking him every few hours, but I am confident that the worst has passed."

"Are you sure?" Mina asked, a hint of quiet desperation in her voice that cut Roger to the quick.

"Quite sure," Father Gabriel said. "No more serious than the wound your husband received in the spring, and I'm sure you will agree that he is quite recovered. It will take some time, however. Sir Albert is not quite as virile as Roger. He will need to rest and keep quiet for a few days—and I do hope, Sir Roger, that you will ensure he abides by my recommendations better than you did under similar circumstances.''

''I will see to it, Father,'' Mina said. ''Now you must be weary after your long journey. Roger will take you to the kitchen for some food, since it is awhile yet before the evening meal.''

It was on the tip of Roger's tongue to ask Mina to accompany them, but in the end, he didn't. She would probably refuse anyway. Besides, he liked Father Gabriel and would enjoy some time in the man's company without worrying about what his wife was thinking.

''This way, Father,'' he said, leading the way out of the room. ''Bredon, you are excused.''

''Aye, sir,'' the huntsman said. He gave a low whistle and Daisy lumbered to her feet, following along behind them, leaving Mina and her lover alone.

When they reached the kitchen and Father Gabriel had been given plenty of hearty stew, a small brown loaf and a measure of ale, the priest turned his kindly yet shrewd gaze onto Roger, who joined him at the table. Around them Thorbert, Hilda and the other servants bustled about preparing the meal, which didn't seem to disturb Father Gabriel at all. "So, tell me, my son, does your head still trouble you?"

"Not at all."

"Something else?"

Was it that obvious that he was deeply distressed? Roger thought. He would have to do better. "Why do you ask?"

"You look tired. Perhaps the worry about Albert . . . ?"

"Yes. Will you be able to stay for a visit?"

"Unfortunately, no. I have to return to the monastery at once. It was only because of my affection for both you and Albert that I decided to come."

"We appreciate it very much."

Reginald strolled into the kitchen, saw Father Gabriel sitting at the table and exclaimed, "You! What are *you* doing here?"

"He came to see Albert, who, I'm sure you'll be pleased to know, is not mortally wounded," Roger replied.

"Indeed I am. Forgive my lack of manners, Father," Reginald said, sliding onto a bench opposite them. "I was startled, that's all. You must admit, the last time we met, the circumstances were not overly pleasant."

That was putting it kindly, Roger thought. The last time Father Gabriel had seen Reginald, the young man had just been released by a band of Welshmen who had kidnapped him so that Dafydd ap Iolo could take Reginald's place and marry Madeline.

"So, Albert is going to get better?" Reginald asked solicitously.

"It will take time, but yes, I believe so."

"How long will you be joining us?"

"I should return to the monastery tomorrow."

"Oh, how unfortunate. So many comings and goings. The baron, Lady Joselynd and now you. I was hoping *you* could stay longer."

Hilda sauntered by, a linen cloth for the high table draped over her arm. She went out the corridor toward the hall. "Well, I must be going," Reginald said quickly. "I trust we'll see you at the evening meal?"

"Of course, my son."

With a jaunty smile, Reginald wandered out of the kitchen, taking the same route Hilda had moments before.

"That is a changed young man," Father Gabriel remarked.

"The power of love," Roger said with more scorn than he had intended to show.

"It is a very influential emotion," Father Gabriel agreed.

Roger didn't want to talk about love. "Tell me all the news of the monastery, Father. Is Jerrald still a thorn in your side?"

Father Gabriel gave a rueful chuckle. "Indeed he is, my son, indeed he is. I was really quite delighted to leave him in charge. Perhaps that will content him for a little while."

"You could say something to the baron. I'm sure he could get Father Jerrald sent elsewhere."

"Oh, there is no need for that. Jerrald has his good qualities, if he does occasionally let his ambition come to the fore."

"You are much more patient with him than I could ever be."

"I am patient with him because I know all men are weak in their own way," Father Gabriel replied. "Even you, my son."

Roger shot the priest a startled glance.

Father Gabriel continued to eat as if nothing were amiss. After a few moments of silence had passed, he said, "You have a most fascinating wife, Roger." He smiled when he saw his companion's face. "Does it surprise you to hear a man of God say so? A priest I may be, to be sure, but I am also human. She is not quite the kind of woman I envisioned you choosing, for I think her qualities are not so readily apparent. I must say I am most pleasantly surprised."

"Her 'qualities' are no reflection of my discretion. It was an arranged marriage, Father, to join our families when Madeline decided to marry Dafydd."

"Ah. You sacrificed yourself, then, for your sister's sake?"

"Yes."

"Love can show itself in many ways, but selfless sacrifice always impresses me. You made your sister very happy, Roger." Father Gabriel lowered his voice. "But what about you? Are you not happy with your decision?"

Roger kept his eyes on his index finger as he moved it back and forth in a circular pattern over the battered surface of the table. "Of course. I didn't mean to imply otherwise."

"You must forgive my impertinent questions, Roger," the priest said kindly. "I ask only because of my concern for your happiness. Do you think you will come to love her, this arranged wife of yours?"

"Enough to make a selfless sacrifice?" Roger asked, trying to sound sardonic.

"Yes," Father Gabriel said.

Roger looked away. "Perhaps," he murmured.

Then he turned back to the priest with a grin. "Now you must tell me the news from the south,

Father. I know you priests at St. Christopher's hear all the gossip.''

Father Gabriel, whatever else he thought, realized that the subject of their conversation had been irrevocably changed, and was no longer to deal with the relationship between Sir Roger de Montmorency and his bride.

## Chapter Eighteen

Nearly a fortnight later, Mina sighed and looked around the bedchamber. She could tell from the disarray that Roger had been here and changed his clothes. She reached for his discarded tunic, reflecting that this was about as close as she ever got to her husband these days.

He avoided her whenever possible and spent his days on other parts of his lands. When he did return, he was gruff and abrupt to her, and to others, as well, with the exception of Dudley.

She had not confronted him about his possible dalliance with Joselynd. Upon calmer reflection, she had decided that it was possible Roger was not as guilty as Joselynd had implied. After all, Joselynd had been angry and upset, and perhaps had misinterpreted Roger's words or actions.

She had spent several fruitless hours trying to decide just how Roger felt about her, but usually gave up in frustration. Sometimes, in her blackest moods, she wondered if he was so surly because Lady Joselynd had packed her baggage and gone, or if he had simply reverted to his usual state.

Mina folded the tunic and put it back in the chest. She sighed wearily, glad to have her bedchamber back although she was once again a solitary inhabitant of the room. Sir Albert had steadily improved and would soon be completely well again. She had tended him with all the time and care she could manage, finding such activity both a refuge and an excuse to stay away from Roger. Feeling as she did now, it was painful to be in his presence, always wondering how he compared her to Lady Joselynd and sure he found her lacking.

No matter how Roger felt about it, the departure of Lady Joselynd was cause for relief to his wife. The aggrieved lady had insisted upon leaving immediately, and neither the celebration of the foot ball victory nor any concern for Sir Albert seemed to affect her determination to follow through with her abrupt change of plans.

The celebration itself had been somewhat subdued, since most of the men of the village liked Sir Albert. Upon hearing Mina's opinion that the wound would not prove fatal, things had gotten more merry. Rumor had it that Reginald had done an astonishingly accurate impression of the hard-to-please Lady Joselynd that had the castle servants rolling on the ground, helpless with laughter. She had also heard Hilda had done a similarly accurate impersonation of Roger, which she wickedly wished she had seen. No one told her if anyone had made sport of the lady of Montmorency Castle. Mina suspected that they probably had, and she hoped she had been portrayed with some kindness. The peasants treated her with deference, respect and genuine affection, something she had yearned for all her life. She would have to learn to be content with that.

Mina adjusted her wimple with swift gestures. As for other aspects of her life, she was used to being alone. It was only since her marriage that she had learned to enjoy company. She had even been pleasantly surprised to discover that Reginald was not a complete simpleton. He had merely been extremely unsure of himself and, therefore, did whatever he was told. He was still rather vain, but she guessed that his concern for his clothes and hair had come from a need to ensure that his outward coverings hid his inner insecurities. Assured by Hilda's good regard, he rarely fretted about his garments these days.

Sadly, if Reginald persisted in marrying Hilda, they would leave the castle, and if Roger continued to be angry about the marriage, who could say when she might see her half brother and his wife again? Once more she would be left completely alone and absolutely friendless.

What did it matter? Being alone was better than depending upon someone else for your happiness.

Being alone was better than being the brunt of a man's unjustified anger. Being alone was...horrible.

Mina sank down onto the stool, desolating loneliness filling her heart, made all the more terrible by her undeniable, undiminished, completely hopeless love for Roger.

Her only consolation had come from talking to Albert. Although she kept her grief private, simply knowing that he had experienced similar emotions helped her. She persuaded him to talk of his Winifred, gently prodding him for details. She had begun her own secret search for Albert's missing love and hoped he would provide some clue that she could use. She said nothing to him of her quest, though, in case it should prove fruitless.

Fritha Kendrick had responded to her first letter, but her news had not been good. No one seemed to know where the merchant's wife had gone, although one of the peddlers who came to Bridgeford Wells claimed to have seen the woman and her son in York some time ago. Fritha knew of a nobleman there who might be able to help, and had provided his name. That had led to another letter, another message of regret, another rumor, and another name, and more letters. Mina could only hope that eventually she would find out something tangible about the elusive Winifred. No wonder Albert had given up the search as hopeless.

There was a sharp rap on the door. "Enter," Mina said, expecting to see Hilda or Aldys arriving to tidy the bedchamber.

Instead, Roger strode into the room, a piece of parchment in his hands. "A messenger arrived today. Dudley was going to bring this to you, but I told him I would," he announced.

"Thank you," she said, reaching out to take the message from him, trying not to show any trepidation at his stern visage.

"What is it?" he demanded.

"A letter from Sir John Delapont, I believe."

"Why has he written you a letter?"

"Is there something wrong with me receiving letters?" she asked, wondering about his manner. His voice was fierce and apparently angry, but his eyes...that was not the emotion in his eyes.

He crossed the room and she noticed how stiff and tense he seemed. "I thought I could deal with this like an honorable man," he said without looking at her. "I thought it didn't matter to me what you did. That it could not touch me. Unfortunately for both of us, I find this is not so." He whirled around to face her. "Is Sir John Delapont willing to receive you and Albert when you leave here?"

She stared at him, dumbfounded. "What...what are you talking about?"

"You are leaving."

She gasped at his words as she crumpled the parchment in her hand. "Are you going to send me away?" she whispered, sickened and hurt. "Do I displease you that much? Has it come to this?"

"If you want to go, I won't stop you."

"I am not planning on leaving this castle unless you cast me out," she said, trying to sound firm and failing utterly.

"I won't be made a fool of in my own home. I won't have everyone pointing at me, the cuckold, and snickering behind my back. If you go, at least most of the shame goes with you."

"Roger," Mina cried, holding out her hands in a gesture of supplication, "I don't know what you are talking about. Who thinks you are a cuckold?" Her eyes narrowed as the full import of his words hit home. "And why?"

"*I* do, and don't play the ignorant maid with me, Mina. I told you when I first met you that I didn't like it."

He thought she was committing adultery! He thought she was betraying him! "With Albert!" she gasped, finishing her thought out loud. "You think I am dishonoring you with *Albert?*" She rose, marched toward him and jabbed her finger at his chest. "You mean to tell me you honestly believe me capable of such a betrayal, and Albert, too?"

His accusation had obviously shocked her. It must not be true, he thought exultantly. She must be faithful to him! No one could be that good at feigning surprise or shocked dismay.

Then came the torture of doubt, which he had lived with for days. Perhaps she was only astonished that he had discovered her duplicity. Perhaps she was amazed that he had guessed what the message from Sir John Delapont contained. "You deceived me before," he noted flatly, crossing his arms as if to protect his already tortured heart.

"How dare you!" Mina cried passionately, glaring at him, the knowledge that he could think her capable of such shameful behavior enraging her, bursting for once and all the carefully constructed wall around her heart, the wall that love had started to crumble. "How dare you accuse me of such a thing!" she cried. "How dare you accuse Albert, your most loyal friend! If there is shame here, it is with you for harboring such base thoughts—and for trying to seduce Lady Joselynd! You, with all your talk of loyalty and honesty! You base, dishonorable rogue!"

"What has that vain coquette to do with this?" Roger responded fiercely. "Do you deny that you care for Albert?"

"Care for him? No, I don't deny it. Do you deny you tried to seduce Joselynd?"

"If I did, it was a fleeting moment of foolishness!"

"Foolishness? Is that what you call it?"

"*I* did not betray my vows. Unlike *you*, I remembered my oath outside the chapel doors!"

"After all your talk, I should hope so. Nor did I forget *my* vows," she insisted. She took a deep breath and lowered her voice, then spoke deliberately. "I care for Albert as if he were the kind older brother I never had. I care for him as a friend. I care for him because...because you do." She could not maintain the comfort of her passionate anger, not with him looking at her as if her sins had wounded him to the soul. "How can you think—"

"I saw you with him in the garden," Roger said, quieter now. "You kissed his hand."

"You *spied* on me?"

"You are my wife. I saw you with him, whispering like lovers."

"Because I had not closed the gate. If I were having a secret meeting with my lover, don't you think I would be more clever than that?"

"Or maybe you were clever enough to leave the gate open, not suspecting that anyone would be walking by at that time."

She saw his struggle and knew that he wanted to believe her. He wanted to trust her, just as she trusted that his contempt for Joselynd had not been feigned, and that knowledge renewed her strength. "Listen to yourself, Roger," she said staunchly. "Your suspicions are ridiculous."

"Then why were you alone with Albert?"

"Because I wanted to talk to him about something."

"What needed such privacy, my lady?" Roger demanded, his voice stern but with a longing in his eyes that touched her soul.

Now was the time, this the place. She would risk humiliation because she could no longer bear the uncertainty of their relationship, because she believed that he had not betrayed her, and most of all because of the yearning she had seen in his eyes. "I wanted to ask him how a person would know they were in love."

He blinked and actually reared back as if her words were a stunning blow.

The die was cast, so she carried on. "I know you don't believe there is such a thing as love, Roger," she said, hoping that she was wrong and he did believe it. "I used to think so, too. After all, what evidence had I to the contrary?

"I married you firmly convinced it would be enough if I could tolerate you. The main thing was, I would be Lady Mina de Montmorency. I would be respected. I would be worth something.

"And then..." For the first time, her determination faltered. She looked at his face and saw, in his eyes, an eager hopefulness that removed the last lingering doubt that she should speak. "And then I discovered that I had married the one man in all the world who could inspire that wondrous feeling within me. Who respected me not because I was

Lady Mina de Montmorency, but for myself alone. Who did not treat me like a child or a toy. Who taught me about passion. But I wasn't sure what I felt was love, so I asked Albert for his help.''

"You . . . you were not going to leave me?"

"No, Roger, I was not going to leave you."

"Oh, God!" he moaned, his voice filled with conspicuous pain. He covered his face with his hands. "Forgive me, Mina. I was . . . I was so afraid . . . everyone I have ever cared about has been taken away from me. And this time, I knew I had no one to blame but myself. I . . . I pushed you away. I tried to believe I didn't need you, or your love. But I was wrong. So very wrong!"

She went to him, putting her arms around him and drawing him into her embrace, exultant at his revelation, touched by his vulnerability. "I was afraid, too, Roger. Afraid that I wasn't the wife you wanted. Afraid that you hated me."

He took hold of her shoulders, his dark gaze searching her face. "I could never hate you, Mina. Even when I had convinced myself that you had broken our marriage vows and I tried to be angry, I felt only sorrow."

"You were going to let us go," she said. "You could have had us imprisoned, but you were going to let us go."

"I could not bear the thought of punishing you for my mistakes."

"Because you love me?" she asked, a glorious smile lighting her beautiful face.

"Because I love you," he answered.

"Roger, Roger, I love you, too. With all my heart."

"Mina!" He sighed. "Mina, my love!" He kissed her face, her eyes, her cheeks. "My dearest love," he whispered.

Mina started to weep, her shoulders shaking as she rested against his hard chest, although why she was shedding tears when she had never been happier made no sense.

He held her thus for a very long, incredible moment as she struggled to come to terms with her riotous, delightful emotions and tremendous relief. The burden she had carried had been lifted.

"I have to ask you," Roger said at last. "Why were you writing to Sir John Delapont? I don't even know him."

"I don't, either." Mina answered. She gave him a brief squeeze and looked up into his eyes. "I'm trying to find Winifred."

"*Albert's* Winifred?"

"The very same."

Roger threw back his head and laughed, a deep, rich irresistible sound that echoed through the stone chamber. She joined him, finding a new release in their shared joy and a confirmation of their happiness. "Oh, God's blood, Mina, I have been a fool. A blind, arrogant, stupid fool!" he said, holding her tightly. "I drove myself nearly mad with jealousy, and you were trying to reunite Albert with his Winifred." He grew more serious. "Have you had any luck?"

"Unfortunately, no. Not so far." She pulled back and gave him a sidelong glance. "Why didn't you ask me about my conversation with Albert in the garden?"

"The great Sir Roger de Montmorency admit his wife might prefer another man?" He gave her a wryly skeptical look. "How can you even ask that?"

"Just as the arrogant, self-assured wife of Sir Roger could not bring herself to admit her weakness, that she was in love with her husband and filled with jealousy."

"You hid it very well," he noted.

"I couldn't be sure. She's so beautiful—"

"She is a silly, stupid, vain creature, and not nearly as beautiful as you."

"Now I know you must be in love," she said with an indulgent smile, "to think I am more beautiful than Joselynd. The minstrels will hate us for starting a new fashion in noble marriages. Imagine—a husband and wife who are in love with *each other*."

"Since we are, and now we know we are, I would like to start our married life anew," Roger said softly, gently caressing her cheek. "With no more hidden fears or jealousies."

"Yes, I quite agree, my love." She took his hand in hers. With a sultry smile, she pressed a kiss to his palm, then slid her mouth down to his wrist and back again to kiss each fingertip.

"God's wounds," Roger muttered breathlessly when she took his other hand and proceeded to kiss it in a similarly provocative manner.

"I did not kiss Albert like that, did I?" she charged seductively, quite unabashedly filled with desire and happiness.

"Thank God, no, or he might have done what I am about to do, loyal or not," Roger said, picking her up and carrying her to their bed.

A short while later, Hilda, accompanied by Aldys, knocked tentatively on the closed bedchamber door. "My lady?" she called out softly.

When she didn't get an immediate response, she looked worriedly at Aldys. "I wonder what she's doing in her bedchamber in the middle of the morning?"

"Do you think she's sick?" Aldys asked.

Hilda knocked harder. "My lady!"

"What is it?" Mina answered, her voice strangely muffled.

The two maidservants glanced at each other. "She doesn't sound quite right, does she?" Aldys whispered.

"We've come to tidy your chamber," Hilda said loudly.

"Come back later!" another voice bellowed.

This time, the maidservants stared at each other with wide eyes. There could be no mistaking that deep, stern voice. Hilda started to giggle, then so did Aldys.

"Go away!" Sir Roger roared.

The two women scurried to the stairs. "Wait until Reginald hears about this," Hilda whispered gleefully. "He's been worried sick!"

# Chapter Nineteen

Over a month later, Roger raised himself on his elbow and gazed lovingly at his naked, sleeping wife. How could he ever have considered her unattractive? he thought, bending down to kiss her silky earlobe. She was vibrant with life, with her incredible eyes, blue or green or gray—whatever color they assumed at the moment. How glorious it was to see them mirror back love and happiness! He was indeed the most fortunate of men, with a wonderful wife who had made his castle a home rather than a mere fortress, and who had told him such marvelous news last night. He was going to be a father.

"Roger?" Mina asked sleepily, rolling onto her back. She smiled at him and drew the coverings modestly higher.

With a lascivious leer, he pulled them lower to expose her satiny skin. "You were expecting someone else?" he asked playfully.

"Roger!" she chided with what was meant to be a frown of displeasure. "I don't find such remarks in good taste, considering."

"I'm too happy to care about any taste but this," he said, bending down to kiss her mouth, delighting as always in her immediately passionate response.

"You're a shameless wench," he said a moment later, reluctantly breaking the kiss. "In your condition, too."

"My condition is all your fault," she observed gravely, her eyes dancing with laughter. "Our child is going to be the most stubborn one ever born, I'm sure."

"Then he will need a firm hand, and I'm sure you are just the mother to provide it."

Her brow furrowed slightly. "I would never strike a child, Roger."

He smiled warmly and touched her cheek. "I know. That isn't what I meant. Heaven forbid he should ever try to persuade you to change your mind, though."

"Or you." She snuggled up against him. "Perhaps it will be a girl."

"Then God help the poor man she decides to marry, if she has her mother's strength of will."

"It is a great pity Albert has no sons," she remarked.

"Or if he didn't still love Winifred. He is not that old a man."

Mina gave her husband a skeptical look. "That is your male vanity speaking, Roger. A girl wants a *young* man. And Albert's heart is already spoken for."

"Have you had any more luck with your search?"

Mina sighed and shook her head. "No, not since that other wool merchant said he had seen Winifred and her son last year."

"Let us not lose hope," Roger replied. "After all, I myself never believed there was such a thing as love until you came into my life, so miracles *can* happen."

"Yes, they can," Mina said slowly, pushing her more than willing body against his naked flesh.

"Mina, you are insatiable."

"We wasted too many nights, Roger."

"Although I agree," he said, giving her a swift caress, "I have men to train. I've been rather negligent lately." He reluctantly climbed out of bed and went to the chest.

"There is also a harvest to oversee." She sighed luxuriantly and snuggled down under the covers.

"Don't you have duties to attend to, wife?" he remarked, pulling on his chausses.

"Dudley has things well in hand, I'm sure."

Roger got a roguish gleam in his eye that Mina was coming to know well. Suddenly he dashed toward the bed and jumped in beside her. "To the devil with my duties. Albert can train the men this morning."

Mina's only answer was a sultry laugh.

Several minutes later, Roger rolled over and wiped his sweaty brow. "God's wounds, you are the most incredible lover, Mina!"

"Better than your others?"

"What, jealous?" he said, smiling at her. "You shouldn't be. I never truly *loved* any of them."

"Good. Now hadn't you better go help Albert or Dudley, or see what Lud has arranged for the hay meadows?"

"You are right as always, my darling." He lifted his hips and slid his chausses back into place with a sigh. "God's wounds, I'm exhausted already."

"You'll recover," Mina said without any trace of sympathy.

"I wish I could lie abed all day," he said, giving her a pointed look.

"How insulting! I don't do that! You know, I think I liked you better before, when you were so harsh and rude. At least then I got some work done." Mina giggled, a sound Roger was coming to enjoy very much.

"Now you've wounded my tender feelings." Roger pouted, getting out of bed and searching for something in the chest. "What have you done with my gray tunic?"

''It's right there.'' Mina pointed to the garment lying in a heap beside the bed. ''Really, Roger, you're going to have to take more care.''

''Then don't make me impatient.'' He pulled the wrinkled tunic over his head.

''You look a mess.''

''Taking after Reginald, are you? Nobody else I know worries about the appearance of his clothes.''

''Speaking of Reginald,'' Mina said, getting out of bed and putting on her shift, which had also been left in a heap on the floor, ''do you think the baron's going to be terribly angry? Maybe we should have delayed the wedding.''

''I daresay we'll find out soon enough. I would have welcomed a delay, too, but Reginald wouldn't hear of it. He's a changed man these days.''

''The power of love, I suppose.''

The couple exchanged amused glances, then Mina frowned. ''In all seriousness, Roger, I think Reginald and Hilda should leave for France soon, although I'll be sorry to see them go.''

''Surprisingly, I think I'll miss the fellow, too. He's vastly improved. My influence, no doubt.''

Mina shook her head as she tried to locate the laces at the back of her gown. ''Still the arrogant nobleman!''

Roger came behind her and grabbed the laces from her, his breath warm on her cheek. ''Mina!'' he warned, his voice filled with laughter.

She leaned back against him. "I like it when you make me laugh," she said.

He bent over her and planted a kiss on her forehead. "You *are* a temptress. But about Reginald, I think it would be wise for him to leave the country. The baron has many friends."

"I suppose, but—"

At that moment there was a flurry of pounding on the bedchamber door. Roger stepped away from Mina so quickly she almost fell over. "What is it?" he demanded, hurrying to the door and flinging it open.

A very agitated Dudley stood on the threshold. "It's the baron! Baron DeGuerre! He's here! In the hall!"

"Baron DeGuerre?" Roger asked stupidly.

"I didn't know what else to do, so I asked him to the hall!" Dudley exclaimed, wringing his hands. "What's he here for? There's no decent meat in the kitchen!"

"Take him some wine and give him our apologies for not being ready to receive him. Tell him we'll be down shortly," Mina ordered. Dudley nodded and scurried away as fast as his stocky legs could move.

Mina swiftly knotted her laces. "Roger, get your black tunic on!"

"Right!" He paused while he was in the process of pulling on his boots. "Do you suppose he's heard about the wedding already?"

"Who knows? I'll have Dudley find Reginald and tell him to stay out of the castle for a while."

Roger halted on his way to the door. "No, Mina," he said decisively. "Reginald hasn't done anything wrong. He should face the baron and get it over with. After all, he *is* a Chilcott."

Mina sighed and nodded, quickly flinging a scarf over her unbrushed hair before shoving a stiffened headband on top. "You know the baron best. I just hope Reginald hasn't fled already."

"We'll find out soon enough."

Hand in hand, Roger and Mina hurried along the corridor and ran lightly down the stairs. Then they halted abruptly.

Baron DeGuerre was seated by the hearth, looking like a very judgmental St. Peter at the gates of heaven. Reginald, pale but defiant, stood before him, holding tight to his new wife's hand. He wore a plain tunic rather like the one the baron had on, and he managed to look both terrified and brave. Hilda, attired in a fine new blue gown that highlighted her fulsome beauty, stood resolutely beside him. Instantly Roger was ashamed for all the less-than-flattering thoughts he had ever had about Mina's half brother. He quickly walked forward, catching the baron's censorious eye.

"So, Roger," Baron DeGuerre said gravely, "you have allowed these two to marry."

"Yes, my lord," Roger answered, making his obeisance. "I did."

"It wasn't for him to give me permission," Reginald proclaimed stoutly. "He is not my liege lord, and neither, Baron DeGuerre, are *you*."

"I know very well who has sworn an oath of loyalty to me and who has not," the baron replied calmly. "I haven't come to condemn you, even if you did insult Lady Joselynd. She was very upset when she reached my castle." He gave Roger the vaguest hint of a smile. "She seemed to think I should comfort her. I regretfully declined. She's left my castle and gone north, to Sir Thomas Tarrant's manor. His son is in need of a wife, or so I heard."

Roger and Mina looked at each other with tentative relief. Reginald and Hilda managed weak smiles.

Aldys, looking extremely self-conscious, arrived holding a tray with a chalice of wine and a goblet. Another maidservant, new to her duties, moved three chairs close to the baron's. "Aren't you going to join me?" the baron inquired of his hosts as Aldys set down the tray, her hands shaking so much it rattled.

Hilda moved quickly to help Aldys, giving her friend a sympathetic look.

"Hilda," Reginald said, his voice only slightly critical. "That's Aldys's job now."

Blushing, Hilda moved away from the table. Aldys dipped a curtsy and said in a high, anxious voice, "I'll fetch more goblets, my lord." She practically ran out of the hall and nearly tripped over a stray piece of kindling in her haste.

"Please, sit," the baron said, unconsciously assuming command of the hall. Roger, feeling magnanimous, decided to let him. "I confess I was not delighted to hear that Lord Chilcott decided to marry. However, he informs me it is a fait accompli, so I shall simply have to accept it. That is not the main reason for my visit. I have recently acquired some additional land, including the manor of the late Sir Guy de Robespierre." The baron's voice was full of contempt, and Roger quite agreed with the sentiment. Sir Guy had been a corrupt and evil man. "It is not my intention to punish anyone," the baron said, obviously not without sympathy for the abused tenants. "However, I need a knight to hold it for me. I realize, Lord Chilcott, that you already have a large estate in France. I came to ask if you would consider taking over this one, too."

"I would have to swear fealty to you, wouldn't I?" Reginald asked doubtfully, looking at Roger, who gave a slight nod of his head in confirmation.

"Yes, you would," the baron replied. "I realize this might seem a step down to you, but I hope you will not refuse. It is important to me to have the very best men for my allies. The times seem peaceable enough, but such things can change within a very short time. It also occurs to me that your wife's... lineage... might prove rather beneficial.

The tenants will surely be more likely to accept you."

"If that's the case, I will say that my wife is not happy with the idea of living in France, so far from her home," Reginald said hesitantly. "I would have to visit France from time to time, of course, but my steward there is a most reliable, trustworthy fellow. I daresay he'll be delighted not to have me sticking my nose in things."

"I will be glad to have you close by, too," Mina said.

The baron smiled with what Mina took to be genuine pleasure. "Then you accept?"

"I accept. I shall do my best to be a good master to them and a good ally to you, Baron DeGuerre," Reginald said.

"I'm sure you will," the baron replied. He eyed Roger pensively. "I must say, marriage seems to be doing you a lot of good, Roger."

"It is, indeed, my lord." Roger glanced at Mina and smiled warmly. "I am delighted to be able to tell you that my wife is with child."

"Wonderful!" the baron cried, rising and giving Mina a kiss on each cheek. "I am happy for you, my lady. You are truly a lucky fellow, Roger!"

There was some sadness in his voice, and Mina could guess why. For all his power, wealth, talent and wives, the baron had no living son to whom he could bequeath his steadily increasing land. "This calls for a celebration," the baron proclaimed.

Mina thought of Dudley's agitation and wondered how quickly they could find or purchase the necessary items of food, as well as how much it would cost.

"At my expense, of course," the baron said. "Perhaps Roger and Reginald will care to accompany me on a hunt to provide the meat?"

Mina wasn't sure if the baron had somehow heard or guessed Dudley's concerns, but it didn't matter, because Roger was always eager to hunt when he was not eager for certain other activities generally confined to the marriage bed . . . or the woods . . . or under that willow beside the river. . . .

"My reeve will have the harvesting well in hand, my lord," Roger said. "I shall be honored to hunt with you."

Reginald swallowed hard. "If you will give me leave, my lord, hunting is not to my taste."

"Even if the food it provides is? Well, you have my permission to stay with your lovely wife, who I hope has forgiven my unconscionable behavior during my last visit."

Hilda blushed and nodded eagerly.

The baron looked around the hall. "A great improvement here, Roger, which I assume your wife is responsible for."

"Yes, my lord."

"I haven't seen Sir Albert since I arrived. I heard of his accident. Is he quite recovered?"

Roger rose with something of a guilty expression on his face. "I think he is overseeing the training of my men."

The baron also got to his feet. "To think I have lived to see the day you are not doing that yourself! Your marriage must indeed be happy, if it can cause Sir Roger de Montmorency to neglect his duties."

"My lord, I—"

"It is a jest, Roger. Come, I would like to greet Sir Albert. You don't have to accompany me, Reginald. I suppose you two newly wedded young people would far rather enjoy your own company. Mina, please join us. I like the camaraderie of beautiful women."

"With pleasure, my lord."

Mina followed behind her husband and his overlord after giving Reginald and Hilda a happy smile. She was sincerely pleased to think they would not be living in France, and perhaps when it was necessary for Reginald to visit there, Hilda could come to stay at Montmorency Castle.

They discovered that Albert had taken several of the foot soldiers and one or two of the lesser visiting knights and their squires to the Lammas lands, the common grazing ground outside the village. When they drew near, they could see why. The men, attired in full chain mail, were busily chasing the inflated pig's bladder, with Albert admonishing them for their lack of speed or clumsiness as he deemed necessary.

Albert spotted the baron, Roger and Mina and made a slight bow. The other men, all of whom were sweaty, some of whom were panting and a few of whom were clearly exhausted, stopped the game until Roger barked at them to continue.

Albert approached and said, "Good morning, Baron DeGuerre. A pleasure to—"

Then he stopped, staring past them as if he had seen a ghost.

Mina, Roger and the baron glanced over their shoulders, then turned to watch a woman on a palfrey riding toward the village. A young man rode beside her. The woman was cloaked, and the young man unfamiliar, yet before they could turn their gaze back to Albert, he had already taken off in a mad sprint down the road. "Winifred!" he shouted, waving his arms, no longer a mature knight, but a young lad again, his voice full of joy and astonishment.

The woman threw back her hood, displaying a face that was not of outstanding beauty, but her smile was dazzling and made up for whatever in her features might be lacking. She dismounted quickly when Albert ran toward her. She held her arms wide and called his name. When he reached her, engulfing her in his arms, she embraced him fervently. Mina could hear parts of their excited exchange, including a mention of a ballad and something about a letter.

She had trouble seeing the young man get down from his horse, because her eyes were full of tears. She was thrilled to think that she had played a small part in this glorious reunion.

"So that is the famous Winifred," the baron mused. "She doesn't look the kind of woman to inflame such tenacious passion."

"Do not underestimate the power of love," Roger remarked, stepping beside Mina and pulling her close. "I assure you, I never will again."

"Nor I," Mina said happily, reaching up to kiss her Norman.

\* \* \* \* \* \*

## Weddings by DeWilde

*Since the turn of the century the elegant and fashionable DeWilde stores have helped brides around the world turn the fantasy of their "Special Day" into reality. But now the store and three generations of family are torn apart by the divorce of Grace and Jeffrey DeWilde. As family members face new challenges and loves—and a long-secret mystery—the lives of Grace and Jeffrey intermingle with store employees, friends and relatives in this fast-paced, glamorous, internationally set series. For weddings and romance, glamour and fun-filled entertainment, enter the world of DeWilde...*

*Twelve remarkable books, coming to you once a month, beginning in April 1996*

Weddings by DeWilde begins with
*Shattered Vows*
by Jasmine Cresswell

**Here's a preview!**

"SPEND THE NIGHT with me, Lianne."

No softening lies, no beguiling promises, just the curt offer of a night of sex. She closed her eyes, shutting out temptation. She had never expected to feel this sort of relentless drive for sexual fulfillment, so she had no mechanisms in place for coping with it. "No." The one-word denial was all she could manage to articulate.

His grip on her arms tightened as if he might refuse to accept her answer. Shockingly, she wished for a split second that he would ignore her rejection and simply bundle her into the car and drive her straight to his flat, refusing to take no for an answer. All the pleasures of mindless sex, with none of the responsibility. For a couple of seconds he neither moved nor spoke. Then he released her, turning abruptly to open the door on the passenger side of his Jaguar. "I'll drive you home," he said, his voice hard and flat. "Get in."

The traffic was heavy, and the rain started again as an annoying drizzle that distorted depth perception made driving difficult, but Lianne didn't fool herself that the silence inside the car was caused by the driving conditions. The air around them crackled and sparked with their thwarted desire. Her body was still on fire. Why didn't Gabe say something? she thought, feeling aggrieved.

Perhaps because he was finding it as difficult as she was to think of something appropriate to say. He was thirty years old, long past the stage of needing to bed a woman just so he could record another sexual conquest in his little black book. He'd spent five months dating Julia, which suggested he was a man who valued friendship as an element in his relationships with women. Since he didn't seem to like her very much, he was probably as embarrassed as she was by the stupid, inexplicable intensity of their physical response to each other.

"Maybe we should just set aside a weekend to have wild, uninterrupted sex," she said, thinking aloud. "Maybe that way we'd get whatever it is we feel for each other out of our systems and be able to move on with the rest of our lives."

His mouth quirked into a rueful smile. "Isn't that supposed to be my line?"

"Why? Because you're the man? Are you sexist enough to believe that women don't have sexual urges? I'm just as aware of what's going on between us as you are, Gabe. Am I supposed to pretend I haven't noticed that we practically ignite whenever we touch? And that we have nothing much in common except mutual lust—and a good friend we betrayed?"

**HARLEQUIN®**

Don't miss these Harlequin favorites by some of our most distinguished authors!
And now, you can receive a discount by ordering two or more titles!

| | | |
|---|---|---|
| HT #25645 | THREE GROOMS AND A WIFE<br>by JoAnn Ross | $3.25 U.S./$3.75 CAN. ☐ |
| HT #25648 | JESSIE'S LAWMAN<br>by Kristine Rolofson | $3.25 U.S.//$3.75 CAN. ☐ |
| HP #11725 | THE WRONG KIND OF WIFE<br>by Roberta Leigh | $3.25 U.S./$3.75 CAN. ☐ |
| HP #11755 | TIGER EYES by Robyn Donald | $3.25 U.S./$3.75 CAN. ☐ |
| HR #03362 | THE BABY BUSINESS by Rebecca Winters | $2.99 U.S./$3.50 CAN. ☐ |
| HR #03375 | THE BABY CAPER by Emma Goldrick | $2.99 U.S./$3.50 CAN. ☐ |
| HS #70638 | THE SECRET YEARS by Margot Dalton | $3.75 U.S./$4.25 CAN. ☐ |
| HS #70655 | PEACEKEEPER by Marisa Carroll | $3.75 U.S./$4.25 CAN. ☐ |
| HI #22280 | MIDNIGHT RIDER by Laura Pender | $2.99 U.S./$3.50 CAN. ☐ |
| HI #22235 | BEAUTY VS THE BEAST by M.J. Rogers | $3.50 U.S./$3.99 CAN. ☐ |
| HAR #16531 | TEDDY BEAR HEIR by Elda Minger | $3.50 U.S./$3.99 CAN. ☐ |
| HAR #16596 | COUNTERFEIT HUSBAND<br>by Linda Randall Wisdom | $3.50 U.S./$3.99 CAN. ☐ |
| HH #28795 | PIECES OF SKY by Marianne Willman | $3.99 U.S./$4.50 CAN. ☐ |
| HH #28855 | SWEET SURRENDER by Julie Tetel | $4.50 U.S./$4.99 CAN. ☐ |

**(limited quantities available on certain titles)**

| | | |
|---|---|---|
| | **AMOUNT** | $ |
| **DEDUCT:** | **10% DISCOUNT FOR 2+ BOOKS** | $ |
| **ADD:** | **POSTAGE & HANDLING** | $ |
| | ($1.00 for one book, 50¢ for each additional) | |
| | **APPLICABLE TAXES**** | $_____ |
| | **TOTAL PAYABLE** | $_____ |
| | (check or money order—please do not send cash) | |

To order, complete this form and send it, along with a check or money order for the total above, payable to Harlequin Books, to: **In the U.S.:** 3010 Walden Avenue, P.O. Box 9047, Buffalo, NY 14269-9047; **In Canada:** P.O. Box 613, Fort Erie, Ontario, L2A 5X3.

Name: _____

Address: _____ City: _____

State/Prov.: _____ Zip/Postal Code: _____

**New York residents remit applicable sales taxes.
Canadian residents remit applicable GST and provincial taxes.

HBACK-AJ3

This May, keep an eye out for
something heavenly from

# SPARHAWK'S Angel

## by Miranda Jarrett

"Delightful...5★s"
—*Affaire de Coeur*

Available wherever Harlequin books are sold.

BIGB96-3

BRIDE'S BAY RESORT

## UNLOCK THE DOOR TO GREAT ROMANCE
## AT BRIDE'S BAY RESORT

Join Harlequin's new across-the-lines series, set in an exclusive hotel on an island off the coast of South Carolina.

Seven of your favorite authors will bring you exciting stories about fascinating heroes and heroines discovering love at Bride's Bay Resort.

Look for these fabulous stories coming to a store near you beginning in January 1996.

**Harlequin American Romance #613** in January
*Matchmaking Baby* by Cathy Gillen Thacker

**Harlequin Presents #1794** in February
*Indiscretions* by Robyn Donald

**Harlequin Intrigue #362** in March
*Love and Lies* by Dawn Stewardson

**Harlequin Romance #3404** in April
*Make Believe Engagement* by Day Leclaire

**Harlequin Temptation #588** in May
*Stranger in the Night* by Roseanne Williams

**Harlequin Superromance #695** in June
*Married to a Stranger* by Connie Bennett

**Harlequin Historicals #324** in July
*Dulcie's Gift* by Ruth Langan

Visit Bride's Bay Resort each month wherever Harlequin books are sold.

HARLEQUIN ®

BBAYG

Bestselling authors

# ELAINE COFFMAN
# RUTH LANGAN

and

# MARY McBRIDE

Together in one fabulous collection!

# OUTLAW
## Brides

Available in June wherever Harlequin
books are sold.

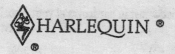

HARLEQUIN ®

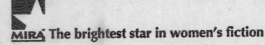